I0602890

ONE BY ONE

The Bishop Smoky Mountain Thrillers
Book 10

LAUREN STREET

STERLING & STONE

The authors greatly appreciate you taking the time to read our work. Please consider leaving a review wherever you bought the book, or telling your friends about it, to help us spread the word.

Thank you for supporting our work.

ONE BY ONE

Chapter One

SHE DOESN'T WANT TO SCREAM BECAUSE SHE KNOWS WHAT will happen when she does, but she screams anyway. It's always that way. She always screams. And the face that is the ugliest face she's ever seen lifts and looks up, sees her there at the top of the stairs. Standing. Staring. Screaming.

The head doesn't snap toward the sound of her screams that have replaced the screams of the silent woman lying on the floor with no face at all anymore. The ugly face turns toward her screams slowly, not quickly in surprise, but slowly, as if it knew she was there all along, watching.

The little girl staggers back, then turns and runs as hard as she's ever run in her life. And even as she runs, she knows she can't escape. She races down the long hallway with doors opening off both sides. And it's dark, not black dark, but shadowy dark. She runs as fast as she can, hears the sounds of her bare feet slapping on the hard wood floor. She shouldn't look back. She can run faster if she just keeps her head forward. But she looks back over her shoulder anyway. And the monster with the axe isn't running after her. It's walking slowly, almost like it's a bride coming down the aisle with measured steps.

The little girl hits the corner of the wall hard, slams into it, and falls backward onto the floor. If she hadn't looked back over her shoulder, she'd have seen the bend in the hallway. But she ought to know that the bend in the hallway is there. It's always there. And she always hits the wall. No matter how hard she tries to make it different, she always hits the wall. She turns over onto her back and sits and watches the monster with the axe approaching. Her throat is raw from screaming. But she screams louder, shrieks, is so terrified that all she can do is scoot backwards on her butt, away from the thing, across the hallway as the monster comes closer and closer. She should leap up and run again, jump to her feet and race away, but she doesn't. She just scoots backward on her butt toward the other side of the hallway, screaming and shrieking.

When she connects with the wall on the other side of the hallway, she stops, watching the monster come at her, knowing she should run but can't. All she can do is scream.

Then the monster's shadow falls over her, a dark black shadow, as if there were a bright light behind it. But there's no bright light in the hallway, it's dim and shadowy, and still the monster's black shadow reaches out to the little girl and covers her. The shadow itself is cold, so cold, it feels like ice water as it runs up over her body, like she could freeze solid.

And then the monster is standing above her, and she's looking up into its face, and she knows that as soon as the monster smiles, it'll lift that axe over its head.

She hears herself forming words, pleading, begging, "Don't hurt me, don't kill me, please don't kill me." The words all run together into one word coming out her mouth, her voice deep and ragged because she has screamed it raw.

She knows it will do no good to beg. It never does any good to beg, but she begs anyway.

The cold of the shadow lies over her like a blanket of snow, so she feels the warmth under her when her bladder lets go and she pees on herself, feels it spread out beneath her like her blood will after the axe comes down.

Then the face, the definition of ugliness and horror, smiles.

The monster lifts the axe up high. The girl's face is turned up toward it, and the blood that's already on the axe drips, and it feels to the girl like she's standing outside when it starts to rain.

Drip.

Drip.

She sees the drips falling off the shiny blade of the axe, watches them come down slowly, one at a time to splash onto her face. She watches the axe lift higher and higher into the air, and then it stops.

There is a pause, a swollen moment in time when it hasn't happened yet, but it's going to. And that swollen moment is the worst of them all. She shrieks — a cry of terror so gut-wrenching that surely it rattled the very throne room of God himself.

Then the axe slices through the air, hurdling down at her upturned face. And one more drop of blood falls—

Drip.

Then she feels the agony as it rips into her nose, chopping her whole face in two, silencing her cry—

"Georgia. Georgia. Damn it. Georgia. Stop screaming. What's wrong?"

Georgia Stump opened her eyes. She was in her bed, Chigger beside her, shaking her. Her throat was sore from the awful sound she just made.

Chigger flipped on the bedside lamp, and she squinted into the brightness as the children raced into the room and leapt on the bed. Their mother's scream had woken them up and scared them to death. She knew she'd screamed. She'd heard herself scream. It was what woke her up. It always did.

"Mommy? Mommy, what's wrong?" Liam's hair was in his eyes in a tousled bedhead.

"Mommy—" cried Connor as he jumped into the bed, followed by Eli, who was silent, his brown eyes huge and frightened.

3

Mason threw himself at Georgia, grabbing her around the neck in a terrified choke hold. "Mommeeeee! Whatsa matter, Mommy?"

Chigger had gotten up out of the bed and was standing beside it in his underwear, looking down at her. His hair was smashed flat to his head on one side, his face a study in frustration and confusion.

"What the hell are you doing? You woke up the whole damn house."

She could hear Mayella now, down the hall, shrieking. She was too little to get out of the bed or she'd be in here, too.

Georgia looked up into Chigger's face, into his eyes, and his face softened.

Sitting down on the bed beside her, he took her into his arms and crooned soothingly. "It's okay. It's okay. It's gonna be all right."

All Georgia could do was cry and cough out, "I'm sorry. I'm sorry. I'm so sorry."

Chapter Two

Sixteen-year-old Hillary Schofield looked into the welcoming face of her iPhone and poured out her heart to the tiny red dot of a camera that was recording it all.

"I'm a damn prisoner, locked up here. Might as well be Rapunzel in a tower." She reached up to pinch a tuft of her platinum blonde hair and held it out from her head. "But my hair's so short I don't have anything to dangle out the window."

She picked up her drink — she'd finally managed to swallow vodka and 7-Up without holding her nose — and took a swig.

She held up the glass to the camera.

"They're turning me into a damned alcoholic."

With an aborted giggle, she said, "You take what you can get when you can't get what you want." She lifted the glass up to the camera in a mock toast before downing another drink.

"Just look at this place!"

Picking up the phone, she turned the camera toward

the room in a pan of the walls, a sweep across dark wood paneling, sixteen-foot ceilings, a dormer above the door frame, and the kind of four-poster bed you saw in a Dracula movie.

"I'm stuck here. I'm going to be stuck here for months. Somebody pleeeeease come rescue me."

Hillary stopped the recording and played it back and saw how screechy and whiny she sounded and that the angle she was holding the phone gave a panoramic view up both her nostrils. And the pan of the room was nothing but a smear.

Hillary sighed. She'd record a better one later. But first, she had to pee. She went to the bathroom with its all-around mirrors, and when she was done, she examined her face. She was pretty, and she could only pray that pretty at sixteen meant she would morph over the next few years into drop-dead gorgeous. She had bleached her hair out to platinum blonde, and it was soft and naturally curly and clung to her head in an abandon of curls. She thought the carefree style made her look a little elfish.

She had beautiful blue eyes, and that had been confirmed on a number of occasions by a number of people, but she probably needed to thin her brows. They were too dark.

And then there were the pimples.

She sighed. God, how she hated pimples. And they were everywhere, on her face, on her chest above her boobs... Leaning over so she could see better, she squeezed hard and popped the yellowish pimple on her right cheek. This wasn't something that Hillary would have admitted to anybody. Not if they tortured her, not if they pulled out her fingernails and put her feet in boiling water... but she liked popping pimples. She didn't like having pimples.

What teenager wanted to have pimples? But she had them, and there was something… satisfying about squeezing and squeezing and then pop, and it splattered on the mirror or sent out some snaky brown tail from an enormous blackhead.

She searched her face for more ripe pimples, found a couple, but there was an art to popping pimples. They had to be ripe, or all you'd do was bruise your face.

She picked up her drink again, took a deep breath, and swallowed three big swallows. Oh, she didn't want to drink alcohol. She never would have picked it. But booze was what she could get, and so she settled for that. Her parents had taken away every other damn thing she enjoyed.

Hillary had had a small stash — some M30s, a handful of benzos and some Adderall. No blow. She enjoyed it, but she wasn't stupid. Anything powder could be laced with fentanyl. Pills were safe, though. She'd had no idea that her Nazi stepmother would search her room while she was at school before they left for the mountains.

She had come home to find that the ugly bitch had laid out her stash on the kitchen table, then Hillary watched her shove it all down the disposal.

She'd managed to keep a good supply of gummies only because she didn't have them in her room. She hid them in the bottom of the sugar canister right there on the kitchen counter. If her stepmother had ever attempted to get a cup of sugar out of that jar, which she never would because the lazy bitch never cooked, she would have discovered that there was only two inches of sugar on the top and the rest were gummies.

Hillary went back into her bedroom to her dresser, picked up the big green bottle of 7-Up, poured some in the bottom of a glass, went to her closet, got the vodka bottle out of the snow boots where she hid it, and topped off the 7-Up. She stirred it with her finger. She'd never liked it, but it was all she had for now. She'd seen that groundskeeper, the one who looked at her in that creepy way, pull a flask out of his hip pocket and she'd screwed up her courage to ask if he would buy her some booze. He'd sniggered like a Neanderthal and reached down to scratch his privates, but he'd come through. She'd wanted bourbon. That tasted good, but her parents would smell it on her breath, and you couldn't really smell vodka, or so she'd heard. Way more important, the creep had set her up with a dealer so she could get something real.

She took another swig of her drink, grimaced as she swallowed it down, and leaned back against the pile of pillows on her bed, wondering for the gazillionth time if there was any possible way she could get out of this but just wasn't seeing a way. Sure, she could run away, but what good did that do? She wasn't seven years old — they'd bring her back.

And then they'd have even more of an excuse for treating her like a criminal.

The story they gave out to everyone was that they had decided to take their children to the mountains where they could all commune with nature or something, breathe pure air and smell the roses.

Her younger brother and sisters were delighted by the prospect. Of course, they were. They were six and seven years old, and being in the mountains was fun if you were that age. It was no fun if you were sixteen and had not a single soul to talk to or hang out with.

And homeschool? Oh dear God in heaven, home-school! For a moment, she almost teared up at the thought that her friends would be starting back to school again at

Bryant High School, while she would be sitting in front of a computer learning remotely. That shit that had driven her nuts during COVID. She couldn't have dreamed up a worse nightmare.

The cherry on the top of it all was the... weird shit. She didn't know what else to call it. Things happened here, like she'd found a broken vase on the floor, but when she went back with a broom to clean up the mess before the littles woke up, it wasn't broken anymore, didn't even have a crack. Strange music, crazy laughter, shimmery things floating...

Bam! She slammed the door on those thoughts, wouldn't let herself think them.

Picking up her drink again, she swallowed, and the room spun deliciously. The vodka was giving her a warm buzzy feeling. She bit her lower lip, and it felt kind of numb.

Then it occurred to her that she should go down to the kitchen and retrieve some gummies from the sugar canister. She didn't know what would happen when mixing marijuana with alcohol, but she was certainly happy to give it a shot and see.

Stepping from her room into the stupid huge hallway of the monstrous house, she headed for the stairs that looked like something out of *Gone with the Wind*. She got to the top of the stairs and swayed and had to grab the big ornate oak post.

"Whoa!" she said. "All I need is to get drunk and fall down the damn stairs and break my neck."

The world was spinning deliciously around her. She closed her eyes to reduce the dizziness and took the stairs one at a time, clinging to the giant banister. Down, down, down. God how many stairs were there — fifteen, eighteen? She could tell she had reached the bottom when she put her foot out and there wasn't another step.

She opened her eyes — and what she saw couldn't be real. Her mind refused to recognize it. This was all wrong. It couldn't be real.

She gasped and stumbled back onto the bottom step, scooting along it on her butt until she hit the wall.

Lying at the foot of the stairs was a body, a dead body with a big puddle of blood on the floor around it. It was a man, and there was a knife sticking out of his chest, a big one, like a sword or a machete or something... and the blood! Oh my god, it was spread out, a puddle of it three feet wide.

Hillary thought she was going to throw up. She couldn't even scream. She slowly inched up to a standing position by sliding her back up the wall. Then she backed onto the first step up, then the second, then the third, never taking her eyes off that body for a second. She'd never seen a dead body before, but he had to be dead.

When she finally got far enough away that the dead body couldn't come to life and grab her, she turned and ran up the stairs, only to stumble and faceplant on the floor at the top. She scrambled to her hands and knees and ran down the hallway to her parents' room.

She didn't knock, thus committing the absolute cardinal sin. Thou shalt not enter thy parents' room without knocking first. That had become a cardinal rule instituted after Hillary had once walked in on them screwing. None of the children was allowed in the bedroom unless they knocked, but she barged right in — didn't care if they were screwing their brains out.

"There's a body, a dead body, oh God, there's a dead body at the foot of the stairs!" she cried, ran across the room and threw herself onto the bed on top of her parents who were wiggling and squirming and cursing.

"What…?" Her father's voice was thick with sleep.

"Hillary, what is the matter with you?" the bitch cried. "What the hell are you doing?"

Her father reached over and turned on the bedside lamp, flooding the room with light, then sat up, rubbed his eyes, and asked, "What's going on?"

"You're such a monster, such a horrible little creature," her stepmother said, shrinking away from her like she was some kind of disease.

"There's a body, there's a murdered man down there, downstairs at the bottom of the stairs."

"What are you talking about?" her father asked.

"At the foot of the stairs. Just go look, Dad, please, just go look."

"You were hallucinating," the bitch snarled. "What have you been taking? I threw all your drugs away, but you found something else, didn't you? You're probably snorting Drano or something."

Her father took her by the arm, dragged her out the door into the big ridiculous hallway. "Where is this body?"

"It's not like you'll miss it. It's lying at the foot of the stairs. He's dead, Daddy, he's dead, and there's a knife in his chest and there's blood all over everywhere."

Her father told her to wait there, but he did look a little reluctant to go down the hallway, and he paused before he turned the corner and started down the stairs.

Hillary leaned against the wall in the hallway, dragging in big breaths of air, feeling the world spin around her, waiting to hear her father's footsteps come running up the stairs as he raced away from the monstrous thing.

She knew now that she had drunk too much. That was

the problem with alcohol. You drank it and drank it, but it didn't hit you until later, so you didn't know when to stop.

It seemed like hours before her father came striding up the stairs and down the hallway. He looked normal. How could you look normal after seeing a thing like that?

No, he didn't look normal. He looked pissed.

Marching in his bare feet and jockey shorts down the hall, he stopped in front of her.

"What in the hell is wrong with you?" he demanded. Then he sniffed. "You've been drinking." As if that was an explanation for everything and the greatest condemnation he could think of.

The bedroom door opened, and her stepmother appeared with a robe wrapped around her. "What is it?"

Hillary's father turned to her. "She's drunk."

Her stepmother looked both horrified and glad at the same time.

"Drunk? We should have known."

"Dad," Hillary insisted, "the body, what about the body?"

"There's no damn body. There's nothing down at the bottom of those stairs."

"But there is. There's a body!"

"You're hallucinating," her stepmother screeched. "What have you taken?"

Hillary had never hallucinated in her life, not even when she took that little pink pill that made everybody else see pink bunnies. "It was a dead body, not a hallucination."

Grabbing her by the upper arm, her father dragged Hillary down the hall to her own room. "You better be glad you didn't wake up the littles," he snarled at her.

He opened the door to her bedroom, then threw her through it. She stumbled and landed on her butt on the floor. "You go take a cold shower and go to bed. And don't you ever… don't you *ever*…"

Her father was so angry, either he could think of nothing to say or didn't trust what he might say. He reached over and slammed the door in her face. But not before he spit out, "What's wrong with you?"

Hillary sat on her butt on the floor, looking at the closed door, wondering the same thing.

What *was* wrong with her?

Chapter Three

YARMOUTH COUNTY SHERIFF MITCH WEBSTER SAT IN HIS office with the door open, holding a small gold key in the light of his desk lamp, examining it. He had stared at the thing for hours but was no closer now to knowing what it unlocked than he was when the key dropped out of the manila envelope onto the kitchen table at Rileigh Bishop's mother's house.

On top of the pile of papers on his desk was the report that he had gotten on the DNA test of the tanned human skin that had been inside the envelope with the key. The man whose skin had been flayed from his back was Santiago Suárez, which explained the intertwined double-S tattoo on the skin that was no longer in its owner's possession. Suárez was a bag man for organized crime on the south side of Chicago, and his body had not been found. So, like the thumb bone and the little finger bone that had previously been sent to Rileigh, the same logic applied. The only person who could have taken the skin from the victim's back was the person who'd killed him.

Mitch hadn't told Rileigh yet about the DNA results.

There were several reasons that he hadn't, but the main excuse he used was that she had forgotten about it. She had gotten over the shock of it. The big date that they had put off for so long was coming up, and that was something to look forward to. Telling her what he'd found out about the DNA results of the skin would send her back down into that dark hole and swirling around the drain.

He was supposed to go to lunch at Rileigh's house today. Her mother was making some strange dish. He didn't remember what, but Rileigh had invited him to come and taste it, and of course he'd said yes. The food was always good there, but even if it had been terrible, it meant he could spend time with Rileigh, which was always worth the price of admission. But the thing was, he felt like a fraud. He was hiding something from her, and that was no way to conduct a relationship. He had to tell her about the report... but just not now, not right before the big date.

He dropped the key into his shirt pocket, then lowered his head and picked up a pen. Every now and then, he'd make a mark on one of the papers in the pile on his desk. If you passed by his open door, you'd think the man was hard at work. And you'd be totally wrong.

Mitch didn't see the reports in front of him. He could see only one thing, a beautiful face with gorgeous jade green eyes — and they were green, they were *not* hazel. They had become green in his mind the night she wore that clingy, slinky green dress on their ridiculous Big Date at Red Eye Gravy, and now Mitch couldn't look at her eyes and see them as hazel anymore. No matter what she was wearing, they were that same dark jade green, and she'd be wearing that dress on Saturday night, along with the matching heels that he'd tried to talk her out of wearing because of her ankle.

Rileigh had sprained her ankle badly coming down

the mountainside on a dirt bike, and he had proposed that she wear flat-heeled shoes that wouldn't be quite so hard on her ankle as the green spike heels. She'd blown him off, told him she was wearing those heels, and secretly he was glad because they went with the dress that went with the eyes that went with the woman whose name was Rileigh Bishop, who'd be by his side Saturday night on the Big Date that had been put off and put off and put —

He heard something of a commotion outside his office and looked up to see a teenage girl barge through the front door, barreling past the receptionist like a stampede of buffalo and into his office.

"You have to come. You *have to*. Please tell me you'll come."

Mitch slowly got to his feet and surveyed the young woman standing in front of him. She was a teenager in the official uniform of teenagedom — a wrinkled tee and cut-off jeans, a small girl with short hair bleached totally white. He suspected she was probably older than she looked.

"Ma'am, could you give me your name, please?"

"My name's Hillary Schofield. Please, you have to come with me *now*."

"How about you sit down, Ms. Schofield."

"I don't want to sit down. I want to tell you about a dead body. Don't you care?"

The dead body part did get his attention.

"A dead body where? Whose dead body?"

"I don't know who. I just know where. And actually, I don't even know where anymore. It's gone."

"Ma'am, you're going to have to calm down and be a little clearer if I'm going to help you."

She took a deep breath and tried to grab hold of her emotions.

"Just come and *see*. At the foot of the stairs, there was a dead body last night. And then…"

She didn't appear to want to finish the sentence so he finished it for her.

"And then it was gone."

She nodded. "But this morning I found the blood! In bright sunlight, you can *see* it. So I can prove there was a body. Please come."

"Ma'am, are your parents here with you?"

"My parents are at home — and if you want to talk to them, take me home and see the place, see the blood for yourself."

"Tell me who you are again and where you live."

"My name is Hillary Marie Schofield, and my parents and I and my sisters and brother are living at the bed and breakfast called Shagbark Manor."

"So your parents didn't drive you here? Did you drive yourself?"

"No, I rode with the guy on the lawnmower."

"The guy on the lawnmower?" Mitch repeated.

"He was the guy who came to trim the bushes and put down the mulch or whatever. He was coming back to town and I asked him to give me a lift. He said he'd take me back home, too, but you have to do it — so you can see!"

The girl sounded like the typical hysterical teenager, but the part about the dead body was something Mitch couldn't afford to blow off. And besides, if this girl had ridden into town with the man who ran Gillespie Lawn Service, which he supposed was who she was talking about, it was not a good idea to let the girl get back into the truck with him.

Mitch reached for his hat.

"Would you wait for me please, out front? I have to make a phone call."

He made it clear she wasn't welcome to stand there and listen, so she walked reluctantly out the door and stood beyond it as he called Rileigh.

"I'm going to be late for lunch today," he told her after she answered.

"Not a problem," Rileigh said. "The goulash will be ready whenever you get here."

Rileigh's mother had decided to cook her way through a cookbook, making each recipe in succession, no matter what it was. Today was Hungarian goulash, and Rileigh had invited Mitch over to "enjoy it" with her. Translate that: taste-test it to see what ingredients her mother had either added to or deleted from the recipe.

"So what's up?" Rileigh continued.

"Teenage girl tells me she's found a dead body."

"Really?"

"I doubt it, but I got to check it out."

"So who's the teenage girl?"

"Her name is Hillary Schofield, and she's a teenager in the family that's staying at Old Shaggy."

"She found a dead body at Old Shaggy. I'm surprised one of the ghosts didn't drag it away before she had time to report it."

"I think maybe they did. I don't believe it's still there, but we'll see. Either way, I won't be on time. You sure that's not going to be a problem?"

"I'm sure. Like I said, the goulash will be ready as soon as you get here.

"Bye."

He sat holding the phone for a minute, savoring the sound of her voice in his ear and feeling like a tenth grader for being so gaga.

Mitch and the girl got into his cruiser, and he pulled out onto the highway.

"Now tell me the story," Mitch started. "What happened?"

She took a deep breath. "I went downstairs last night to get..." She stumbled there, so that was a clue. "I went to get something to eat, and there was a dead body at the bottom of the stairs."

"You do realize how crazy that sounds?"

"Do you realize how crazy it *was*?" she snapped. "It's a nightmare." She sank back into the seat and heaved a dramatic sigh. "It just keeps getting worse and worse."

"And what would that be?"

"My life," she moaned. "My whole life."

"Could you get a little more specific than that?"

She cut her eyes to him quickly to see if he was making fun of her or simply making a joke.

"All right, *specifically* — I've been dragged here from home where all of my friends are together having summer fun *without me* by my wicked stepmother who screws around on my dad with anybody whose pants zip in the front — she doesn't know I know that — and my father, who only demanded custody of me to get back at my mother. And we're going to stay here for months in that horrible house, and all kind of crazy shit has happened."

"Such as?"

"You won't believe me. My parents don't."

"Try me."

"Okay, the portraits have... eyes. The faces — sometimes the eyes in them look at you and follow you when you walk away. And things are broken, and then they're not. Like a broken vase that's suddenly un-broken, not even a crack. There's this weird sound like somebody crying that you can hear when you walk down the hallway, but you can't hear it in any other room in the house, and

I've looked and looked for who's crying and I can't find anybody. And then there's these shimmery things."

"Shimmery things."

"Just… it looks like a heat wave in the desert."

"And where are they?"

"Different places. In a doorway or at the end of the hall or the top of the stairs. But when you go to see what they are, there're gone."

"But you've never seen anything like a dead body there?"

"Of course I've never seen anything like a dead body! Until last night."

"I'm surprised your parents didn't come with you to report it."

"They don't even know I'm here, and boy are they going to be pissed when they find out."

"Pissed that…?"

"Pissed that I came into town and told the truth."

"What are your mother and father's names?"

"My mother's name is Leanne, but she's dead. The witch who now lives with my father's name is Tabitha, but she goes by Tabby." The snarl and disgust were thick enough to spread on toast. "My father's name is Paul.

"What does your father do?"

"Whatever Tabby tells him."

"I meant by occupation."

"He's an investment banker. He plays with other people's money like it's Monopoly money."

"And the rest of your family?"

She smiled then for the first time.

"I have a brother and sister who are twins, Sage and Sam. They're eight. And Liza is six."

They turned into a long, winding drive lined with shag bark hickory trees that led to the huge old mansion. There really wasn't anything that could have prepared Mitch for the sight of Shagbark Manor. Tall and creepy, with dark windows that stared down at the drive like malevolent eyes, it looked like the picture that would have been beside "haunted house" in the dictionary — all it lacked were broken windows, shaggy bushes, dead flowers, and rotten porch steps to complete the picture. And of course, it had none of those things. It was a bed and breakfast that somehow managed to keep the ambiance of a haunted house and also meet all the fire codes. It was three stories tall and looked like some gothic house that Jane Eyre would have lived in. Obviously, whoever ran the bed and breakfast had capitalized on both that look and all the rumors about the place to convince those who came to stay that they might be sleeping in a haunted house.

Mitch made a mental note to ask Rileigh how in the world a place like this had come to be here. Why had somebody built this deep in a hollow in the Smoky Mountains?

"Are you going to be staying here long?" Mitch asked Hillary.

"Until Christmas!"

Most of the customers of a bed and breakfast only stayed for a weekend or perhaps a week. They'd drive up from Nashville or Knoxville and there were always tourists who wanted to get away from the hustle and bustle of Gatlinburg and Pigeon Forge.

"It's a nightmare." Hillary looked absolutely desolate. "You don't know what it's like when terrible things are happening to you and your parents don't believe you and won't do anything about it!" Actually, Mitch did know what that was like. *Exactly* what that was like. "What do you do when the people who are supposed to help, don't?"

What you do is learn to look after yourself, even though

you're too young to. You learn how to take care of those you love even when you're not really big enough or smart enough or strong enough to do it. ,

"I mean... what if something happens to the littles?" she continued. "It'll be my fault."

Those words punched a hole in Mitch's belly. How many nights had he stared at the ceiling of his room, trying to figure out how he could protect his little brother and keep him safe?

As he pulled his cruiser into the driveway and wound his way down towards the house, he caught sight of a man who took one look at the police cruiser and immediately turned his back and hurried off in the other direction. Then he noticed small children, a little boy and two little girls, playing at the edge of the woods. He pulled up in front of the house and looked at his passenger. Hillary Schofield had become quiet and morose the closer they got to the house.

"Let's go see if we can find that dead body," he said.

She cut her eyes toward him and sighed. "When my parents see you, I am in so much trouble!"

With that, she hopped out of the car and went up the walkway leading to the house. It was lined with flowers. He suspected it was no accident that all the flowers were blood-red roses.

Hillary had not closed the door behind her, and he stepped inside and immediately heard the sound of angry voices — women yelling. Hillary had gone off somewhere in the house and he followed the sound of the voices, out of the huge vestibule with its wide staircase sweeping down from the second floor. He passed through a room that looked like a library out of the eighteenth century, with shelves of books reaching all the way from the floor to the ceiling, a stretch given that these appeared to be sixteen-foot ceilings. That room led to another, a "parlor" perhaps, where three women were engaged in a shouting match.

No, only two of the women were shouting. Both of them were yelling at the third.

Chapter Four

Rileigh Bishop was peeling potatoes to go into Mama's Hungarian goulash when she heard her phone ring in the next room. When she dropped the potatoes into the drainer and hurried to answer it, she was rewarded with the word "Mitch" on the caller ID screen.

"Hello there, stranger. How are you today?" she greeted, then he told her about there being a possible dead body at the old bed and breakfast. She kept peeling as they talked.

Mama had planned to make shrimp creole for the FBI agent, Lamar Devereux, who had stayed at their house. Okay, who *had hidden from killers* at their house. She'd bought all the ingredients, but the agent had died before she'd had a chance to make the dish. Nobody else in the family was interested in eating it, so Mama had made the shrimp creole and taken it to the county senior citizen's dinner for them to serve at lunch.

The thing was, Mama had enjoyed chasing around and getting the ingredients and making a dish she'd never made before. And she announced at some point that she intended to make all the untried dishes in the recipe book where she found the recipe for shrimp creole. Rileigh and her sister Jillian had figured she'd forget all about it, but you never knew what was going to hang on a nail in Mama's head. She could ask you what Sunday's sermon topic had been ten different times and not remember that she'd asked you the other nine. On the other hand, she could decide to cook her way through an entire cookbook on a whim and remember it as if it were her Social Security number.

She smiled after they hung up. Mama's first new recipe out of the cookbook had been a raging success. It was meatloaf, but not the way she'd ever made it before. All kinds of different ingredients she'd never put in a meatloaf. Rileigh and Jillian had been steeling themselves to bite into it and discover that Mama had either left out some key ingredient or added one or more new ones of her own. But both of them were pleasantly surprised to discover that it was good. It was really good. And when they told Mama that, her cook-through-the-recipe-book determination became engraved in granite. So lunch today was to be Hungarian goulash, and Rileigh was peeling the potatoes for it. She didn't know what other ingredients the dish might require. The potatoes were her contribution, the job she'd been assigned, and she was glad of it because peeling potatoes was one of those gloriously mindless tasks that let you disengage the higher order thinking centers of your brain and go on autopilot. Which meant that those higher-order thinking centers were free to consider other thoughts. And her other thoughts were of the man who was going to be about an hour late for lunch. She thought of Mitch's smiling face and broke into a broad smile of her own.

"What you grinning at?" Mama asked. Only then did

she realize she'd been standing in the dining room, holding her cell phone in her hand and grinning like an idiot.

"I was thinking about how good this goulash is going to taste."

Mama cocked her head to the side.

"You think I buy that? You was thinking about Mitch, wasn't you?"

Damn, how she hated the way Mama could sometimes read her thoughts.

"I was considering our date, yes," she said as she returned to her potato peeling.

"I ain't never been to Ruth Chris Steakhouse. But I've heard two things about it — it's really good food and it costs an arm and a leg."

"I hope you're correct at least on the first count."

Both she and Mitch agreed that — drum roll please! — the *big date* was worthy of that kind special occasion restaurant. Her mind bounced to the first date that wasn't, the one that was set for a Gatlinburg restaurant that had caught fire and burned to the ground before they arrived, and they wound up at the Red Eye Gravy Diner. The night of a murder.

She shook off the thought and continued peeling potatoes.

"Mitch said he's going to be late for lunch today," she told her mom.

"Something come up?" Jillian asked. Rileigh hadn't heard her enter the kitchen.

"Yeah, a teenage girl and a dead body."

"Oh, no." Jillian and Mama said the two words with the perfect unison of a Greek chorus and all three of them laughed.

"It's a teenage girl reporting a dead body, and Mitch hopes it will turn out to be absolutely nothing."

"Who's the teenager?" Mama asked.

"I didn't ask her name. Mitch said that she and her family were staying at Old Shaggy."

"Old Shaggy…" Mama said pensively, as she chopped red and green peppers on a cutting board. "I've often thought I'd like to go up there sometime and spend the weekend."

Both Rileigh and Jillian gawked at Mama.

"What?" Rileigh asked.

"Why in the world would you want to do that?" Jillian asked. "You're no tourist. You live here."

"It seems like such an intriguing place, is all. And I've lived here my whole life and I ain't never seen the inside of it — I'd sure like to. And I think it would be fun to be chased up and down the halls by an axe murderer ghost, don't you?"

Jillian and Rileigh laughed.

"I can think of things I'd rather do," Jillian said.

"Like get a root canal without Novocain," Rileigh added.

"Aw, come on. You girls is wrapped too tight. It'd be entertaining."

"David told me a couple of weeks ago that he had been hired as a personal trainer for some guy who was going to be staying at Old Shaggy for several months. Maybe it's the same family."

The mention of David put a bit of a chill on the room, because Mama and Rileigh didn't quite know what they should and shouldn't say to Jillian about David Hicks. After the death of the FBI agent, Jillian had sat down with David and explained to him why she had been being so mysterious and why she couldn't tell him about the agent's presence in the house. And oh, by the way, why she had taken his four-wheeler over the mountain and that Rileigh had just about destroyed his dirt bike. But in the process of that conversation, she had a let's-get-real discussion that she didn't realize she needed to have until Agent Devereux had come into her life. She told David that they needed to put the brakes on what was going on between them. It was too much too fast, and she was not in any emotional shape to get into a serious relationship.

Rileigh was proud of her for having the backbone to have a hard conversation and speak a hard truth. But she had to admit that she missed seeing David around. Since Jillian had come home, he had become just about as much a fixture at their house as Mitch was. Now, it felt like there was a vacant space at the table where he should have been sitting.

"So are you all set for the big date?" Jillian asked, changing the subject adeptly.

"Are you kidding me? I've been all set for the big date for months!"

"You reckon that 'cause you've been looking forward to it for so long and 'cause it's been put off so many times, that no matter how good it is, it's going to be a letdown from what it's been built up to be?" Mama asked.

Rileigh looked her dead in the eye. "Not a chance, Mama. Not a chance in hell."

Chapter Five

IT APPEARED TO MITCH THAT THE WOMEN WERE RELATED, sisters, perhaps. They had a family resemblance. Two of them were blondes and the third might have been, too, but it was impossible to tell because her hair was what Rileigh's mother would have called a Sears color — "a color you could buy out of the Sears catalog, but ain't nothing that looks natural." It always seemed to Mitch that hair colored pink or green or blue looked like hair on a doll, not a human being, and he'd never preferred it. But he had to admit that the hair on the woman who was currently screaming at the smaller of the three was attractive. It was shades of green and blue and blue-green weaved together in such a way that it reminded Mitch of a tropical fish. The tropical fish woman was smartly dressed, stylish, with lots of makeup — a pretty woman who knew it and capitalized on it. The other of the two women who was screaming at the third had yellow-blonde hair, the color of butter, and large colorful tattoos on her arms. The third woman in the altercation, the one the other two were yelling at, was slight and delicate and had the kind of pale blonde hair that you usually didn't see on people older than age two. She was a cotton-top toddler whose cotton top had stayed cotton, and she stood literally with her back to the wall as the other two women yelled at her.

"Damn it, it's what we agreed on!" yelled the tattooed woman.

"All *three* of us agreed," the other one chimed in. "You're the one who backed out."

"It's not a crime to change your mind," said the woman with her back to the wall.

"No, it's not a crime," said the tropical fish woman, "but it is a *betrayal*, and damn it, we were all agreed."

"Can we stop talking about what we agreed to thirteen years ago?" said the beleaguered woman.

"It matters," said the tropical fish woman, getting up in the third woman's face. "The three of us were united, and then *you*—"

The woman with tattoos all up and down her arms pulled her away. She seemed to have gotten hold of her temper and was trying to modulate her tone of voice.

"Look, Carly, this place is not a viable option to make a livelihood. It's just not."

"Well, I've managed fine so far, kept it afloat during COVID when half the other places like it went under."

"And you did that with borrowed money! How are you going to pay that back?" shouted the tropical fish woman.

"I *am* paying it back. I make payments to my creditors every month, never miss."

"As soon as you do, they've going to come after you with an army of lawyers and sue you—"

"They can't sue me as long as I make payments."

"What happens if you *can't?*"

"I've told you before — I *can* make payments. If I keep the place occupied, it all works. And I have a five-month rental, a single family — they want the *whole place* for five months. I can take care of them myself. With no maids and cooks to pay, there's hardly any overhead. For five months, I don't have to drum up business. I put a 'No Vacancy' sign on the website!"

"And if the five-month people bail on you, and you have no other rentals in the pipeline — what then?" sneered the tropical fish woman. "It'll take you a couple of months to get the flow established again, and the sharks will smell the blood in the water."

The tattooed woman had lowered her tone of voice, at least an octave, but she suddenly gave way to screaming again. "Dammit, Camille is right, Carly. You're just living hand to mouth, never getting ahead, and one of these days—"

The tropical fish woman took the handoff. "This place is going to cost a fortune. And there's no way there's enough money in the maintenance and repairs account to pay for all the things you're going to have to pay for, and I will be damned if I will pay an assessment on this monstrosity."

She began ticking items off her fingers.

"The HVAC for this place — I can't imagine how much it cost to retrofit this mausoleum with thirty-plus rooms and the high ceilings. It had to have been millions. And that unit is now ... what?" She looked at the tattooed woman. "Twenty years old, maybe?"

The tattooed woman replied, "At least twenty-five, maybe more than that. It's going to go, Carly, and when it does, how in the hell do you think you're going to pay to replace it?"

The tropical fish woman pointed toward the ceiling. "And the roof? Holy shit, Carly, I can't even imagine what a roof for this place would cost."

"The roof doesn't leak," said the woman, whose back was still against the wall, the others standing too close.

"It might not leak now, but it will eventually. And then what will you do?"

"I'll fix it if it leaks."

"You'll have to replace the whole damn thing. You can't *fix* a roof like that."

"This is all what-ifs. What if the HVAC goes? What if the roof goes? None of those things have happened."

"But they're going to," said the tropical fish woman. She turned and looked like she wanted to pull out all that blue-green hair. "Aggh!" It was the cry of one barely holding onto her temper with her fingernails. "Don't you get it? Can't you look ahead? They're going to, and when they do, this place is going to be an albatross around our necks, pulling us down instead of being the windfall it could be if you'd just listen to reason."

"The windows, what about the windows?" the tattooed woman blurted out. "I remember how bad they leaked. It was freezing on the second floor."

"We survived," said the smaller woman.

It occurred to Mitch that she was the only one of them being calm and reasonable. The onslaught of the other two crashed against her like the sea against the shore and washed away, leaving her standing composed, facing down the other two.

"I *know* I can sell this place. I know it. Even in this economy."

The money phrase in that sentence was "in this economy." Translate that: it'll be a long shot.

"I mean… I may have a buyer."

"What will they do with it?"

"If they buy it, what difference does it make what they do with it?"

32

"They want to tear it down, don't they?"

"I don't know. What do you care?"

"They want to tear down Shagbark Manor, bulldoze it, and build… what? Condominiums?"

"What does it matter what they—"

The smaller woman cut her off. "It matters because this is our heritage."

The tropical fish woman rolled her eyes. "Please, dear God in heaven, don't tell me you think the ghosts of our ancestors are here."

"Riiight," said the tattooed woman, "sailing up and down the hallways, little girls with pieces hacked off running from a madman with an axe."

The mention of the family heritage and the ghosts seemed to have hardened the demeanor of the smaller woman, but she didn't care, plowed doggedly ahead.

"Do you know what you could do with the kind of money we will make off selling this rat trap?

"It's not a rat trap."

"Think what you could do with the money," said the tattooed woman. "We could all use it! I could buy out my partner in Brews and Giggles, and Camille could do whatever she needs with Trendy Threads—"

"Keep it afloat!" the woman snarled. To the smaller woman, she said, "You could start your own business. You could buy some small place somewhere."

"Small?"

The woman lost it. "If you're so damned determined to get up every morning and cook pancakes for strangers, I'm sure Waffle House is hiring."

"It's our home," the smaller woman fired back.

"Dammit, Carly!" the tropical fish woman said, and Mitch saw she'd finally lost her battle with her temper. She lunged at the smaller woman, knocking her into the wall, and the tattoo woman was about to back her up when Mitch stepped forward.

"Excuse me."

All three of the women froze. The tropical fish woman whirled on him. She was so furious he suspected if he hadn't been wearing a badge, she'd have taken him on. As it was, she wrestled her rage under control and said tightly, "Appears we have company."

"Official company," said the tattooed woman.

The third woman, the smallest, stepped between the other two and walked to Mitch.

He noticed in that moment that she reminded him of Hillary. In fact, Hillary could have been the fourth sister! She looked more like the smallest than either of the other two. Of course, a large part of the similarity was the hair that was a blonde so light it was almost white. Hillary's was artificial — whatever color it once was had been bleached out. But the hair color of the Marilyn Monroe-blonde woman crossing the room toward him was real. It was obviously long and straight, piled on top of her head in what hairstylists called a "messy bun."

"You've walked into the middle of a family spat. I'm sorry that you had to see that. My name is Carly Farrington. And I'm the housekeeper here at Shagbark Manor." She held out her delicate hand and he shook it. "To what do we owe the honor of the presence of the Sheriff of Yarmouth County?"

"I've come—" he started, but before he could finish, he heard a commotion behind him and turned around.

A tall, balding man was barreling toward Mitch like a runaway freight train. He probably was Hillary's father. Mitch braced himself for the impact.

Chapter Six

THE TALL, BALD MAN WAS TRAILED BY AN ALMOST EQUALLY tall woman. She had to be at least six feet, and her face had a look of even greater anger than his.

"I can't believe Hillary did this!" the man said as he reached where Mitch stood. "She went to the damn sheriff. I am so sorry."

"She's crazy," said the tall, dark-haired woman who had followed him into the room. "That girl is nuts. She needs to be locked up!"

Hillary came in after them, not exactly defiant, but certainly not meek, either. She had known she was going to get in a lot of trouble for doing what she did, and she'd done it anyway, which sent some kind of message to Mitch; he just wasn't quite sure what. Though not the brazen, cocky teenager who had shown up in his office earlier, she didn't seem to be cowed by the situation.

"And you are…" Mitch began.

"I'm sorry, my name is Paul Schofield. This is my wife, Tabitha. We're Hillary's parents." Mitch saw Hillary cringe at that and remembered her remark about how Tabitha was her stepmother.

"Your daughter came to me earlier," Mitch said, "and said she had found a dead body here in the house and I'm here to investigate."

"I told you, she's crazy," the woman standing beside Schofield said. She had an unusually unpleasant voice, high and grating, a fingernails-on-a-blackboard sound to Mitch. Her face had large features — wide plump lips and big eyes — that were striking rather than pretty. "She's absolutely lost her mind. I mean, really — a dead body, a damn *dead* body. What kind of lunatic would say that?"

"There was a dead man here!" Hillary cried. "I don't know what happened to the body, but I can prove it was here."

"Was where?" Mitch asked.

"At the bottom of the stairs," Hillary said and turned back toward the vestibule.

Mitch and her parents followed. Mitch saw that the housekeeper had followed along, staying out of the way. Her sisters had already tired of the show and left.

Hillary pointed to a spot at the bottom of the steps and said, "There was a big rug there when we first got here." She glanced at the housekeeper, Carly. "Last night I came downstairs and there was a man lying there on the floor. He was dead. He had to be dead. He had a knife sticking out of his chest and there was a huge puddle of blood around him. It was this big." She spread her arms out in a wide circle. "And that's what I can prove — that there was blood on the floor."

"Hillary, for god's sake!" her father said, more in angst than in anger.

"Look for yourself." Hillary got down on her hands and knees on the hardwood floor.

"I came down this morning and looked — see, right here." She pointed to the cracks between two of the flat boards. "In the bright sunlight, you can see. If you look close, you can see there was blood dripped here. Somehow the blood got cleaned up but—"

"She said last night she saw a body and blood everywhere," Tabitha said, "and Paul came down minutes later and it was gone. How could you clean that up, a big puddle of blood in just a few minutes?"

"But you can see it," Hillary said, pointing to the crack. "Get down and look."

Both her parents remained upright. Mitch dropped to his hands and knees and looked where she pointed.

"Can you see it?" She whipped out her cell phone, turned on the flashlight app, and pointed it toward the spot. "See."

Mitch leaned close to the boards and saw where something dark had dripped down between the boards and stained them.

He straightened up to his knees. "Let me see that flashlight," he said.

She handed him the phone and he stood, moved away from the bottom of the stairs into the middle of the foyer, and got down on his hands and knees again. He shone the light on the boards there, then looked up at Carly.

"Come and take a look at this," he said.

Hillary went to him and got down on her hands and knees.

"See, there's a stain here just like the one at the foot of the stairs."

She shone the flashlight on the crack, got down close, looked, and sat back up with a look of stunned confusion. "But, but how can—?"

"That's not blood. It's wood stain. When they renovate

these old houses, they usually sand off the hardwood floors and stain them new."

He looked up at Carly Farrington, who nodded and pointed to the high gloss of the boards in the vestibule. "I just had a new coat of gloss put down."

"But, but—"

"Young lady, you go to your room right now," pronounced her stepmother.

Hillary only glared at her and didn't move.

"Hillary, go to your room," her father said, in a softer, kinder voice. She looked at him with disappointment, then turned and raced up the stairs in tears.

"That girl needs to be sent off somewhere," Tabitha said. "She's crazy."

"Tabby, would you excuse us, please?" Paul said. "I'd like to talk to the sheriff privately."

"Tell him all the things she's claimed to have seen. Tell him about the lights and the bad smells."

"I will tell him, Tabby."

The woman shrugged and stormed off into another room. The man sagged. "I'm sorry you got hauled out here for no reason, Sheriff," he said. "I apologize. If we'd had any idea that Hillary intended to go report... She went to bed last night after I showed her there was no body, and I thought it was over. She seemed fine." He paused. "But then, I think she'd had quite a bit to drink."

"Drink?"

He sighed. "Hillary's a handful, okay? As you surely picked up on, Tabitha is not her birth mother. Her mother and I divorced seven years ago, and I married Tabby. We have three small children. And until about six months ago, Hillary lived with her mother, and I had visitation rights. I was always there, never missed spending time with her. Came home early from business trips just so... And every time I went to see her, the house was in absolute chaos. Where she lived was such—"

He held up his hand. "I don't mean to claim that Valerie is a drug addict or anything like that. She's just too scattered and self-absorbed to take care of a child. Hillary practically raised herself. When she's with her mother, she does whatever she wants. There's no discipline. She could drink openly in front of her mother, and Valerie would smile and say it was just part of growing up.

The man began to pace.

"I finally went to court and fought for custody. It was ugly, but finally the judge granted me temporary custody for six months. And Hillary's the reason we're here." He gestured around at the big house. When he continued, he spoke softer. "I convinced Tabby that it would be good for the littles — that's what we call the younger children — that it would be good for the littles to come and spend a few months in the mountains. But the real reason was Hillary. I had to get her out of that environment."

He rubbed his hands over the top of his head and seemed only then to realize he'd been pacing and stopped in front of Mitch.

There was no more anger, just an anguished look on his face.

"This is my last shot. She's sixteen years old. If I lose her now, she's gone forever. And not just she's gone as my daughter or our relationship is gone. If she goes back to live with her mother, she'll be into drugs. She'll be into sex. She'll be into whatever she chooses to be into. I've got six months to try to turn that kid around."

He shook his head. "I never dreamed she would come up with something like this. I guess I wasn't prepared enough for how badly she wanted to stay where she was."

"She's a sixteen-year-old kid," Mitch said. "Their lives revolve around hanging out with their friends."

"I didn't realize how bad... Hillary has done everything she can think of to spoil our time here and to get me to send her back to her mother."

"Like what?" Mitch said.

"She keeps making up stories, scaring the littles. She says she sees lights. She sees ghosts. When she learned this was a 'haunted house,' I think she actually bought in, believed it. I'm not sure she's lying. I think maybe she really does see... If she can scare the littles into not wanting to be here, then we'll all leave. Or if she can make us mad enough with all her insane claims, maybe we'll send her back. At least I guess that's her plan."

The man shrugged. He tried to smile but couldn't pull it off. "But you didn't need to get dragged into this, Sheriff. I'm really, really sorry."

Mitch stood for a moment in thought. "You know, either your daughter deserves an Oscar for her performance, or she really did believe there was a dead body here. All of her bluff and bluster aside, the reason I came was that I've got a pretty sensitive bullshit meter. And whatever else she might be, she seemed sincere to me."

The man sighed even heavier then. "She sure did last night when she came running into our bedroom. She was hysterical, throwing herself on the bed, screaming there was a dead body at the foot of the stairs and blood everywhere. She had me about half convinced there was."

"So you came to investigate?"

"Of course, I did. There was no body. No blood. She must have made it up or hallucinated. Maybe she's taking drugs. We thought we got rid of everything. She had stashes of I don't even know what in her bedroom in Nashville and we cleared it all out. But I suppose we could have missed something. We haven't been here long enough and she doesn't know anybody, so she couldn't have gotten new drugs here."

"I wouldn't bet the rent on that," Mitch said. "When I was a camp counselor years ago, you'd bring in two or three busloads of kids from different cities, and it was scary how quick the drug kids found the other drug kids. I never knew what it was they saw, and I tried to figure it out. Maybe Hillary has hooked up with somebody here who's supplying her drugs. Hallucinogens maybe."

The man sighed. "Maybe so. It seems preposterous to me. She hasn't gone anywhere. She doesn't know anyone. She hasn't seen anybody."

"But she managed to hook a ride into town with the landscaper," Mitch said. He didn't mention that he noticed the scruffy-looking man when he and Hillary drove up the driveway, the man who'd turned his back and walked away when he saw Mitch and the cruiser.

"Yep, she's a pretty resourceful kid." He shook his head, clearly flummoxed. "Again, I'm really sorry that she hauled you into the middle of our family drama."

Mitch held out his hand. "It was good to meet you, Mr. Schofield. And I wish you luck with your daughter. If you ever need my help, give me a call."

"I'll do that, Sheriff."

Chapter Seven

RILEIGH HEARD THE CRUNCH OF TIRES ON GRAVEL AS someone pulled up in front of the house.

"You can start dishing out the goulash, Mama," Rileigh called into the kitchen. "Mitch is here."

Then she went down the stairs to greet him as he came in. Mama came out from the kitchen as well. Jillian was still upstairs in her studio, but they'd call her when it was time to eat. Mama, of course, hugged Mitch in the basic greeting hug of all Southerners, and Rileigh could do no more than that, though she wanted to hug him and pretty much hang on, she simply smiled up into his face. God, he looked good.

"Well, I want to hear all about the dead body," she started.

"Can we talk about something else in this house besides dead bodies?" Mama said as they followed her into the kitchen

"What is that I smell?" Mitch said.

"It's Hungarian goulash," Mama said. "I don't know

nobody Hungarian so I ain't got nobody to ask if I done it right. But if it tastes good, guess that don't matter."

She went to the stove and stirred the pot, where steam and a glorious mouth-watering aroma rose into the air.

"If it's good, I'm going to take some to the Dalai Lama," Mama said, and Rileigh saw Mitch almost choke at the mention of the Dalai Lama. Rileigh didn't even know Mama knew who the Dalai Lama was or if there even was such a person. She couldn't figure out where she'd chanced upon it, but Mama had latched onto the name and the thought and had yesterday gone to Red Eye Gravy while Rileigh grocery shopped and pronounced when she came out that she'd spent a wonderful time talking to the Dalai Lama there.

Rileigh could see Mitch struggling to keep a straight face when he asked, "So the Dalai Lama likes Hungarian goulash, does he?"

"Now how would I know a thing like that? I just told him I was going to make it. He said to bring him some and he'd see if he liked it. Maybe he don't like it at all. Them monks eat strange things."

Jillian came into the room then and went to the sink to wash her hands.

"Hello, Mitch." She held out her paint-splattered hands as an explanation for why she didn't hug him.

"Come on Mitch, I want to hear about the dead body," Rileigh said.

Jillian turned around. "Rileigh said you were investigating a dead body at Old Shaggy."

"Turns out, there was no dead body," Mitch said.

As Mama set out big bowls and spoons and looked in on the cornbread she had just put in the oven, Rileigh said, "Come on, just tell us the story."

"There's nothing to tell. A teenage girl named Hillary

Schofield barged into my office this morning, demanding that I come with her because there was a dead body at the foot of the stairs at Shagbark Manor. When I pressed her on it, she admitted the dead body wasn't there anymore, but she could prove there'd been one there last night. She had also mentioned that she rode into town with Ryerson's lawn service."

"She what?" Rileigh asked. Ryerson's lawn service did groundskeeping for houses all over Yarmouth County, most of them rentals where tourists came and spent a week during the summer. It was run by two brothers, Charlie and Pete Ryerson. There had been complaints about them now and then that they had worked at a house and tools were missing out of the garage when they left, things like that. Nothing was ever proven, but Mitch thought that they were not the most trustworthy of people, and he didn't like the idea of the teenage girl riding into town with them.

"Her father went down to check and there was no body."

"So why did she come to you today?" Rileigh asked.

"Because she went downstairs the next morning and thought she saw blood between the boards and the hardwood floor."

"And was there?"

"No, it wasn't blood. There was a brown stain, but it was the flooring stain."

"And her parents let her come back."

"Her parents didn't let her do anything," Mitch said. "They were more than a little upset with the kid for bothering the sheriff."

Mitch took his usual spot at the table. Rileigh and Jillian sat down, while Mama ladled out steaming bowls full of goulash and set them in front of each place. Mitch and Rileigh and Jillian didn't like that Mama waited on them, but it was the order of the universe, unchallengeable, sacrosanct. Then Mama put on two mittens and opened the oven door, and the aroma of warm cornbread filled the kitchen. She pulled out the tray, set it on the countertop, cut big hunks of the cornbread for each of them, and set it all on the table beside a dish of fresh churned butter.

Mitch took one bite of the soup and almost spit it back out, it was so hot. "I *think* that was wonderful," he said, "but it's hard to tell with a burned tongue."

"Blow on it," Mama said as she sat down to her own bowl and demonstrated as if Mitch couldn't figure out how to blow on a spoonful of hot liquid to cool it off.

"Tell me about Shagbark Manor, Mama," Mitch said as he slathered butter on his piece of cornbread and watched it melt and soak in. "What's the story on that place?"

"Which story?" Mama said. "There's dozens of 'em."

"Stories about what?"

"All kinda strange things. Folks seeing ghosts and such flying around in there, people disappearing without a trace, things like that. You know how people talk, exaggerate things."

"No, I mean the original story, whatever happened that made people think it was haunted."

"Axe murders was what happened. Nothing like a bloody axe murder to churn up stories about ghosts."

"Somebody was murdered with an axe in the house?"

"More'n one somebody. A whole family — the mama, papa, and two little girls was kilt. Well, not the whole family. One little girl, the youngest, musta been five or six years old, survived — Jocelyn Farrington. The woman who's the housekeeper there now — Carly, I think her name is — that little girl who survived grew up to be Carly's Grandma Josie."

"Grandma Josie's who turned the place into a bed and breakfast, made a business out of it years ago," Rileigh added.

"A whole family killed by an axe murderer..." Mitch said. "That'll preach."

"Oh, it preached all right," Mama agreed. "And ain't nobody sure who done it neither, but there's all kinda theories about it. That got everybody's tongues to waggin'."

"They never found the murderer? What happened?"

"That kind of depends on who you talk to, but the best I remember it, them little girls was dressed for bed, in their nightgowns. The parents musta still been up when it happened. Somebody, don't nobody know who, went into that house and for reasons that I also don't know, decided to take an axe and kill the whole family, and they come close to doing just that."

Mitch almost choked. "Seriously?"

"Well, that's *one* of the versions of what happened," Mama said. The took a big bite of her cornbread and frowned. "Needs more salt."

Mama never measured anything. It wasn't a half teaspoon of this or a full tablespoon of that. She just put ingredients in the way she'd been doing it for 50 years and it always came out the same. That's why cooking through the cookbook was an adventure. She was making things she'd never made before, had to buy new ingredients she'd never cooked with and follow the directions in the recipes.

Rileigh had been certain she wouldn't be able to do it, that whatever she cooked would be inedible. But the chicken parmesan she made night before last and the meatloaf she made for Sunday dinner were delicious, and this goulash smelled wonderful. If there was one thing you could aways count on about Mama, it was that there was absolutely nothing you could always count on.

Mitch was shaking his head. "I can't believe they never caught the killer."

"Might be that was because the killer was already dead."

"Huh?"

"The way I hear it, their papa come home from somewhere and musta found a killer with an axe chasing his little girls around the house, hacking at 'em, and when their mama tried to protect them, she got all hacked up her own self, hacked all to pieces. Course if that's what happened, why wasn't the two of them able to stop the killer? Less maybe Papa was the killer."

"How could Papa be the killer if he was killed, too?"

"I said their Papa *died*, but might be it was something else that killed him."

"His whole family was chopped up with an axe, but *he* died of something else?"

Mama shrugged. "I never said the stories made any sense, but that's what people said. The papa's name was something strange. Last name was Tillman, but it was like Crawford Tillman or something like that, and the mama, I don't remember her name, but she died, too, and wasn't no doubt getting hacked up is what killed her, wasn't hardly nothing left of her." Mama took another bite of goulash. "That there tastes good even if I do say so my own self."

"So, the youngest little girl, Carly Farrington's grandmother, wasn't home at the time?"

"She was home alright, she just didn't get hacked up like everybody else in the family. Folks figure she musta hid somehow, seen what happened, though, but she didn't remember none of it afterwards, which I am sure is a blessing."

Jillian and Rileigh exchanged a look, knowing full well that being unable to remember a bad thing was in itself a bad thing. And Dr. Al Masri, Jillian's psychiatrist, would definitely agree.

"I went to school with Carly," Rileigh said, "but I haven't seen her in years. You must have met her when you took that teenager back to Old Shaggy to her parents."

"Yeah, I walked in on a family feud," Mitch said.

Rileigh looked at him quizzically. "What were her parents fighting about?"

"Oh, it wasn't her parents who were going at each other. When I came in, Carly Farrington was in a knock-down, drag out battle with two other women whom I'm assuming were her sisters."

"Nothing like a good catfight," Mama said.

"If I hadn't been there, I'm sure at least one of them would have turned violent."

"What were they fighting over?"

"The gist of it, I think, is that the two older sisters wanted Carly to agree to sell Shagbark Manor. Apparently, they had reached some agreement that they were going to sell it, and then Carly backed out and they were pissed about it. How did she come to be running the place?"

"Carly's mama was Jocelyn's daughter Sarah, who got killed in a car wreck when Carly was just a little bitty thing, six or seven years old. Both her parents was in the car. That's when she and her sisters — they was a lot older than her, best I remember — came to Shagbark Manor to live with their Grandma Josie. And Carly helped Grandma Josie with the bed and breakfast till Grandma Josie died, and now she's running it."

"She wouldn't be if her sisters had anything to say about it," Mitch said.

"The annual Bluegrass Festival is in Gatlinburg next

week," Mama said excitedly. If you weren't careful, you'd get mental whiplash trying to follow Mama's shifting train of thought. "Me and Mildred already made plans to go." There was little in life that Mama liked better than bluegrass.

They finished lunch. Mama and Jillian insisted on doing the dishes, while Rileigh walked Mitch back out to his cruiser.

"You certainly had a more exciting day than I did," she said. He was walking by her side down the sidewalk and she felt like he was about to take her hand, but he never did. He opened the car door and turned, stunned her by taking her into his arms and kissing her. She was flabbergasted, so shocked that she almost didn't respond. Well, it took her a second or two before she did, and then she melted into his arms like that butter on hot cornbread. When he finally pulled back, he looked down into her face.

"I've been wanting to do that for six months."

"That's about how long I've been wanting you to," Rileigh said.

Mitch got in his car and drove away, and Rileigh floated on a cloud back into the house.

Chapter Eight

MADISON MONTGOMERY AND HILLARY SCHOFIELD HAD been besties for years. It would have ripped Hillary's guts out to leave Nashville and Madison if things had been the way they used to be between them. But Madison booed up with Lucas and they were getting it on hot and heavy all the time, and Hillary almost never saw her anymore. She was surprised when Madison answered. She almost always screened her calls and only took the ones she wanted. Apparently, she wanted to talk to Hillary.

"Hey, Hills, how's it going?"

"I hate it here."

"That's what you said the last time I talked to you. I thought things would be better by now."

"How in the hell can they be better? It's miserable. I just want to scream. I want to run around in circles and jump up and down and…"

"Tell me what's going on," Madison said.

Hillary paused. She told her parents all the strange things she'd seen and her parents had blown her off, culminated in them telling her she really didn't see the dead body at the foot of the stairs that she was a thousand percent certain she *did* see. But she hadn't told anybody else about the other things. Would Madison think she was cracking up?

Well, she had to tell somebody. *Somebody* had to believe her.

"This is the creepiest place you've ever seen in your life. There are shutters on the windows, and they rattle even when there's no wind outside."

"So?"

"That's not the worst of it. The other day I walked past the china cabinet, and all the china was broken."

"What do you mean broken?"

"How many things can broken mean? I mean it was all shattered. There were pieces of bowls and plates and cups. Everything was broken. And I knew who did it. It had to be Sam or Sage — more like the dynamic duo working together. So I went looking for them, little idiots pull something like that and they best go fess up before they get caught. I dragged them both back into the house, and..."

"And what?"

"The dishes weren't broken anymore."

"What?"

"I said they weren't broken anymore."

"You mean you were mistaken, they never were broken in the first place?"

"No, I didn't say that. They *were* broken in the first place. But then..."

"Then what?

"Then they... I don't know, maybe Tabby found them like that and replaced them."

Hillary realized how crazy that sounded and for the first time since she got here, she faced the stark reality that her parents were not crazy for not believing her. She could tell Madison didn't believe her, either. So where did that leave Hillary? She had seen the crazy things she'd seen. She knew she had. But no one else saw what she saw... what did *that* mean?

"So are you sure about that?" Madison asked.

"Biblically sure, I swear. And there's other creepy things like... there was a door. I found this door and it opened, but all that was behind it was a brick wall."

"As old as that place is... what did you say? A hundred and twenty-five years? Who knows how many times it's been renovated. Stuff like that happens when you renovate a house."

"And at night, the floors creak like somebody's walking on them. But there's nobody there."

"Hillary, old houses *always* creak. My grandmother's house moans and groans. I'm always afraid it's going to fall in on us. That's just the way old houses are."

Hillary let out a breath. "Well, then there are the smells."

"Smells."

"I walk into the dining room and it smells like cigar smoke. It's choking."

"What's so strange about somebody smoking a cigar in the dining room?"

"Nobody smokes cigars here. Nobody."

"Well, somebody did. Some hired hand or handyman or something. You told me there was a handyman, the guy who hooked you up with the dealer."

"But he wouldn't have been in the dining room."

"You don't know that."

"And the perfume. I go in my bathroom and it smells like perfume. You know I never wear perfume. It gives me a headache. I'm not talking about Bite Me or Vera Wang or Fox in the Flower Bed, either. I'm talking cheap cheesy perfume, the kind fat women in Walmart wear."

"That's the whole point of perfume, isn't it? That it doesn't fade away? That you can keep smelling it for a long time?"

"Sometimes in my bedroom, the stink is so bad I have to leave."

"I thought you said the smell was in the bathroom."

"Not perfume. In the bedroom, it smells like... like *rotting* things. Like a dead dog smell... roadkill. You know how awful that stinks."

"Hillary..." Madison began, paused, then continued, "Hillary, are you listening to yourself? Because if you are, and you're hearing what I'm hearing, you sound delulu."

"There's nothing wrong with me. I just hate it here."

"Have you told your father and"—she sneered—"your stepmother, Jobu Tupaki, about this shit?"

Hillary almost smiled at Madison's reference to the villain in *Everything Everywhere All at Once*.

"I've tried. They don't listen. They never listen. They just blow me off."

"Well, I'm not blowing you off," Madison said. "But I do have to jump off. Lucas is here. We're boutta go to see *Furiosa*, that Mad Max movie. Olivia saw it and she said it was bussin'! Keep it 100."

Hillary sat on the edge of her bed, looking at her phone. She punched favorites. And clicked on Emma. Emma answered on the first ring.

"Hillary. Hey G. How you doing?"

"I'm miserable. That's how I'm doing. RIP me."

"I'm sorry. I'd kill myself if my parents hauled me off into the woods so they could commune with nature. Put me in home school? I'd off myself, no shit."

"The thought has crossed my mind."

"What do you do all day?"

"I wander around this creepy old house where the rooms have names."

"Like 'the kitchen' and 'the bathroom'?"

"No, the guest rooms. There's the Bluebell Room and the Magnolia Room. I'm in the Willow Tree Room. I've looked in them all... and I see things that nobody believes I've seen." But she was becoming leery of talking about the things she'd seen. She didn't want all her friends to think she was delulu, as Madison clearly did. "Oh, I play with the littles a lot and I go for walks in the woods. Listen, I'm sorry. Sam and Sage are into it again. I gotta go. Smell you later, Emma."

Hillary hung up and tried to shake it off, tired of letting the awful live rent free in her head. Leaving her room, she started down the ridiculously long hallway to the stairs... and that's when she saw the letters on the wall. The big blank wall where surely family portraits had once hung. Now, there was nothing on the wall. Except there was. It was written in red like somebody had stuck their finger into a bucket of red paint and wrote with it on the wall. Except it wasn't paint. She knew it wasn't paint. It was blood, dripping. Fresh, hadn't dried.

The words? "You die."

Hillary staggered back and turned to go downstairs to find Dad to come and show him the wall. That's when she looked down and saw the pentagram on the floor in the hallway. It had been etched there in chalk right beneath the bloody words dripping down the walls. She stifled a scream, turned and ran down the stairs, almost tripped at the bottom and dashed into her father's study.

"Dad, you have to come look. Oh, God, Dad, you have to come see."

He looked up from his computer screen, took his glasses off, and rubbed his eyes as if he was really tired.

"Not right now, Hillary. Give me a few. Later, after dinner, maybe."

"No, you have to come *now!*"

"Look at what?" he said.

"There's blood on the walls."

Her words hit her father like a drop of water in hot grease. He father slammed his palm down on his desktop.

"Dammit, Hillary! This is getting really old."

"It's true. Just come and look."

"Like the dead body was true? "

"The dead body was there, too, Dad. It really was. And there's blood on the wall upstairs. Somebody wrote 'You'd die' in blood on the wall and there's a pentagram on the floor."

"Stop it. You sound like a raving lunatic. It won't work, Hillary. We are not going back to Nashville. I am not going to take you back to your mother's house so you can do whatever you want. Drop the act. Pretending to see crazy things in a haunted house is not going to rescue you. You're staying here with us. So just stop it."

Hillary didn't move. "Dad, *please,* you have to help me, because this is real. It really is real."

Her father shook his head and turned back to his computer monitor. Hillary backed out of the room. Could hear the voices of Sam and Sage and Liza squealing as they ran in from outside. And suddenly, it hit her. What an idiot! Go take a damn picture, moron! Then you can prove it.

She turned and raced toward the stairs.

"And where do you think you're running off to?" Tabby said as she came out into the foyer.

"I'm going to take a picture."

"Until you've finished that assignment in geometry, you're not going anywhere."

Hillary rolled her eyes. They had set up something like a mini schoolroom for her with a big computer monitor and everything she needed to take online courses. Hillary hated every second of it. And she ducked out as soon as she could. That geometry assignment was probably still blinking on the monitor.

"I'll go back to it later."

"You come back down those stairs right this minute, young lady."

Tabitha loved to use her size to intimidate. She was a big woman, had played basketball and had a swagger that she could turn on and off like a faucet. When her father was around, she acted positively demure.

Hillary ignored her, turned and started up the stairs.

"I'm talking to you! I told you—"

"I don't give a shit what you told me."

Hillary ran on up the stairs, knowing that Tabitha was at that very moment rushing to tell her father how *his* daughter had disobeyed and been disrespectful. She got to the top of the stairs and pulled her phone out of her pocket, tapped the photo app, took a deep breath and stepped into the hallway. Raising the phone up so she wouldn't have to look at the bloody words for very long...

She stopped. There was nothing on the wall. The blood was gone. The chalk marks of the pentagram on the hardwood floor were gone, too. She stood gawking at what looked normal but shouldn't.

Her father called from downstairs.

"Hillary, come down here. We need to talk."

Hillary Schofield wanted to cry.

Chapter Nine

RILEIGH PULLED UP IN FRONT OF GEORGIA'S, AND THE children playing outside dropped what they were doing and flocked to her car. Rileigh loved watching them come running. She loved the kids, of course, all of them, but she had a special place in her heart for little Mason, who had saved her life by being disobedient, but that's just how he rolled.

"Aunt Rileigh!" cried Eli and Liam.

Mason flung himself at her, grabbed her around one leg, and told her passionately, "I wuv you, Aunt Wiley."

Even Mayella was playing outside. She didn't often play outside because she liked being in the house, close to her source of bananas, of course. The only little girl in the herd of rowdy boys hugged her too.

"You bwing May-May nanas?"

"Well, Mayella, as a matter of fact," Rileigh said. She closed the car door and then turned and opened the back door, picked up the grocery sack off the seat, and headed into the house with it, Mayella nipping around her heels like a dog at feeding time.

The boys went back to playing outside. Rileigh knocked, opened the screen door, and called in, "It's me, Georgia."

"In the kitchen."

Rileigh took the grocery bag and Mayella into the kitchen and found Georgia sitting at the table with a cup of half-drunk coffee in front of her. She looked exhausted.

Rileigh pulled the bunch of bananas out of the grocery sack that she had brought of items Georgia meant to pick up in town but forgot, or items Rileigh thought she would remember that she needed right after Rileigh left.

Peeling a banana, Rileigh handed it to a gloriously happy Mayella, then sat down beside Georgia.

"You look like death on a cracker," she said.

Georgia looked at her and grimaced. "You're ugly and your mama dresses you funny," she responded, which was their response as children to all insults.

"I didn't mean that as an insult, just an observation."

"An accurate one. I not only look like death on a cracker, I feel twice as bad, which, I suppose, is double-dead on a cracker."

"Or dead squared. How come?"

"Haven't been sleeping well lately."

"Something wrong?"

"No."

Rileigh leaned back in her chair. "Oh, that is so *not* a no I believe," she said. "Want to try again?"

"Okay, I've been having nightmares."

Rileigh looked surprised. "I didn't know you had nightmares."

"Actually, I had nightmares when I was a kid."

"Well, if you told me about them, I don't remember."

"I started having nightmares the summer you and mama went visiting all the national parks in the country, right before she became the manager of the visitor center at the park."

"The park" being the Great Smoky Mountains National Park. Rileigh's mother started out working in the Cade's Cove Visitor's Center there, and gradually moved up the ladder. Oconaluftee, Clingmans Dome, and finally at the biggest one, Sugarlands. Eventually, she ran the whole Backcountry Information Office for the park, which issued permits for all manner of activities. If you wanted to get married in the park, or scatter Uncle Herbert's ashes there, go fishing or spelunking or stage a war protest, Lily Bishop had to issue a permit for it.

"I remember that summer," Rileigh said, smiling, and leaned back in her chair. "It was one of the best summers of my life. We went to Yosemite. We went to Glacier National Park. We went to the Grand Canyon. We went to everywhere any kid ever wanted to go, and Mama got the red carpet treatment when we got there because she was part of the staff."

"That was not exactly a banner summer in my life," Georgia said grimly.

"How come?"

"Well, duh. You were gone the whole summer. I didn't have anywhere to go, anybody to talk to."

"I'm sorry," Rileigh said.

"I think there's a statute of limitations on apologies. After twenty-five years, they don't count."

"You started having nightmares that summer — why? And what does that have to do with you having nightmares now."

"Well, they started up again — the same dreams I had over and over as a kid — after I picked up Eli and Connor at Vacation Bible School. There were kids in their classes I didn't know. Their last names were Schofield — Sage and

Sam, twins. They were eight, in Eli's class. And a cute little six-year-old named Liza in Connor's class."

"New family in town?"

"Kinda sorta. They're staying at Old Shaggy."

Rileigh perked up and asked, "The people who are staying at Old Shaggy — their names are Schofield?"

"Yeah. How do you know about them?"

"Because Mitch met the sixteen-year-old in that family, Hillary, under rather bizarre circumstances. She came barging into his office and told him there was a dead body at the bottom of the stairs at Shagbark Manor. That got his attention."

"I'll bet it did. Was there a body, or was it just another one of those Old Shaggy hoaxes?"

"Well, there was no body, so I guess she made it up, which qualifies as an official Old Shaggy hoax. Mitch said she didn't like being here and was probably trying to scare her parents so they'd go back home to Nashville."

"Did Mitch meet Carly Farrington? And by the way, do you want a cup of coffee?"

"I'm coffeed out, thanks."

"Good, because we're out of creamer."

"I got you some. It's in the bag."

"I owe you my very *being*!"

"Don't get sloppy. What were you asking about Carly Farrington?"

"Wondered if Mitch met her."

"He did. Got me to thinking about her, remembering her in school — or at least I tried. But I swear I didn't have but about two memories that she was in."

"She showed up sometime during elementary school, right?"

"Yeah, her parents were killed and she came to live with her Grandma Josie. The first day of middle school, I think. She was in line behind me coming back from the lunchroom and Ralph Lott threw up all over her shoes. But that's one of only a couple of memories. She graduated with us. Do you remember her in high school?"

"I remember her as wallpaper," Georgia said. That was the label applied to all the quiet, introverted, shy teenagers who merely formed a backdrop for the big shot loudmouths — more kindly described as extroverts. Like Georgia and Rileigh. "I remember her in some crowd scenes. She was in the choir, wasn't she?"

"How would you know? You weren't in the choir."

"I seem to remember her standing up there singing at assemblies. Do you remember that?"

Rileigh nodded her head. "The one thing about Carly Farrington you couldn't miss was that blonde hair, long and straight, down to her waist. So if she was in a group, you could spot her."

"And then after high school, she became wallpaper in town," Georgia said. "You went off to the army, so you don't remember. But I saw her now and then in the grocery store, either shopping with Grandma Josie or for Grandma Josie. I don't think she ever left Old Shaggy. Carly just went to work there helping her grandmother run the place, and then took it over when Grandma Josie died."

Georgia shook her head. "I do remember, or at least I seem to... that Old Shaggy got more and more prominent over the years, and I believe that in her own quiet way, Carly was a marketer. She glommed onto the 'haunted house' schtick of Old Shaggy and ran with it. Like the people in Roswell, New Mexico did with aliens."

Rileigh smiled, remembering the only time she'd ever been there — the flat, featureless expanse of prairie. She had been surprised by how the people in Roswell had taken their own lemon and made it into lemonade. Suspected of being the one place Martians or other alien life forms had landed on Earth—and the government had kept it secret—Area 51 near Roswell became infamous. Or maybe the aliens were supposed to still be alive there. Or there was still a spaceship under wraps there, or maybe there were just dead aliens floating in formaldehyde. But whatever it was, Roswell embraced the notoriety. They painted aliens on their park benches and the benches inside bus shelters. They advertised alien burgers at Hardee's and on the sign out front of the grocery store — alien tomatoes on sale.

"It's not like I ever talked to Carly about it," Georgia said. "It's just — I noticed. Ads in the paper and brochures that played up the haunted house, axe murders theme that I think Grandma Josie always tried to downplay. Years ago, it was just one of dozens of B&Bs in the county. Now, it's the most famous one of all. Sure, COVID sank a lot of the others, but I always see cars parked out front."

"Well, there will be only the cars of the Schofield family parked at Old Shaggy for the next six months."

"Six months?"

"Yep, that's what Mitch said. He said the family was going to stay there until Christmas."

"Good god. No wonder the sixteen-year-old is losing her mind."

Chapter Ten

After finding the dead body at the foot of the stairs, Hillary Schofield stopped drinking. She stopped doing edibles, stopped everything else, too. *Something* was making her see things nobody else could. What other explanation was there? Was she supposed to believe there really were ghosts in the damned house? That was crazy. No, maybe what was crazy ... was Hillary.

She spent as much time as she could with the littles, because they kept her grounded, anchored to reality. She hated her stepmother, Tabitha, but her hatred did not in any way diminish her love for the little babies that the woman had brought into her life. She had loved playing mama to them whenever she had the chance during her visitations with her father. She pretended Sage and Sam, the eight-year-old twins, were her babies, and she rocked them and fed them and changed their diapers — loved them unreservedly, even though their mother was a monster. And Liza, who was six, had Hillary wrapped around her little finger. The child was so adorable, big, wide, brown eyes, and at six, no teeth in front, so everything she said was a lisp. Hillary found she could be glad to be in the mountains just for the littles because they adored it. Every morning, they would run out and play in the creek. Who gets to play in a creek in Nashville? Sam caught frogs and chased Sage around the yard with them. Hillary had to sit down with both children and make sure that Sage wasn't afraid of the frogs in some ridiculous female way and that Sam wasn't being "toxically masculine" by poking them at her. Turns out Sage wasn't afraid, just grossed out by them. With their big eyes bulging out, she thought they looked like roadkill.

Hillary took the children on long walks in the woods. She had a book of plant identifications that she got at the Welcome Center at the Great Smoky Mountains National Park and they would try to figure out what kind of tree they were looking at, or what kind of wildflower they had found.

It was delicious time, but she couldn't spend every moment with the children. And whenever she was by herself, she was circling the drain, every moment tensed for a blow. And while the blows didn't come every moment, they came often enough to stagger her.

Hillary came into the house from outside where the kids had made a full kitchen with Tabitha's pots and pans and were cooking up all manner of mud dishes. She was on her way upstairs because Monster Woman, the bitch of the universe, had flown in on her broomstick to where the children were playing and, of course, had to spoil everything for everybody. That was her *job*, and she ate and left no crumbs.

She was going to make the children go inside because Liza was getting her good shoes muddy until Hillary volunteered to go upstairs and get Liza's plastic minion flip-flops that had cost $1.98 at some souvenir store.

There was a front staircase and a back staircase connecting the three floors of the house. The whole front part of the third floor was closed off. The housekeeper, the little shadow of a person Hillary saw now and then doing some kind of domestic task or cooking something, lived in that portion of the third floor. Hillary almost never saw her because Hillary never got up for breakfast, and that was the only meal the woman provided to the family.

As she went up to the second floor, Hillary heard a sound and paused. It was the sound of a violin playing and seemed to be coming from that back staircase from the second to the third floor. She supposed that maybe the woman, the housekeeper, Carly Whatever-her-last-name-was, had some music playing, but it didn't sound like taped music. It sounded like somebody was actually playing a violin. Then she realized it couldn't be Carly, because Hillary'd seen her as she walked out the house and to the garden to pick tomatoes.

Hillary walked slowly to the back stairs entrance and looked up. That was a mistake. She should have let well enough alone. She should have turned around as soon as she heard the sound rather than going to investigate, like all those idiots in slasher movies. But had to see what it was. And when she did, she was sorry. Floating in the air in the stairwell was a violin, and it was playing the most beautiful music Hillary had ever heard. She stood transfixed in wonder; horrified at the same time, horrified down to the marrow of her bones - because that violin was there and the music it was playing was real.

Then the bow held by an invisible hand lifted off the strings and hung suspended above the instrument for a second, maybe two. When the bow came back down on the violin, the sound it made was so different that Hillary covered up her ears — terrible squawking, raucous

65

screeches, awful sounds. With her hands over her ears, she ran back down the hall to the littles' bedroom to get the flip-flops for six-year-old Liza.

She could hear the squawking still, but it was muffled by a kind of roaring sound in her ears that grew louder and louder. She didn't look right or left, just picked up the shoes and went back out into the hallway and started to go down the stairs. That's when she saw the red dress. There was a rack of coat hooks at the top of the stairs on the other side of the wall, and a dress was hanging on one of the hooks. It wasn't a dress she'd ever seen. It was too big to have fit Liza, even too big for Sage, but it was too small to have fit Hillary.

She looked at the dress and cocked her head to the side. The roaring sound had grown louder and louder, and now it was the rumble of a waterfall. As she watched, the dress slowly lifted off the hook. It hung limp in the air, then slowly got plumper, as if there was a body inside that you couldn't see. Then the dress began to dance. It moved and flitted in the air to the tune the violin had begun to play. It was no longer making raucous sounds in the stairwell, but beautiful waltz music. And so the red dress danced to the waltz music, spinning so that the shiny taffeta fabric spun out away from the invisible legs of the invisible person dancing, making a big fan of swirling color.

She stared at the dress and then forced herself to close her eyes, squeeze them tight shut, then opened them to look at the floor. She refused to hear the music that she could hear, which was growing louder even with the roaring in her ears. She refused to turn and look at the red dress on the invisible body dancing in the air. Clutching the plastic flip-flops she was taking down to Liza so tight in her fingers they were cutting into her palms, she walked slowly — not fast, *slowly*, she didn't run — down the stairs, refusing to acknowledge that she'd seen anything. When she got to the bottom of the stairs, her father was coming out of his office. And he smiled at her.

"Having a good day, sweetheart?" She looked at him as if he'd lost his mind. "I saw you out playing with the littles in the mud."

He approached her with a kind smile on his face.

"I know you don't remember this, but when you were a little girl, five or six, maybe, I used to make mud pies with you. It's not like we lived in a place with a lot of dirt to make mud pies with. We lived in an apartment building on the fifth floor. You remember? That place on Fort Couch Road? Everything was asphalt and concrete. But one day when your mama wasn't home — because she didn't like to clean you up when you got dirty — I took you by the hand and we went down in the elevator out to the court-yard and dug dirt out from under the lone tree in the courtyard. We put it in a bowl, added some water, and stirred. Do you remember that?"

Hillary had heard everything he said, but she'd had to concentrate because what he said was coming from some great distance through a roaring in her ears and the sound of the violin. She looked at him blankly.

"Daddy, do you hear music?"

"No, why? Did you leave some playing upstairs?"

"No, I mean an instrument, a violin."

"Are you asking me if I hear a violin playing?"

She saw the confusion in his eyes and that was answer enough.

"Nothing, I just…"

"Are you all right, beanie girl?" He reached out his hand and cupped her cheek. "You'll always be my little beanie girl, you remember that?"

She did remember that. He always called her beanie

girl because one day he had brought home a bag of jelly-beans and she had eaten almost all of them, smeared the colors around her mouth, and on her fingers… and then threw up most of the night.

"Yeah, Daddy," she said softly, "I remember being beanie girl."

He glanced in the direction of the door that led outside to where he could hear the kids playing.

"Sage doesn't like jellybeans. Did you know that?"

"No, Daddy, I didn't know that."

"I tried and I tried with Liza, too, and she likes jelly-beans, but only the licorice ones that turn her tongue black."

Hillary realized how hard her father was trying to be kind, trying to relate to her, and she might have responded. She almost dropped the façade — the angry, narcissistic, snotty teenager. If only she could have heard his words without that roaring in her head.

She looked down at the shoes in her hand and told her father, "I went to get these for Liza. She needs them. She's making a mess of her shoes."

She started to turn, and he touched her arm.

"You didn't answer my question, sweetheart."

"What question?"

"Are you all right?"

She looked up into his eyes and wanted so desperately to be Daddy's little beanie girl living in a world where nothing was wrong.

"No, Daddy, I'm not all right. I'm not all right at all."

Chapter Eleven

RILEIGH WAS PUTTING ON HER MAKEUP IN FRONT OF A makeup mirror in her bathroom when she spied Jillian, standing in the doorway, leaning on the door jamb.

"Do you remember my senior prom?" Jillian asked.

"No, I don't think so," Rileigh said. "I would have been, what, six years old?"

"Well, if you did remember," Jillian said, stepping into the room, "you would recall that you came and stood in the bathroom and watched me put on my makeup and you wanted to know why I was painting my face. And I said I wasn't painting my face, I was putting on makeup and you said it looked like paint to you."

Rileigh stopped what she was doing and grinned at Jillian. "Are you making this up?"

Jillian made a cross sign over her heart and held up two fingers. "If I'm lyin', I'm dyin'."

"So I thought you were painting your face?"

"Oh, it gets worse than that. You said that in kindergarten, you were learning about Native Americans and the teacher said they painted marks on their faces before they went on 'the warpath,' and you didn't know what a warpath was, but you wanted to know if I was about to go on one."

Rileigh had turned back around to face the mirror. "You're making that shit up. I don't believe a word of it."

"Seriously, you said that."

"If I did, I must have been a very entertaining child."

Jillian barked out a laugh. "You were a lot of things as a child, and entertaining was definitely one of them."

The sisters settled into companionable silence.

"There are all kinds of questions buzzing around in your head, but you're too polite to ask them," Rileigh started.

Jillian cut her off. "No, not too polite, just..." She paused. "Okay, too polite."

"Well, I'll tell you what I do know. I found out from Georgia that Ruth Chris Steakhouse was where her father took her mother on their 50th wedding anniversary. And according to Georgia, her mother had better food that night than in all the other forty-nine years of anniversary dinners leading up to it."

Rileigh put down a powder brush.

"I wear makeup so seldom that when I do, I always wind up putting on too much. Is this too much?" She turned around and let Jillian inspect.

"All there is, is a little... what? Blush, eyeliner, and mascara. I think you need some eyeshadow."

"Eyeshadow? What color?"

"Well, duh. Green. Here, let me help you."

Jillian dug around in Rileigh's drawer until she found the palette of twenty-four different eyeshadow shades, opened it up, and wiped a little on the tip end of the sponge brush. "Close your eyes."

Rileigh obediently closed her eyes. Jillian dotted some

green eyeshadow above her eyeliner and mascara and then gently blended it in.

"Okay, turn around. See what you think."

Rileigh turned around to the mirror. "Oh my, I like that," she said. "Mitch will like it. He likes everything that makes my eyes look green."

Rileigh had naturally curly hair and it was cut short. She could hop out of the shower, shake her head and go as soon as it dried into curls. But it had been cut in a style that her mother had called Mary Lou Retton, like Rileigh would know who that was. Rileigh Googled the Olympic figure skater and noted how her hair instantly fell back into place again after a spin or turn. To make her hair do that tonight, Rileigh had to blow it dry over a hairbrush to straighten some of the curl out. She had done that after her shower, and now she whipped her head back and forth to watch the chestnut hair fall back into place.

Jillian stepped back and looked at her younger sister. "You look gorgeous."

"I'll settle for at least pretty so people don't look at Mitch and me as a couple and wonder what he sees in me."

"Not a chance of that happening, sweetheart," Jillian said. "Not a chance."

Rileigh had considered staying upstairs in her bedroom so that she could make a grand entrance down the staircase when Mitch arrived, as she had accidentally done the night of their first 'big date' — aborted when the restaurant where they'd had reservations burned down. Bahama Mama's had never built back, and she and Mitch had ended up in the diner called Red Eye Gravy, their evening capped off with a dead body.

They were going to Knoxville tonight. No chance of an interruption.

She considered gliding down the stairs just as he came in the front door tonight. But this time she'd be calculated, and it had been an accidental Kodak moment before.

She examined her fingernails. Bright red, not some ridiculous silver or orange or purple-striped color. Fingernails and toenails should be red if you painted them at all, and she never did. So should lipstick, and she never wore that either, but she had that on tonight.

Mama let out a wolf whistle when Rileigh walked into the kitchen, balancing well, she thought, on her high heels and praying to the Dear Lord not to let her twist her ankle again. She wasn't used to walking in heels, but she didn't feel clumsy, didn't think she looked like a little kid staggering on stilts.

She had examined her body in the full-length mirror after she got out of the shower, and it certainly wasn't the pristine body of some high school teenager on prom night. Rileigh had scars. She'd earned all of them. She had been shot several times. She had had surgery on her shoulder after a bad break, and that had left a scar, as had the bullet wound that almost killed her the night of the last big date fiasco when a waitress, whose name was not Cookie, had come to the house to kill Mama and Rileigh had walked in on it. Rileigh had intended to stop her, of course. Instead, she'd taken a bullet that almost killed her. It had been Jillian who had stopped her, had killed her with one shot.

Rileigh had reminded herself as she stood in that steamy bathroom looking at her reflection that Mitch had seen what she looked like with no clothes on before — the day he had stripped all of her clothes off when he found her on the riverbank suffering from hypothermia.

She stopped, one thought coming to such an abrupt halt that all the thoughts behind it slammed into it and then fell over on their sides, derailed. She was considering how she looked with clothes off in anticipation of a date with Mitch — which meant "Hold onto your shorts, Mildred" — but she was assuming that at some point, she'd take her clothes off.

Yep, that's what she was assuming, alright. And the assumption made her feel warm all over.

Mitch came to the door and knocked while Rileigh was in the kitchen drinking Mama's lemonade. She didn't make the grand entrance down the stairs that she had made before, but he didn't appear to mind. He just smiled at her, and his smile lit up the whole room.

"It's that green dress again," he said, holding his hands in front of his face as if shielding himself from a bright light. "Your eyes look like two emeralds."

"They're not green, Mitch."

"Yes, they are."

"No, they're not. We've had this conversation before. They're hazel."

"Oh, they're definitely green." He held up his hand before she could protest. "Come on, let's get out of here. I'm hungry."

He told Mama and Jillian goodbye and actually took Rileigh's arm, led her down the porch steps and opened her car door

Yeah, this was definitely date behavior. They were going actually going on the big date. It was about damned time.

Chapter Twelve

Sage, Sam, and Liza were bouncing off the walls. Hillary loved seeing how excited they were, and it made her even more indignant that she was grounded. Dad was taking the rest of the fam, the three littles, to see *Despicable Me 4*, which had just come out in the theaters in Gatlinburg. All the Despicable Me movies were fire, but Hillary wouldn't be seeing this one.

"I want to be a minion on Halloween," said Sage.

"Me too," said Sam, and then realized what he'd said. "Wait, no, I don't. I'll be the guy with the pointy nose."

Sam hated the look-alike twin routine his mother put him through so often. He didn't like looking just like his sister. It offended him in some very fundamental way that Hillary could understand and was proud of him for. Sage in a blue skirt and red blouse, walking beside Sam in blue pants and a red shirt, looked absolutely adorable to Tabitha, and it blew right past her that her children, at least one of them, hated it. Sage didn't care one way or the other.

"No, you can be a minion, too, just not the same

minion as me," Sage told Sam, and Hillary realized that apparently the little girl had figured out her brother wasn't into being one piece of a matched set. "The one who has one brown eye and one green eye, you can be that one, and I can be the one that only has one eye in the middle."

Liza bounced up and down.

"We can all free be minions," she lisped through her missing front teeth. "They all look the thame, but they're all different, too."

Hillary leaned against the door frame watching her siblings get more and more excited while Hillary was getting angrier by the minute that she wasn't allowed to go with them. She had been grounded by the Hateful Hag because she had disobeyed when Tabitha had told her to "come back down those stairs right this minute, young lady" and Hillary had said she didn't give a shit what Tabitha had told her. Tabitha had immediately gone to Dad and pleaded her moany-groany case.

Hillary had heard her through the door. "She doesn't respect me and she will never respect me unless you *make* her respect me. If you let her get away with—"

Yada, yada, yada.

Tabitha totally didn't get it. Her father couldn't *make* Hillary respect her. Hell, an act of Congress couldn't make her, a decree from the Pope... the voice of God Almighty speaking out of a burning bush couldn't make Hillary respect her stepmother. There was absolutely nothing there to respect, and absolutely everything to loathe.

Hillary acknowledged she was being totally irrational, but she embraced the paradox of her feelings just the same — she would give *anything* to go back home to Nashville, but she'd be *damned* if she'd let the witch from hell drive her away.

In the end, Dad had caved. He always did. He'd

grounded her so she couldn't go to the movie — like that sacrifice would magically repair her relationship with her stepmother. If that's your plan, this ain't it, chief.

Tabitha had already left the house and wouldn't be home until later tonight. Hair appointment. Riiiiight. What hairdresser fixes your hair at night? Maybe men didn't understand those things, but it was clear to anybody with opposable thumbs that the hairdresser was *not* Tabitha's destination tonight.

What woman takes a shower and puts on perfume to go to her hairdresser? Seriously, Dad.

Hillary said nothing, though — for two reasons. One, because she was afraid her father wouldn't believe her and he would side with Tabitha, and that would break Hillary's heart. And two, sometimes ignorance is bliss. Though she could not understand why on any level, Hillary knew that her father loved her stepmother, and she couldn't bear to hurt him the way it would hurt him to find out that Tabitha Schofield would screw anything in a jock strap.

But then Tabitha had landed a barb as she walked out the door.

"Sorry you're going to miss the movie. You need to learn how to behave or face the consequences."

Hillary couldn't stop herself. "You need to learn how to keep your legs together, or you'll face the consequences."

Tabitha looked like Hillary'd slapped her. And when Hillary saw how devastated she was, she couldn't stop herself.

"You're not going to a hair appointment. You're going to a booty call. I *know*, Tabitha. I saw your texts. And as soon as Dad gets home tonight, I'm going to tell him *everything*."

Tabitha opened and closed her mouth a couple of

times, looked like a fish on the dock gasping for air. Hillary loved it.

The kids came running into the room then and she said nothing, just stalked out the door and slammed it behind her. *That* was worth the price of admission. Why hadn't Hillary thought of it before? She'd never rat Tabitha out to Dad, but Tabitha didn't know that. Hillary had a weapon now.

"I've got a dragon and I'm not afraid to use it," she said aloud in her best Eddie Murphy imitation.

Liza cried, "That's what Donkey said in *Shrek*!"

Hillary smiled.

"It sure is, sweetheart. It sure is."

Hillary stood at the front door and watched her father drive away with the kids, closed the door, and turned back around in the foyer. She looked up the big staircase, at all the grandeur, and tried to figure out what kind of person would build a place like this *to live in*. She shook her head. She was a minimalist, and this kind of opulence actually made her teeth throb. She went quickly up the stairs to her bedroom and slammed the door behind her without looking from side to side. She had learned that sometimes she saw things out the corner of her eye, but when she turned around to face them, they were gone. And such sightings were unnerving.

She went to her closet, took out her pair of snow boots, and removed the vodka bottle from one of them and the bottle of 7-Up from the other. She took them to the bathroom and mixed herself a drink in the bathroom glass.

Yeah, she had sworn off alcohol, drugs, even weed in an effort to figure out what was making her see *mysterious* things that weren't there. Well, all those mysterious things were outside her room, and she planned to stay inside her room all night watching movies on her iPad.

An hour later, Hillary was well on her way to being drunk… so drunk, in fact that she'd pulled up the list app on her phone to record every possible synonym for being sloshed — no fair using the thesaurus — in an effort to take her mind off *why*.

Hammered, wasted, plastered, smashed, tanked, trashed … what else?

It was hard to think.

Bombed. Ripped. Wasn't drunk in England called getting pissed?

It wasn't working. Listing words for drunk was not distracting her from dwelling on her situation, and the more she considered it, the angrier she got. Oh yeah, the standard storyline of a stepmother who hated her and was constantly trying to cut her out of her father's life and the overlay of being stuck out in the middle of nowhere when her friends were back home in Nashville having a good time — those were enough to make anyone furious.

But Hillary found herself getting angrier and angrier at the damned *house*.

Shagbark Manor *sucked*.

There was some real physical explanation for all the shit she'd seen. There had to be. It occurred to her in her muddled state that maybe the root of all that evil was the same as the root of all the rest of the evil in her life.

Tabitha.

The more she thought about it, the more it made sense. Tabitha was behind all the fake scariness. Of course, she was! She wanted to get rid of Hillary. What better way to do it than to either make Hillary seem crazy or make her father so angry at her he'd send her back to her mother.

That was it.

Well, the bitch was *not* going to get away with it.

Hillary stood up quickly. That was a mistake, because

the room swam around her. She looked down at her drink and realized the glass was empty, so she poured the remainder of the vodka into the glass, skipped the 7-Up entirely, then took a big gulp and shuddered at how awful it tasted.

Unsteady on her feet, Hillary went to the door of her room and out into the big hallway. It was dark outside now, and the sconces on the walls must have 25-watt bulbs in them, or maybe 10-watt if there was such a thing. Why put lights on the walls unless you want them to illuminate the hallway? And if you want to light the hallway, why put teeny tiny little bulbs in the sconces? Another reason to hate Shagbark Manor.

Leaning her head back, she yelled out at the top of her lungs.

"Hey ghosts, come and get me!" She found herself laughing maniacally, sounded like a lunatic. "You think you scare me? Well, you don't. It's a trick. It's all a trick."

She staggered down the hallway with her drink in her hand, shouting as loud as she could. "Whatsamatter? You scared of a little teenage girl? You should be. I'm gonna ruin your life just like you've been ruining mine — I'm going to rat you out! I'm gonna tell Dad *everything*."

She found herself running then, or staggering rapidly, splashing the drink out of her glass. Forcing herself to stop, she took big gulps and finished the drink, then she tossed the glass on the floor and continued her attack. She'd read the brochures and the little self-published book on the "ghost alcove" in the parlor, knew the bullshit tale about an axe murderer attacking a family here, and how the ghosts of that family remained, forever tormented. Made a good story. Now she called on them by name.

"Hey Lenora. You there, Lenora? Come out, come out, wherever you are! Got a bunch of dead little girls, do you?

I'm soooo sorry your precious little ones got their heads chopped off."

The big gulp of vodka hit Hillary hard then, and she had trouble standing. But she stayed upright, kept running up and down the main hallway upstairs, yelling for the ghosts. Taunting them.

"Eee-lizz-abeth! Is that you playing the violin? You suck at it. Sounds like your hands got chopped off."

That struck Hillary as riotously funny, and she laughed so hard she had to lean against the wall for support.

And then she was standing in front of the last door in the hallway, all the way down at the end. The Persimmon room. Hillary remembered when they'd discovered it in their first wandering tour of the house after the family arrived. The bedroom was filled with dolls, dozens and dozens of them, most large and old. They were lying on the bed, sitting on tables, and arranged along the baseboards on the floor and the top of the dresser and the dressing table. Some were baby dolls that spoke a tinny "Mama" when you moved them — lying in a wooden cradle, or wrapped up in soft pink and blue blankets. Others were beautiful dolls with long flowing hair, blonde, black, brown, wearing satin and lace dresses, their angelic faces painted on. She'd reached out and touched the face of a newborn in a pink blanket. Tabby'd said they were called china dolls because their heads were made of porcelain. Then she'd warned Sage and Liza on pain of death not to touch them, that they were fragile and very valuable and had belonged to the three little girls who'd once lived in the house.

The *ghosts'* dolls!

Hillary flung open the door, staggered into the room, picked up a baby doll out of its cradle, and smashed its glass head against the wall. It shattered, sending shards of glass pinging around the room like shrapnel.

"Like your dollies, do you?" she cried out to nobody. "Well, I don't. I think they're as ugly as you are." She swayed and stumbled, caught herself on the bed. "Hey Victoria, E-liz-a-beth, Joc-e-lynn. Yoohoo. Come watch. I'm going to break your precious dolls and...*you... can't... stop... me.*"

She went into a staggering, stumbling frenzy then, picking up dolls and hurling them at the mirror, shattering it, too. She smashed their glass heads on the floor and the bedposts and the furniture, ripped the old fabric of their bodies open with her fingernails and scattered the stuffing until the air was full of a white haze. She grabbed a double armful of them and took them out into the hall, hurling them like hand grenades at the walls. When she got to the top of the stairs, she flung the remaining dolls over the railing to shatter on the floor below, laughing like a lunatic.

Then she found herself downstairs — and Hillary didn't remember going downstairs — in the room with all the books beside the front door, calling for "Vic-torrrr-ia, where are you?"

Things smeared then. Time fell off the rails. Hillary had no idea how long she'd been yelling at the fake ghosts, only knew it must have been a long time because her throat was raw.

Then she found herself slumped on the bottom step of the big staircase, leaning against the railing. Her neck was stiff and her butt numb, so she'd been there for a while. She must have passed out. Did she fall down the stairs? Surely, she'd have remembered falling down the stairs. She tried to rise, the world spun, but she clung to the banister for support to remain upright. She needed to pee, like really bad, and started across the entryway toward the downstairs powder room. She was halfway across the open expanse when she heard a sound behind her. She turned and glanced over her shoulder, and what she saw stopped her cold. Turning slowly around, Hillary stood gaping at the thing.

Someone was dressed for Halloween in a reeeeally bad costume. White — like a little kid in a sheet. It was wearing a Halloween mask — a doll's face, perfect and serene, missing one eye and its nose, with gore oozing down across it from a split-open skull above. To complete the effect, the figure was holding a huge axe with dried brown blood stains on both sides — the axe that had been hanging on the rack above the mantel.

Well, Hillary had Tabitha's number now. She wasn't going to fall for this shit. Spreading her feet apart so she could stand without weaving Hillary announced to the apparition, she said, "You want me? Come and get me."

The creature standing in the doorway made no move.

"I don't know how you're doing it, but I got it figured out." She turned and yelled to the house at large, "I know what's going on. It's all a fake. Shove all these tricks up your ass, Tabitha — they don't work anymore."

The apparition moved toward her then, taking small steps, holding the ridiculous axe. And there was a smell that wafted from the creature. The smell of death maybe, of a crypt, of rotting bodies. Hillary'd had a lot to drink on an empty stomach, and that stink was more than she could stand. She began to gag.

"Get away from me, I'm gonna throw up!"

She turned, staggered to the stairs, but stumbled and face panted on the bottom step. When she turned over, the apparition was standing over her.

"I'm not buying it!" she screamed.

The thing lifted the oversized axe high in the air above

her. At the sight, she felt a cold chill, like ice water was dripping slowly down her spine from one vertebra to the next.

"You broke my dolls," the figure said in a little girl voice.

When Hillary focused, looked into the eyes of the apparition peeking out through the doll mask, she could tell the face inside was smiling. It was all a joke.

"It's not real!" she yelled into the face of the thing holding an axe above her.

She realized she was mistaken when the axe fell and chopped off her left arm. Hillary screamed, *shrieked*, the agony was breathtaking. This couldn't be happening. Blood squirted from the stump of her arm.

"No!" she cried, then the axe fell again, caught her in her right shoulder and tore all the way through it. She heard the *thunk* sound as the axe dug into the wood of the stairs beneath her.

Hillary understood then that she was going to die.

And in those few seconds, while the apparition raised the axe again to come down into her chest, Hillary realized how much she didn't want to die. She was only sixteen years old. She wanted to *live*.

"Please..."

She begged with her eyes, watched in horror as the axe began to fall. Hillary felt the agony of it slicing into her chest and through her heart, but the agony lasted only a moment.

Chapter Thirteen

Rileigh wanted to tell Mitch that she liked his aftershave, but that felt like a cheesy thing to say. She did like it, though. Not that she was a connoisseur of men's cologne. She just knew for lead pipe certain that he didn't wear aftershave or cologne when he was on duty, because she'd sat in this cruiser beside him on many occasions and he had never smelled so good.

"I like that perfume," Mitch said, and Rileigh burst out laughing.

"What's so funny? It smells good. Like flowers. What's it called?"

"A Kiss from a Rose."

"Why did you laugh?"

"Because I was sitting here thinking how much I like the smell of your aftershave."

"Seriously?"

"Yeah, and I didn't say it because I thought it sounded cheesy."

"So that means you think my comment about your perfume is cheesy."

"No. I think it was sweet."

He looked at her and smiled and she melted in a puddle in the front seat.

They had agreed that they would not talk shop. That there would be no mention of dead bodies in any form or fashion. And so they talked music. Mitch liked country music. Rileigh did too, so long as it wasn't what she called yee-haw music, that being music that when you heard the first stanza, you felt an irresistible urge to leap to your feet and yell, "*yee-haw!*"

Mitch's favorite country musician?

"Hard to pick."

"Just one."

He thought. "Okay, Alabama. But right up there at the top — I'm old school, by the way — Nitty Gritty Dirt Band, Charlie Daniels Band, Gatlin Brothers."

"And individuals?" He ticked them off his fingers: Garth Brooks, Reba McEntire, Keith Stapleton, Jason Aldean, Tim McGraw, Faith Hill.

Rileigh broke in. "Tim McGraw and Faith Hill were wonderful in that TV mini-series, *1883!*"

"You saw that?"

"Binge watched the whole series three times. I bet that showed as close as you're likely to get to the way life really was on a wagon train heading west."

Mitch dragged the conversation back to music.

"So you're not a Swifty?"

Rileigh wrinkled her nose.

"Good god, no!"

"What don't you like about Taylor Swift?"

"Everything! Okay, not everything. I just… I am just so sick of her singing about all the men who dumped her or she dumped, lamenting what slime bags they are. I always think, 'Hey sweetheart, if you've been through a dozen different serious relationships before you turn thirty-five, maybe you ought to look in the mirror to figure out why they didn't last. The only constant in those serial breakups is you.'"

She paused. "I mean, if you were Travis Kelce, wouldn't you be counting the days until she dumps you and writes a song about how devastating it was?"

They moved from country music to classic rock, which Mitch also loved, and Rileigh did too. They'd never talked about it before.

"I love the Beatles. I love the Beach Boys, the Eagles, the Rolling Stones. Guns N' Roses, the Grateful Dead. Makes me sound like a boomer, doesn't it?"

"I'm still stuck on trying to picture you as a Deadhead. Actually, I'm the one who sounds like a boomer. I think Paul Simon was one of the most talented song writers who ever lived. Simon and Garfunkel... there's no equal."

And so it went. Discovering things about each other that they'd never known because they'd never taken the time to have casual conversations like other men and women did when they were together. However, other men and women together were on dates, and they had always been chasing down some horrible killer, but *this* was a date. And it felt *good* that it was a date.

They got to the restaurant. Mitch hopped out of his car, came around to her door, and opened it for her and offered her his arm. "Reservations for two," he said when they went inside. "The name's Webster."

"Ah, yes. This way, please," said the waiter.

Rileigh followed him as he weaved among the tables. All with crisp white tablecloths, and most of them occupied, but the place wasn't jammed. Conversation was quiet and muffled. Music was playing in the background. She didn't know what it was, couldn't quite identify it because it wasn't loud enough to hear clearly, but she was sure it wasn't country western, and absolutely certain it wasn't yee-haw.

Mitch pulled out Rileigh's chair for her and she sat down in it, looked up at him and smiled. He went around to the other side of the table and sat.

They talked.

They ordered and then they talked some more.

Nothing heavy, but it was several levels deeper than chitchat. He wanted to know why she had joined the military and she told him. She wanted to know why he hadn't served in the military and he told her. Mitch asked about her deployments — no specifics, just what was it like. Rileigh asked about his early years as a police officer. The waiter came with wine. Mitch tasted it, then smiled and nodded. Their salads were served, and then dinner. Through it all there was the pleasantness of having a conversation with this wonderful, good-looking man that had nothing to do with murder, death, and mayhem.

They laughed a lot. Mitch told her about a time when he was in college and had picked up a girl at a pricey boarding school and they had gone to a costume party dressed as Darth Vader and Princess Leia. When they returned, the front gates to the pricey school were locked as a safety precaution. There was a code on the gate, of course, and she knew what it was. Or she had known it when she was sober. She punched in what she thought was the code but it was wrong and the panel beeped and flashed red. She tried again and again and after three tries, the system was locked down and she could not enter any more codes.

"What did you do?"

"We decided to climb over the gate. Not the smartest decision I ever made. Picture the scene: Princess Leia is standing on Darth Vader's shoulders with one leg hiked over the top of the gate ... when the spotlight comes on and the security guard yells, 'Freeze.'"

He stopped.

"And...?" she prodded.

"And Darth Vader froze, like a good little Boy Scout. Princess Leia, on the other hand, ignored the order and kept climbing. She made it over and was on her way down the other side when she got hung."

"Hung?"

"Her dress snagged on the grillwork. Left her dangling upside down, screaming. They had to use one of those telephone basket trucks to get her down."

They talked about the present as well as the past, about how life had changed for Rileigh since Jillian came back.

"She has put things on hold with David. Is that right?" Mitch asked.

"Yeah."

"Because of Lamar Devereaux?"

"More or less. She had some feelings for him, I think, though she's never talked about it. The whole incident was kind of a wakeup call, a realization that she had rushed into a relationship with David just because he was David, the guy that she'd left at the altar. But that wasn't a good reason to get in so deep so fast."

"And she told him that?"

"She did."

"How did he take it?"

"She said he was kind and understanding."

"And how did she take his kindness and understanding?"

"I think it made her feel even more pressured. I think she might have preferred for him to be angry about it. To show something besides goodness. He's Sir Lancelot, too good to be true."

Rileigh and Mitch lingered over dinner, content to sit and be together and enjoy each other's company. But as the meal wound to a close and dessert was about to be served, Rileigh was saddled with the perennial question: now what? All that had ever been discussed in the many discussions about the big date was that they would go out to dinner in a really nice place.

There had never been any talk about what would happen *after* dinner.

Rileigh had certainly had plenty of daydreams and fantasies about it, but—

"Would you like to go back to my house and have a drink?" Mitch asked.

Rileigh found a knot in her throat, but still managed to choke out, "I would like that very much."

THE DRIVE back to Yarmouth County from Knoxville seemed to take forever. The trip there had been so full of glad-to-be-together conversation that the time flew by. The trip back was more mellow. For starters, both of them were stuffed. As they were walking out to the car, Mitch commented, "Good thing it wasn't turkey, or we'd both be sound asleep from tryptophan poisoning."

But perhaps it was the anticipation of what the "let's have a drink at my place" most certainly meant. That made both of them quiet and sober.

They pulled into his driveway, and he turned off the engine. Rileigh started to get out and Mitch said, "Uh uh, remember?" So she closed the door back and sat back in the seat so that he could get out and come around the car and open the door for her and offer her his arm. They walked into his house through the front door because he had parked behind his cruiser. The few occasions when Rileigh had been to Mitch's house for one reason or another, they had come in through the kitchen door, but tonight Mitch led them into the living room. The light was dim and music was playing.

"You turned that on before you left?"

"Like it?"

She listened and then burst out laughing. It was a golden oldie. Alabama's "Feels So Right."

"I picked it before I knew you liked country music. Good guess, huh?"

Good indeed. It was one of her favorite songs. She knew all the lyrics, including the words floating into the room now about promising that you'll stay and keep me warm tonight.

She shivered.

"Have a seat and I'll make you that drink."

Rileigh planted herself on the couch, her heart pounding, her breath coming shallow. She grabbed hold of her thoughts and anticipation. Don't get out in front of your headlights, girl. She forced herself to live in the moment.

This is now. Enjoy every second of it.

Mitch came back into the living room with drinks. A Tom Collins for Rileigh and a bourbon and water for him. He handed her the drink and sat down on the couch beside her. Close. Their legs were touching.

Rileigh found she couldn't think what to say. Didn't have anything to say. The silence lengthened until Mitch set his still full glass down on the coffee table. He took Rileigh's drink from her hand and set hers beside his. Then he turned her face to him and kissed her. Rileigh fell into the glory of that kiss. The warmth of it. The tenderness.

The aching longing behind it you could feel through the softness.

She put her arms around his neck and drew him close to her. The kiss deepened. The hunger both of them had been keeping at bay for so long finally burst free, and Mitch pressed his mouth hard into hers, kissing deeply. Rileigh arched up to meet his desire. He opened his mouth and—

Bam, bam, bam, bam!

Mitch jumped, and Rileigh almost choked.

What in the world?

She opened her eyes and only then noticed that there were car lights shining in the picture window. Someone had parked behind Mitch and left the lights on.

Mitch was angry. He sat up, breathing hard, got up from the couch and marched to the door. Threw it open, ready to make whoever was out there regret that they had come here, but he never had a chance. The man literally grabbed Mitch's arm and cried, "You've got to come, Sheriff. She's *gone*."

Rileigh had no idea who the man was or who the "she" was who had gone missing. But it was clear the man was distraught. She could hear the incipient hysteria in his voice, in every word he spoke.

"Mr. Schofield, what are you doing here?"

Schofield? Wasn't that the name of the couple who were staying at Old Shaggy?

"You *told* me... you said if I ever needed your help, you'd come. That's what you said. *Remember?*" He probably didn't realize he was shaking Mitch as he spoke. "Well, I need your help. My daughter's gone. Hillary is *gone.*" He drew in a ragged breath, and his next words rode a sob out of his throat. "And there's blood *everywhere!*"

He let go of Mitch then, just stood in front of him,

desolate. Rileigh got to her feet and crossed the room toward them, stood behind Mitch as he spoke calmly.

"What do you mean by 'gone?' You have to tell me what's going on."

"We went to the movies. The littles. I took them to see *Despicable Me 4* and we came home and... oh God." He froze then. Even in the dim porch light, Rileigh could see his face turn white. "We came in the door through the kitchen as we always do. The littles stopped to grab a bag of chips and I went on. I would have stopped them if I could have. I didn't want them to see..."

"See what?"

"The blood. Dear God, I've never seen so much blood. It was... everywhere, all over the floor in front of the stairs and on the stairs, splattered on the walls, *everywhere*. And I yelled, 'Hillary, Hillary, where are you?' But she didn't answer. The littles came running, and then they stopped. And they all three started screaming."

The man had been able to hold it together until that point but he lost it then. Put his face in his hands and sobbed. Mitch turned helplessly toward Rileigh with a pleading look on his face. She didn't know if he was begging her with his eyes to grant permission for them to abort yet another attempt to be together, or if he was begging her to stand her ground and demand that he stay. Either way, the call was hers to make.

"We have to go, Mitch," she said, then glanced down at her bare feet. "Just gimme a minute to find my shoes."

Chapter Fourteen

RILEIGH AND MITCH CALMED MR. SCHOFIELD ENOUGH
that he could tell them what had happened, that when he
couldn't find his daughter, he had roused the housekeeper,
Carly Farrington, got her out of bed, and together they
had searched everywhere, but Hillary was nowhere to be
found. He said that his wife had gotten home from her hair
appointment in the middle of the search and taken the
little children up to their rooms, and Mr. Schofield had
called the numbers on the refrigerator, *all* of the numbers
on the refrigerator.

There was a standard emergency call list printed out by
the sheriff's department and placed with magnets on the
refrigerators of every rental property or any other place
that might house tourists. It listed the numbers to call for
all emergency services.

"I dialed 911," Schofield said, "and told them what
was wrong, and then I called the other numbers."

"You called the other numbers?"

"Yes, all of them."

Rileigh and Mitch exchanged a look over his head.

Most people were satisfied with 911, but he had called everybody. They put Mr. Schofield in the back of the cruiser. He was in no condition to drive. It was a miracle he made it to Mitch's house alive.

"Why did you come here?" Mitch asked.

"Because you told me if I ever needed your help to call... and because I could tell you cared. I could tell the day we talked that you felt some kind of connection to Hillary's situation, that she touched you somehow."

"Where did you get my address?"

"I didn't have your address. I just stopped at the convenience store and asked. Everybody there knew where the sheriff lives."

Mitch let it go at that.

When Rileigh and Mitch and Mr. Schofield arrived at Shagbark Manor, it looked like the circus had come to town. The rescue squad was there, the fire department, the ambulance service, three sheriff's department vehicles. They had all responded to Mr. Schofield's frantic, desperate calls for help — and had arrived to find nobody to rescue, and no one in need of medical care. All they'd found was blood.

Paul Schofield leapt out of the back seat of Mitch's cruiser and rushed up the front walk but was stopped by Deputy Mullins, who wouldn't let him go any further. Rileigh had never put her shoes back on and went into the house barefoot.

When Deputy Mullins saw Mitch, he asked in surprise, "What are *you* doing here?"

"It's a long story."

"Seriously, you're off tonight. Go away."

Mitch offered a resigned sigh. "It is what it is. I'm here now, so tell me what's going on."

The deputy explained what they had done since they

had arrived, which was search the huge house for the missing sixteen-year-old girl. And they had put up police tape to preserve the crime scene inside.

Mullins led Rileigh and Mitch into the house through the front door into the entryway, with its fine chandelier glittering high above a scene that looked like a pig had been butchered. Mr. Schofield had not been exaggerating. There was blood *everywhere*. A huge pool of it was puddled right beneath the first stair tread. Gus had told her once that there was a gallon, maybe a gallon and a half of blood in the human body. It looked like there might be that much pooled on the floor and splattered on the walls and the stairs.

"Where's Tennessee's most famous coroner when you need him?" Mitch said to Rileigh, nodding to the mess. Gus Hazelton was not in town. He had left three days before on a two-week trip to photograph mountain goats in the Andes Mountains. A medical examiner would be called in from Gatlinburg.

What Schofield had not described was what was all over the entryway besides blood — broken glass. It took Rileigh a moment to figure out what the glass was. It was pieces of a china doll's head. Pieces from more than one doll — half a dozen broken dolls littered the stairs and the floor, with broken heads and bodies ripped open, stuffing trailing out.

When Deputy Mullins saw Rileigh notice the broken dolls, he said, "There are a lot more of them upstairs in the hallway and in one of the bedrooms — all destroyed."

Why would Hillary have destroyed a roomful of dolls? Or if Hillary hadn't destroyed them, who had?

Deputy Rawlings had herded Mr. Schofield upstairs to his wife, who was waiting for him in the children's bedroom, and Mitch asked Mullins, "So we're sure the girl's not anywhere here in the building?"

Making a grand gesture to take in everything around him, he said, "We looked, but this place is," he shook his head, "enormous, hallways and rooms leading into other rooms leading into other hallways. But I guess she could be."

"Are you telling me she could be somewhere here that you didn't find her?"

Rawlings shrugged. "I'd like to say not. I'd like to say we looked in every crook and cranny, but there were only three of us and we could have missed something. If she is here, she's hiding. We called and called for her."

"Are you saying she's still here alive somewhere here?" Rileigh asked.

Mitch shook his head. "I told you about it — that she said she's been seeing all kinds of crazy stuff and she was desperate to get away from here. It's possible she staged this so she could run away."

"Is that what you think? She staged it?"

Mitch shook his head. "Nope, I don't." He gestured at the mess all around. "Where did she get all this blood? But it's not a possibility we can rule out at this point."

"I'm going to go have a look in Hillary's room," Rileigh said. She went into the kitchen and asked Mr. Schofield which one of the dozens of bedrooms in the house belonged to Hillary. It was on the second floor, and he showed her to the back stairs that led up to the second and third floors from the kitchen, the route the house-keeper took to her apartment on the third floor. Rileigh went up the stairs to the second floor and walked down the long hallway, looking at doors opening off each side, the high ceilings, the massive woodwork ... and broken dolls on the floor at the other end of it. It looked like some

English manor house. She decided she was going to find out who built it and for what purpose when she had the time, but right now she needed to go through Hillary's room.

There were clothes strewn everywhere, a typical teenager room. She didn't even have to look for the alcohol. There was an empty bottle of vodka and a half empty bottle of 7-Up sitting beside it on the counter in her bathroom, and in the bedside table she was surprised to find a journal. She didn't think kids these days wrote anything in longhand. Everything was digital. But this kid had apparently put her thoughts down on actual paper.

Rileigh sat down on the edge of the bed to read it. Normal kid stuff — boyfriends and girl drama, smoking weed and "doin' the deed."

Rileigh flipped to the back and read through the final pages, the part written after Hillary had come to the mountains with her parents. The entries beyond that were bizarre. She made it abundantly clear in that diary how much she hated being here, how much she hated her stepmother, and how badly she wanted to get away. Those were the beginning entries after she arrived. But subsequent entries described bizarre occurrences that she had seen and that her parents refused to believe existed.

In one entry, she'd written, *There's a whole roomful of dolls! Not Barbie dolls, but the old kind, baby dolls and big ones with pretty faces painted on the heads and long hair. We found it the first day and Tabby told the littles not to even touch them. I went into the room to take a closer look and suddenly the dolls' eyes opened, all of them. I just stood there, surprised and scared. When I started to back out of the room, their eyes followed me. Then they started making sounds — old-doll sounds — "Ma-ma, Ma-ma." They all were making the same sounds and it got louder and louder and louder. But nobody believed me when I told them about it.*

Rileigh flipped through pages where Hillary described seeing "You die" written in blood on the wall. One of her last entries reported that she had come into her bedroom and found all of her underwear and nightgowns ripped up and blood smeared on them.

Rileigh read the last entry. *Nobody believes a word I say. I saw a dead body at the foot of the stairs with a knife in its chest and not a soul believes that I saw it but it was there, I swear to God it was there. Now I'm scared to be here. The balls of light that you always see at the other end of the hall and when you look at them directly they're gone. The thing that floats through my bedroom at night, a little girl in a pink nightgown crying. No one believes I've seen any of this but it's true. Morgan commented on my Instagram post, the selfie I posted three days after we got here. She pointed out that there was something in the background, some kind of blurry face and she wanted to know if it was a joke. It was no joke, but everybody laughed when I said it wasn't, that anybody who'd ever spent more than ten minutes with Photoshop could have put it there.*

Rileigh sat for a while looking at the diary. If the kid was telling her parents lies, trying to get them to leave or send her away, making up shit that she said she saw, why would she put it in her diary? Who was she trying to fool there?

Hillary was not particularly adept at hiding her drugs. Rileigh looked in the base of the lamp and in the tank of the toilet, on the top closet shelf and in shoes and coat pockets, and finally found what she was looking for when she unscrewed the spindle on the cannonball bed and looked into the hole in it. She pulled out a baggie with other baggies inside. There was a baggie of weed and one of cocaine and another bag with pills of different sizes and shapes. Rileigh recognized benzos or bricks, street names for Xanax, and M30s, which was oxycodone, either real or synthetic. It was hard to tell the difference. The rest, though, Mitch would have to get analyzed to find out everything the girl was taking. Her father had told Mitch that they'd cleaned out her stash of drugs in Nashville and he swore she'd brought none with her. So where had these come from? If she'd gotten these drugs since she got here, it begged the question: who was her pusher?

Chapter Fifteen

THE FIRST ORDER OF BUSINESS IN DETERMINING WHAT HAD happened to Hillary Schofield was to find out for sure that she was nowhere on the premises, and that meant a thorough search.

That met with resistance from Carly Farrington, the housekeeper, when he explained what he wanted to do. It was very clear, very fast, that Carly was not at all in favor of having a bunch of strangers tromping all over her house.

"But there are places in this house that are closed off," Carly said, sputtering, "rooms and whole sections of one floor you can't get to."

"If it is somewhere that a sixteen-year-old girl could have gone to hide, then we have to search and make sure she isn't there."

"But those rooms are locked."

"With the key on the door frame above the door?"

She nodded reluctantly.

"Even if they're locked up with a chain and padlock, I

want to see what's inside. Do you have any kind of blueprint of the layout of this place?"

"Well, there are some blueprints on the wall in the library that show the original outline of where rooms were, but there have been many renovations since then."

"I'll take what I can get," he said.

He gathered up his forces — Rileigh, of course, and his three deputies. He pressed the Fire Chief Pete Brady and three firemen and three members of the rescue squad into service. The ambulance crew had already left by then. That made twelve searchers — fourteen if you counted Carly Farrington and Paul Schofield.

He gathered them in the beautiful room called the library. Mitch didn't seem to be terribly impressed with Shagbark Manor, but Rileigh was positively gobsmacked. Maybe it was just that Mitch was focused on his job. When Mitch had a case, he got tunnel vision; he saw nothing but his job in front of him, and that was to find this girl, hopefully alive, likely not, and find out what had happened to her. Things like the most beautiful building and rooms that Rileigh had ever seen in in her life didn't make any impression on him at all.

Rileigh was surprised that she had spent her whole life in Yarmouth County and had never known what an incredible treasure Shagbark Manor was. She had heard about it from various people over the years, that it was gorgeous inside, that it was like a palace or a mansion or a castle. But seeing was believing, and walking through from one room to another in the stately building was awe-inspiring and humbling.

They'd passed through the sitting room directly off the wide entryway on their way to the library, and Rileigh paused there while the others went on to look over the house plans.

On one wall was a huge fireplace with a large axe resting on hooks above it beside a placard that identified it as "the" axe, the original one that had been found beside the dead bodies who'd been hacked to death in the house in 1926. Even with a lake of blood in the entryway, it was too early in this investigation to declare that Hillary Schofield was dead, but the inescapable conclusion was that someone had removed that axe, used it on Hillary, and then returned it to its "place of honor," since the blade was covered in dried blood and there was a small puddle of it on the mantel. Mitch left it as he found it for the forensic guys to bag up as evidence.

On the opposite wall was a huge family portrait of the Farringtons — father, mother, and three stair-stepped little girls, standing stiff and unsmiling, dressed in what was high fashion in the 1920s. The portrait was so large, the people in it were almost life-sized, and Rileigh was struck by how much Carly Farrington looked like her grandmother, Jocelyn, when Jocelyn was a little girl, with that cottony blonde hair. The hair of the other two girls in the portrait was dark like their father's. Only Jocelyn had her mother's hair, so blonde it looked white. Lenora wore hers pulled back in a dignified bun at her neck, while Jocelyn's lay in fat braids on her shoulders.

On the other walls of the room were dozens of photographs, all variations of the same picture, just with different people. Like what you see in a bait shop — pictures of dozens of people standing in the same place holding out the fish they'd just caught. This was a staged souvenir photo of different families that had stayed at the bed and breakfast. Rileigh thought it was ghoulish, but the place was billed as a haunted house, after all. Every photo showed couples, families, or individuals holding a small box in a stylized pose beneath the chandelier in the entryway with the grand staircase in the background...

and a ghostly, gauzy figure that had a split-open skull and a white face like a painted doll, standing on the stairs above them, holding the "murder axe."

In the corner of the room was a small sitting area, a comfortable chair, a table and a lamp — and stacks of Shagbark Manor memorabilia on shelves nearby, newspaper stories, magazine stories, even a couple of books about the house, the murders... and of course, the ghost sightings.

When Rileigh entered the library where the others were gathered, Mitch was asking Carly about the security cameras, positioned in the corners of some rooms near the ceilings.

He wanted to know about the footage from those cameras, and Carly ducked her head.

"I'm afraid there is no footage. The cameras are just props. They're not real, they don't connect to anything." She spread her hands and shrugged. "I couldn't afford to hire somebody to operate a security system like that, monitor the images from thirty-four different rooms. I just put the cameras there for effect, to discourage anybody who might decide to take home a souvenir from the house."

The room where Mitch and the others were now bent over framed drawings of the layout of the house had a large oak desk in one corner and books from the floor to the ceiling all around. The "to the ceiling" part was significant, since these were at least twelve- and fourteen-foot ceilings.

"We're going to form into four teams," he told the searchers. "I've divided the house into four quadrants, and you'll each be assigned to one. The teams will switch after you search your assigned quadrant. The people searching quadrant A will move to quadrant C. The people who searched B go to quadrant D. Rileigh, Carly, and I will search all four quadrants. In the end, that will mean at least eight people have searched every square foot of this residence. Make sense?" Everybody nodded.

Rileigh knew now wasn't the time or place to say this, but she was fairly certain they wouldn't be searching every square foot, not if the stories she'd heard about secret passageways and doors that she had heard were true.

"Let's go," Mitch said. Carly looked very uncomfortable, taking Mitch and Rileigh up the stairs to the second floor to the rooms that were the most commonly used for the bed and breakfast. It was where the Schofield family was staying.

The three small children had one room that opened off a huge bedroom where their parents were staying. Hillary was in a different bedroom, several doors down the hall.

The children had been taken to their room and their mother was in there with them, so they didn't invade their privacy, but they searched everywhere else. The bedroom where Tabitha and Paul Schofield were staying, one of many master bedrooms, was at least as big as the first floor of Mama's house, and maybe larger. It had a huge boudoir where the bed sat in stately manner against one wall, with curtains hanging from rods that stretched from one of the eight-foot bedposts to another. There was a desk, a full office, and a sitting area, and the team split up and looked under, around, behind, and in every piece of furniture, crevice, crack, and cranny. They moved on to the next bedroom, which was closed off because no one was staying in it. It wasn't quite as large as the master suite, but it was close.

The hallway was littered with the pieces of broken dolls, and Rileigh had to be careful not to step on a piece of glass in her bare feet. The doll room at the end of the hall looked like Hurricane Katrina had blown through it, with broken dolls, stuffing, and overturned furniture.

For Rileigh, the rest of the night became a confusing blur of walking barefoot on hardwood floors that glistened in the light down one dark hallway and another, opening up one hand-carved door with a brass knob and brass fittings after another. They looked in closets, they looked under beds, they looked in window seats and shower stalls. A couple of the rooms were used for storage, where she saw cleaning supplies, extra linens and a pile of ornate rugs.

Rileigh had absolutely no hope of finding the girl alive anywhere. She was pondering the logistics of getting rid of such a bloody corpse without leaving a trail of blood. She had leaned over to Mitch when they first stood staring at the roped-off area of blood at the bottom of the stairs and pointed to marks on the steps.

"That looks like where somebody hit that step with an axe or a hatchet — recently," he said. "You can see the bare wood where a splinter chipped off, and there's no varnish on it."

"You know what I'm picturing?" Rileigh said.

"What?"

"The same thing you're picturing. Somebody used the axe on that girl with such force that it went *through* her and cut into the wooden step beneath."

The back stairs led down to an open area beneath the kitchen where the basement door was located. It had an old key-pad combination lock.

There was a huge fan behind a grate inset in the wall beside the door.

"I am the only person who knows the combination to this lock, and the door's always locked," Carly said.

"What's in there that's so valuable?" Mitch asked.

"Nothing but Christmas decorations. It's storage."

"Then why the elaborate lock?"

Carly shrugged. "I don't know. I didn't build it. Maybe there used to be something valuable in there, but not anymore."

She punched in a series of numbers and opened the door. Rileigh was surprised by the basement, not by how big it was but by how small. It wasn't much bigger than Mama's basement, and given the house above it, she expected it to be four times that size.

They stepped into the dark interior of the room and suddenly there was a clicking sound and Rileigh jumped, looking around to see what it was. About thirty seconds later, the clicking sound was followed by a *whump.* It was the big fan coming to life, starting slow but gaining speed until it was moving a huge amount of air.

"That's the cold air return," Carly told them. "The HVAC unit is complicated. I don't understand anything about it. There are several fans like this around the house — this is the biggest. The fan turns off and on automatically based on… I have no idea what, but they're necessary to keep the air circulating and cool."

The basement was more storage — shelves full of Christmas decorations and what must have been ten thousand Christmas lights. Rileigh had seen the place lit up at Christmastime and was always grateful she didn't have to climb up on the roof of the place to hang those lights.

A line of Christmas trees stretched across the back wall, along with a life-sized nativity scene… but no Hillary.

They searched Carly's living quarters, which were in a closed-off section at the back of the house on the third floor that she reached by the back staircase that came up from the kitchen. Carly stood first on one foot and then the other, fidgeting as they dug through her closets and

checked out the contents of her window seat — just about
every room had one. There was nothing out of the ordinary except the computer equipment. She had three
different computers hooked to a huge monitor. When she
saw Rileigh looking at the setup, she said she had it to
watch movies on. Then why was it sitting on a desk instead
of positioned in front of the couch and lounge chair in the
living room? She did not like them searching through her
personal items, but that was only obvious from her
demeanor, because she never said a word of protest. From
what Mitch had said, Rileigh figured the little blonde
woman was way into passive-aggression and didn't like
confrontation.

It was near dawn when the house had been thoroughly
searched. The forensic pathologist team from Gatlinburg
had arrived about three hours in. When they were finished,
they told Carly that she could have the site cleaned up
tomorrow morning. Paul Farrington had been omnipresent
in the search of the building, going from one group of
searchers to another, up and down stairs, asking, pleading,
"Have you found anything yet?"

Rileigh felt sorry for him. From what Mitch had told
her, she understood his angst. Paul had brought the girl
here in a last-ditch effort to bond, and now she was
missing.

Rileigh got back into Mitch's car, exhausted, and
leaned back against the headset. Mitch got in beside her,
and she realized, but did not point out, that he hadn't
stopped to open the door for her. It was odd, no, not odd,
just *interesting* to note how their relationship shifted like the
gears of a car. When they were in dating mode, there was
cologne, aftershave, doors opened, chairs pulled back.
When they were in official mode, she was just one of the
guys.

They pulled up in front of Mama's house when it was dawn out on the flat. The sky was beginning to lose its pitch-black color, the stars fading, and Rileigh burst out laughing.

"What's so funny?"

"What's so funny is that when I go in that house, nobody is going to ask me where I've been or what I've been doing. It will be the elephant in the room that I stayed out all night and nobody will even mention it. And when I do finally tell them about it, they're going to be sorely disappointed."

He lifted an eyebrow.

"Oh, come on, I know they have been wondering aloud ever since we left whether or not I'd come home at all tonight."

Mitch sat very still after she said that and turned to her. When he spoke, it wasn't an official voice at all.

"I hoped that I wouldn't be bringing you home until breakfast," he said and looked deep into her eyes. His blue eyes pinned her to the spot, and she suddenly found she didn't know what to say.

As she fell into his gaze, she found herself just blurting out the obvious. "I hoped I wouldn't come home until noon."

Chapter Sixteen

WHEN RILEIGH FINALLY GOT OUT OF BED ABOUT lunchtime, she watched Mama's and Jillian's faces fall when she told them she'd been investigating a missing teenager all night long. They tried to hide it, of course, but it was clear they'd been assuming Rileigh was engaged in an entirely different activity and were disappointed to learn it didn't go down that way.

Rileigh went by the sheriff's department midafternoon — to get the green high heeled shoes she'd left in Mitch's cruiser the night before — and invited Mitch to dinner to try out the Mediterranean meatballs Mama had made from the recipe that was next in the cookbook after the Hungarian goulash. She'd informed him that she believed it was his civic duty as an elected official to test every one of Mama's recipes, and he had given her a mock salute and said, "Ready as ordered."

The meatballs, while not a rousing success, were way up the ladder from "just edible," but Rileigh suspected Mama'd left out or put in some random ingredient. Rileigh had just completed as detailed a description as she could summon of the inside of Shagbark Manor and Jillian was as gobsmacked as she had been.

"I never dreamed it would look like that inside. I thought it was yet another big old house, creepier, bigger maybe, but I never imagined that," Jillian said.

"No wonder it's been such a success as a bed and breakfast," Rileigh said.

"Oh, I think you need to give the credit for that to Carly Farrington and her marketing campaign," Mama said.

"That's what Georgia said."

"I had no idea you knew what a marketing campaign was," Jillian said to Mama.

Mama drew herself up. "I know a sight more than you do about a lot of things, baby girl," she said with as much haughtiness as she could muster, which wasn't much. "I know you think you got to see all there was to see of Shagbark Manor, but I am here to tell you there's a lot more to it than the casual observer ever sees."

"Meaning what?" Mitch said, picking at the last of his meatball on his plate.

"You know it was a magician who bought it after it got all run down, don'tcha?"

"No, I didn't, but I do now."

"I hear tell he had all kinds of secret rooms and secret doors and passageways installed."

"Do you believe that?" Rileigh asked her mother.

"Of course I don't, not entirely. You know, maybe 45 or 50 percent of it's true."

"Whoever did the renovation work on it was a master craftsman," Mitch said. "When you go into an old place and have to retrofit all the electric lines and the plumbing, make it work around the floors and the walls as they have been constructed, you can usually tell, but I couldn't see a single place where I would have said it looked like it had been redone. How did it wind up back in the Farrington family? Given the dispositions of Carly's sisters, I can't imagine they purchased it."

"I used to know what happened, but I can't remember anymore exactly what... it was something about it being a private sale to the Farringtons. Wasn't no loan from a bank or nothing like that, and when he couldn't make the payments, the estate got it back."

"I want to go back to those secret passageways," Mitch said. "You said you believed that maybe part of it was true."

"I do. I've heard tell over the years of people who've seen some secret door or some passageway or some such and talked about it after. I'm sure that's how all them people turned up missing."

"All *what* people turned up missing?" Mitch asked.

"Oh, all kind of people's gone missing from that place."

"Mama, those are just rumors," Rileigh said.

"Well, something happened that started the rumors."

"If people had regularly turned up missing from Shagbark Manor, there would be a record of it," Mitch said.

"Not if them people was tourists," Mama said. Mitch's head came up. "If the people who turned up missing was from away from here and they just didn't show up back home, how would anybody here have ever known?"

"Tell me what you've heard"—Mitch held up his hand to stop her before she started—"that you thought was a *credible* story."

"I *know* this is credible 'cause I met the woman my own self."

"What woman?

"Years ago, Rileigh," Mama began, "you was in

middle school maybe? I don't know. I was in that funnel cake shop in Pigeon Forge, Funnel Heaven, the one everybody liked so much 'fore it burned down. I bumped into this woman, and I mean literally bumped into her and knocked her funnel cake out of her hand and it went flying, powdered sugar going every which way. She was an old lady with her white hair in a bun"—Mama stopped and smiled—"maybe even as old as I am right now! I apologized and apologized, made her let me buy her another one, and while they was making it, we got to talking. She said she was staying out at Shagbark Manor. I never thought another thing about it until about three or four months later, I was back in Funnel Heaven getting one for Daisy and some tourists was in there with a picture and they was showing the clerk and I seen it and it was her! I told 'em I had run into her in the store. Turns out the people with the picture was her son and his wife and they was looking for her. They said she never come home to Arizona from her trip to the Smoky Mountains."

"Did they report her missing to the police?"

"He said they did but wasn't nothing done about it or wasn't done to his satisfaction. It was complicated, reporting a missing person in all the different states she traveled through from Tennessee to Arizona — 'cause she coulda gone missing in any one of them. He didn't think they tried all that hard, so he decided that he and his wife would retrace her route, figure all the places she was likely to have stopped, and talk to people — and she dearly loved funnel cakes. I told him when I seen her and he was disappointed, was hoping maybe I'd seen her *after* she left the bed and breakfast. He was hoping maybe she'd hung around for some reason. But I seen her the day *before*. She called him and said she was on the way home, told him she had a surprise for him, and I guess that was the last time he ever heard from her."

"She told him she had left the B&B already, or she was just 'on the way home'?" Rileigh asked. "You could say that if you were still there and loading up your suitcases."

Mama shrugged. "I don't know. All I do know is she never got there. And she was just one. They was others. I can't remember rightly when, but they was others."

Mitch sat back in his chair and had that look on his face that Rileigh recognized as *I'm considering.*

"So you're telling me Hillary Schofield is not the first person who has disappeared from Shagbark Manor?"

"I'm telling you that other people disappeared, but they didn't make a bloody exit like she did or everybody would have known about it."

"I wonder how many police reports were filed about missing people?"

"Probably not many, if they went missing after they left here."

"But I bet there were some. I'm going to look."

Rileigh took another helping of the salad Mama'd made to go along with the meatballs. She, Jillian, and Mitch had eaten more salad than meatballs.

"So Shagbark Manor has gotten more and more popular over the years?"

"Oh yes. Years ago it was just this little place you heard about sometimes. It was after Carly took over running it. That was, oh, fourteen, fifteen years ago maybe. She put ads in newspapers and magazines and such. Called it the 'haunted mansion.' Said there was ghosts and strange happenings and a lot more people showed up. That was something new and different. Let's go to a *haunted* bed and breakfast."

Rileigh remembered the display in the corner of the

sitting room with a comfortable chair, a table and a lamp — and stacks of Shagbark Manor memorabilia on shelves nearby. There were copies of magazines that ran stories about haunted houses. Guests who claimed to have seen little girls in bloody nightgowns running down the hallway. That was a good way to prime the pump. Tell your guests what other people have seen, then make the lights and the fans blink on and off, pipe in some creepy music. People's imaginations would take care of the rest.

Rileigh walked Mitch out to his cruiser and asked him what his game plan was for the investigation. He told her that he planned to track down the handyman that Hillary had described to him, the fellow who gave her the creeps. He had been nowhere around when they had arrived in the middle of the night at the crime scene. He was also going to dig back through old police records and see if he could find any evidence of former guests of the Shagbark who had gone missing.

"I'm going to have a talk with Mrs. Schofield, too. What was her name? Tabitha?"

Rileigh nodded.

"Hillary told me she didn't like Tabitha."

"Confirmed by Hillary's diary!" Rileigh put in.

"Hillary said it was mutual and that her father didn't know that Tabitha was screwing around on him." Tabitha had not come home until much later than Paul and his children from the movie that night. Her husband had told Mitch that she'd had an appointment to get her hair done.

Rileigh remembered catching sight of Tabitha when they'd been searching the house for Hillary. Even with just a brief glimpse, it was clear to Rileigh that the woman had *not* just had her hair done. In fact, she'd looked completely disheveled.

One By One

"What hairdresser cuts hair at night?" And what man is so dense he believes a story like that?

Chapter Seventeen

RILEIGH GOT INTO MITCH'S CRUISER THE NEXT DAY FOR the drive out to Old Shaggy, took one look at him, and said, "You didn't get any sleep at all." It wasn't a question.

"Oh, I got a little."

"Bullshit. Your head has not hit the pillow. I can tell."

"How?"

"The dark circles under your eyes and the lack of a sheet crease on your cheek."

"When have you ever seen a sleep crease on my cheek?"

"Never. But not having one is a sure sign you didn't go to bed."

"That's illogical."

"You'll get no argument from me."

They rode along in silence for a minute or two before Mitch asked, "You know, you never did tell me what your mother and your sister had to say about your late/early return from our big date."

Rileigh chuckled.

"I wish you could have seen it. It was precious watching them squirm."

"Squirm?"

"Well, they weren't about to ask what I'd been doing all night. That'd be rude and embarrassing, and besides, they thought they knew. On the other hand, they couldn't pretend like it was no big thing at all that I stayed out all night. I let them wiggle on the end of the hook for a little while before I told them. And boy, were they disappointed."

"Not nearly as disappointed as I was," Mitch said.

His words hit her in the belly like a blow.

Then he quickly changed the subject, and she was grateful that he did. They had to keep a line, a space, a distance between their personal and professional relationships. Actually, they needed something like a moat. Maybe one with alligators in it.

"According to my notes, the man we're looking for's name is Rick Spriggs. Carly said he had worked at Old Shaggy for years and was a dependable employee. By the way, I didn't ask her that."

"Ask what?"

"About him being dependable. She volunteered it."

"When Hillary got here, perhaps she already had drugs, but I doubt that. Her father seemed very convinced that they found her whole stash, which means…"

"Which means she bought drugs after she got here."

"Right. And how did she find a dealer in a place where she knew nobody?"

They both said the same words at the same time. "The handyman."

"It'd be my guess that he either provided the drugs to her or he hooked her up with a dealer. We need to find out which."

They turned off the lane and drove down the winding driveway to Old Shaggy, where they saw a man in a pair of ragged jeans and a t-shirt working in the garden. When he saw them pull up, he immediately turned and was walking toward the side of the house when Mitch pulled to a stop in front, got out, and called out, "Excuse me, is your name Rick Spriggs?"

The man stopped reluctantly and turned around.

"Yeah, I'm Rick Spriggs. What can I do for you?"

Rileigh and Mitch walked across the grass to where the man stood. He was probably mid-thirties and was good-looking in that rakish way some men had where the fact that they looked mildly dangerous was attractive. He had a slouch to the way he stood, an indifferent insolence, and it was clear that he didn't want to talk to Rileigh and Mitch.

The two introduced themselves, then Mitch asked the man, "Would you give me your full name, please?"

"Rick Spriggs."

Mitch waited. The man gave an exaggerated sigh. "Richard David Spriggs."

"Let's see your license."

"Left it at home."

"You a local?"

"No, I moved here from Nashville."

"We're here because of what happened night before last at the manor."

"Then why do you want to talk to me? I don't know anything. Miss Carly told me about it, and it sounds awful."

"Where were you when Hillary Schofield went missing?"

"What time was that?"

"Sometime after her father and mother left, about six o'clock."

"Well, I get off at 5:30."

"Where'd you go when you got off?"

"Home."

"Is there anybody at your house who can verify your whereabouts, that you came home at 5:30?"

"No. I live by myself."

"So there's nobody who can back up your story?"

"Story? You're acting suspicious. You think I've done something to that girl?"

"Did you?"

"Hell no. I didn't know the girl. What would I have against her?"

"So you stayed home all night last night."

"Yeah, I stayed home all night. Didn't see nobody. Didn't talk to nobody."

"How well did you know Hillary Schofield?" Rileigh asked.

"Know her? I didn't. I seen her around just like I seen all the other guests."

"So you never had a conversation with her?"

"Not that I recall."

Rileigh produced her cell phone out of her purse and held it out to the man.

"This is Hillary's school picture. Is this the girl you're talking about?"

He took the phone and looked at the picture, then handed it back to Rileigh. "Yeah, that's her, but I didn't know her no better than I knew anybody else who stayed here."

Mitch had watched the exchange between Rileigh and the handyman. It was clear he didn't understand why she wanted him to identify a picture. Then he noted how carefully she took the phone back from the man, and she thought he'd figured out what she was up to.

"We found drugs in Hillary Schofield's room. Would you know anything about that?" Mitch said.

"Why would I know anything about drugs in her room? Like I say, I never even had a conversation with the girl."

"So you didn't sell her some weed? Bars, benzos, M30s, blues?"

"No, I didn't sell her drugs."

"Did you maybe hook her up with a dealer who would sell her drugs?"

"No. Why are you asking me all these questions?"

Rileigh held up her cell phone, careful to touch it only on the sides, and said, "So when we run this fingerprint that you left on the screen of my phone, we will find out that your name is Richard David Spriggs and that you moved here from Nashville. Is that right?" Rileigh watched surprise morph into a seething rage, and he dropped any pretense of being civil.

"All right. Damn it. That's not my name."

"What is your name?"

He said nothing.

"We're going to find out when we run these prints. So sooner or later, you pick."

"My name is Richard David Stevenson."

"And you moved here from Nashville? Is that right?"

"Yeah. Well, I've moved around a lot."

"I'm sure that Carly Farrington ran a criminal background check on you before she hired you. But she ran a check on the wrong name, didn't she? Let's see your driver's license—the real one."

He took his wallet out of his pocket and grudgingly handed it over. Rileigh compared the picture to his face, but couldn't tell much since he was now clean shaven, more or less, and the license picture showed a full beard, but the name was Richard D. Stevenson. She jotted the number on the license in her notebook.

"You going to tell Miss Carly that I'm a criminal?" Richard asked.

"Are you?"

"I've been busted a time or two."

"For what?"

"Property crimes. I ain't never hurt nobody. But that was years ago when I was a kid. I ain't done nothing like that in years. Look, I like my job here, and I'd just as soon you didn't ruin it for me."

"Well, we're obligated to tell Mrs. Farrington that you lied on your job application and whatever we find out about your criminal background," Mitch said.

"Of course we would like to be able to tell her that you fully cooperated with us when we asked you questions about Hillary Schofield," Rileigh added.

"I am cooperating," he said. "I'm telling you everything I know."

"Either you sold her drugs, or you hooked her up with somebody who did. Which was it?"

The man squirmed. "Look, alright, damn it. The kid come to me and said she wanted a little weed. What's the harm in that? Hell, it won't be long before it's legal in every state in the country."

"It's not legal in Tennessee."

"So that's all you got her? A little weed?"

"She wanted some other things too."

"So who did you hook her up with?"

The man ran his fingers through his hair. "Look, I ain't done nothing wrong. I don't know nothing about what happened to that girl. And if you go snooping around trying to find her dealer, that chicken's gonna come home to roost in my barn."

"Either you sold her drugs or you sent her to somebody who would sell her drugs," Mitch said. "It is one or the other. If you didn't set her up with a dealer, then you're the one looking at the drug charges."

The man spit the next words out. "Scooby."

The name rang several alarm bells with Rileigh. He was a known drug dealer with a rough reputation.

"Scooby who?"

"I don't know his last name. Just Scooby. And I don't know what she told Scooby she wanted. I don't know what she bought from him. You go talk to him if you want to find that out. Just don't bring me into it. I don't want to have nothing to do with him."

"We'll talk to him," Mitch said. "I want to circle back around to your relationship with Hillary Schofield."

"Relationship? I didn't have no damn relationship with that girl. I've seen her around, that's all. I've just seen her around."

"Well, you must have had some kind of relationship, if she felt comfortable asking you to recommend a drug dealer," Rileigh said.

The man let out a big sigh and ran his fingers through his hair again.

"Look, I was working on the gate hinge. It broke off in the back, and I was fixing it, and she come out on the back porch and down the stairs and struck up a conversation just, you know, like you do with strangers."

"And somehow the basic what's your name where are you from how do you like the weather, became hooking a teenage girl, a minor, up with a drug dealer."

"It wasn't like that."

"What was it like?"

"Look, that was one pushy damn kid. Did you ever meet her?"

Mitch nodded.

"If you met her, she know how pushy she was. She was a girl used to getting whatever she wanted."

Mitch didn't say anything, but he had pointed out to Rileigh that Hillary Schofield was indeed assertive.

"We was talking about the hinge on the back gate, and the next thing I know, we're talking about weed and did I smoke and what kind did I like and where did I get it and next thing I know, you know…"

"So did she tell you what she wanted and give you money and…"

The man backed up and put his hands up in front of him.

"Hell no, I done told you. I wasn't in no drug deal with her. Ain't you listening? I just hooked her up with Scooby. I don't know where she met him. I don't know how they got together. I gave her a cell phone number, and that's all I know."

"You do know we're going to check all of this out, including your criminal record."

"I told you the truth. I've been busted some, but it was a long time ago. I ain't been busted in years. You can check that out in my record. And when I was busted, it wasn't my fault. Them girls said things about me that wasn't true."

A fire alarm rang out shrill in Rileigh's head.

"What girls?"

He shook his head. "Just them girls. They said I've done things I didn't do."

"What things?"

"Look, I ain't been convicted of doing anything but stealing a stereo system and heisting a car and cutting it up into parts and selling them."

"You ran a chop shop?"

"I didn't run nothing. I just took a car apart, sold pieces

of it, got caught, but that's all. That's all I've been convicted of. You can check."

"Oh, we'll check all right."

Mitch looked at Rileigh, and she shrugged.

"That's all we have to ask for the time being," Mitch said, "but hang around. Don't leave the county. We may want to ask more questions."

"I ain't going nowhere unless Miss Carly fires me after you talk to her. Can't you just let that one ride?"

"I think she has a right to know that the guy in her kitchen unclogging her drain has a criminal record. Don't you?"

Richard spat in the dirt, then turned and walked away.

Mitch and Rileigh turned and headed back across the grass and up the porch steps.

"That cell phone trick was the bomb," Mitch said. Rileigh grinned.

"Clean off the front of a cell phone and nothing will give you a better, clearer fingerprint."

"You're full of tricks."

"When I was a cop, I was real good at my job."

"You're still a good cop even if it's not your job anymore."

When Mitch told Carly Farrington that her handyman Rick Spriggs was actually a convicted felon named Richard Stevenson, she looked surprised but not shocked. Like maybe she didn't know that particular thing about him but had figured out he was the kind of man who tiptoed along the edge of the law.

"You did run a criminal background check on him, didn't you?" Mitch asked.

"Of course I did. I run criminal background checks on anybody who comes to work here. When you have guests in a place, there's state regulations you have to follow."

"You don't seem upset that Mr. Stevenson lied on his job application form."

That rattled her.

"Oh, I am. I mean, I don't like it that I..." She sort of lost her voice and stopped talking. And Rileigh realized that standing before her was a true introvert. A person who absolutely was uncomfortable in the presence of others and would have preferred not to interact with anybody at all. So why had she decided to run a bed and breakfast where she spent all of her time dealing with guests? But that was a question for another time.

"About Mr. Stevenson," Mitch began, but Carly held up her hand.

"I'm going to go have a talk with him, but I just want you to know that he is a reliable, hardworking employee. I would hate to have to find somebody to replace him. I mean, he does a really good job."

She wasn't a particularly good liar. There was more to her defense of him than what she was saying.

"Is he your only employee?"

"Right now he is."

"But in the past, you've had others?"

"Oh, my yes. Lots of others."

"I'm sure you could not possibly take care of the number of guests that could fit in this house all by yourself."

Carly chuckled. "Oh, I don't rent out all the bedrooms out. I limit the guests based on the number of people I can cook for and care for properly with a very small staff."

"But what about all the other bedrooms? You don't rent them all?"

She smiled. "Oh, they're just for show. They're window dressing."

They got up to leave and Mitch said, "May I borrow some baking powder and a roll of tape, please?"

Carly Farrington looked surprised, but gave him what he asked for.

Rileigh and Mitch started back out to their car. Mitch had already sprinkled baking powder on the surface of Rileigh's phone and used a piece of tape to lift the fingerprint that showed up there. As they were walking out, Mitch paused at the foot of the stairs.

"I've been thinking about what your mama told us, trying to make it all work out in my head… so the parents come home from somewhere one day and just happen to stumble into an axe murderer killing their children?"

"Not both parents. Just the father. Remember, the mother was home."

"Fine. Daddy comes home and finds somebody chasing his small daughters around with an axe, chopping at them. Mommy's trying to save them, so both of them get chopped up, too."

"Not both of them, just Mommy. As I understand it, Daddy didn't have a mark on him and nobody's sure exactly how he died."

Mitch gestured to the staircase.

"Right where we're standing, maybe they all three struggled for the axe and the bad guy won."

"Maybe he won because Papa had a heart attack."

"Just dropped over dead? That sounds a little too convenient and contrived for my tastes."

"It was well-known he had a serious heart condition. Fighting with an axe murderer is a lot of exertion. Or maybe he blew an aorta chasing his daughters around the house with an axe? Chopping two little kids to death would tire you out."

Mitch was still picturing the scene in his head.

"Mama said Crawford and Lenora Tillman were found at the foot of these stairs, dead. Mama was chopped into little pieces with an axe."

He paused.

"Think about that. All that blood... just like the blood that was left here *in the same spot* when Hillary disappeared."

Rileigh nodded to the fresh cut marks in the wood of the steps, where an axe had obviously come down on that spot. Recently. Since Hillary's blood was on it, maybe the axe had hit the step after it had hit Hillary... maybe it went down *through* Hillary. She shuddered.

"Does all this strike you as maybe a copycat?"

Rileigh cocked her head. "The disappearance of this girl is a copycat crime?"

"Well, sort of. The method of it, anyway. I mean, if somebody wanted to kidnap Hillary Schofield, why cut her up when she almost bleeds to death first? If they wanted to kill her... there are a lot of cleaner, neater ways to commit murder. If she was murdered with an axe, that was a deliberate choice the killer made. Why? I think it has to be connected in some way to the axe murders here almost a century ago."

"Well, Shagbark Manor is supposed to be 'haunted' by the ghosts of a family butchered with an axe." Rileigh paused as her glance fell on the window seat by the front door. "Maybe while the youngest watched."

She walked over to the window seat, lifted the lid, saw that there was nothing inside. It was just a wooden box. Perfect for a little kid to hide in.

"It all seems tied together somehow, don't you think?"

"What are you driving at?"

"I just wonder if it might be a plan to do some poking around, see what we can find out about what really happened."

"What really happened almost a century ago?"

"Yeah. Find out the real story... without all the glitz and glamor and rumors."

"Well, I've always been curious."

"They happened in, what, 1925? — no, 1926 — but I'm sure there are old records. We can look up information in the library and maybe the back issues of the newspaper. This was a national story. There must have been newspaper reporters everywhere. Almost all big newspapers have their archives online."

"Right. But I think the place we ought to *start* is local."

"The local newspapers and library?"

"No. Local people. I'm thinking of one local person in particular. Her name is Thelma Rittenhouse, and she's older than Mama, high nineties."

"She's not dating the Dalai Lama, is she?"

Rileigh rolled her eyes and sighed.

"I never said Mama was *dating* the Dalai Lama. She just met him for a cup of coffee, that's all."

"Oh, well, that changes everything."

"Seriously, this old woman has a memory like a steel trap. She would remember what it was like here in the years after the crime, when everybody's memories were still fresh."

"Let's have a talk with her soon. Sounds like you know where to find her. I hope that drug dealer, Scooby, is also easy to find.

"To quote the Dread Pirate Roberts, 'Get used to disappointment.'"

Chapter Eighteen

WHEN PAUL SCHOFIELD SAID THAT HIS WIFE HAD BEEN getting her hair done at the time Hillary disappeared, all the normal alarm bells went off in Rileigh's head. Rileigh had seen her that night, just a glimpse, but with only a glimpse, it was clear she was not a woman who had just come from the hairdresser. In fact, she'd looked disheveled.

The name of the beauty salon, according to Paul Schofield, was the Hair Affair, and it was on one of those side streets in Gatlinburg where the tourists didn't go. It, like a select few other businesses, was supported by local people.

It was what you'd call a mom-and-pop hair salon. It wasn't some fancy thing with ten chairs and ten hairdressers whose own hair color was a glaring Sears color, cut in every strange style that happened to currently be popular, serving a clientele that enjoyed and expected to be in a place with lots of mirrors, lots of chrome, comfortable chairs, and a manicurist to do their nails while the hairdresser worked on their hair. That was the kind of place where Rileigh had had her hair cut in Mama's designated figure-skater style, but Rileigh had come to a place like the Hair Affair with her mother when she was a little girl.

A bell dinged on the door when Mitch and Rileigh stepped inside. There were three hairdressers working on three women. All three of the hairdressers, and their customers, were middle-aged women who looked mostly normal, with the kinds of hairstyles you'd expect a middle-aged woman to wear. The girl who had cut Rileigh's hair had one side of her head completely shaved all the way down to the skin and the other side had maybe two dozen long braids.

"May I speak to the manager please?" Mitch said.

The hairdresser working on the woman in the middle chair said, "That'd be me. My name's Constance Krueger. What can I do for you, Sheriff?"

"You can tell me if you or one of the other ladies has a customer named Tabitha Schofield."

"I do," said the hairdresser on the end. "She's come in a couple of times."

"When was the last time you saw her?" Rileigh asked.

"Several days ago. She likes highlights in her hair and she thought they'd gotten kind of dull and called to see if I could work her in to brighten them."

"Did you see her yesterday?"

"No, she didn't have an appointment yesterday."

"May I ask why you're asking all these questions?" the manager said.

"It's part of an ongoing investigation," Mitch said. "Thank you, ladies." He tipped his hat, then he and Rileigh went back out to his cruiser.

"So much for Tabitha Schofield's alibi. Let's go have a talk with the lady," Mitch said.

They drove back out to Shagbark Manor, saw no sign of the handyman gardener on the grounds, and went inside. Carly greeted them in the foyer while drying her hands on a dish towel.

"Do you have more questions for me this morning?" she asked as if steeling herself for that unpleasant eventuality.

"No, actually we'd like to speak to Tabitha Schofield."

"She's in her room, the Hollyhock room," Carly said, "but Mr. Schofield has taken the small children out for the day. Those are pretty traumatized little kids, I can tell you."

"Of course they are. Who wouldn't be?"

Tabitha Schofield was seated at the big desk in the Hollyhock room on the phone and quickly ended the call when Mitch and Rileigh appeared at her open door.

"We'd like to talk to you, Mrs. Schofield," Mitch said.

"Do you have any news? Do you know anything about Hillary?" She wrinkled her nose. "If you ask me, she staged it all. She's like that. She's the ultimate drama queen. I wouldn't put it past her to come up with a stunt like that just so she can go back to Nashville and live with her crazy mother and do whatever she wants. And that would *not* be a bad thing. She's not a good influence on the younger children."

"Mrs. Schofield, you said you were getting your hair done the night Hillary disappeared. Is that correct?" Mitch said.

She was instantly uncomfortable. "Yes, that's right."

"Your husband said you were at the Hair Affair beauty parlor in Gatlinburg. Is that also true?" Rileigh asked. You could tell she was afraid she'd been outed.

"Well, yes … more or less."

"Actually, Mrs. Schofield, it isn't true at all, either more or less. We just came from the Hair Affair beauty parlor and the stylist who does your hair said you didn't have an appointment that night."

Tabitha Schofield's eyes darted around like maybe she was looking for somewhere to hide.

"Well, you know, I mean, I said I was getting my hair done and I *was* getting my hair done, just not at that place. I didn't tell Paul the right place."

"And what might the right place be?" Mitch asked.

"Oh, well, I was in town and I saw this girl who had a really good color job and I asked her where she got her hair done and she said that a friend of hers does it for her in her home, so—"

"How about we cut the bullshit," Rileigh said, "and you tell us the truth. Where were you that night? Because we're going to track down whatever stupid alibi you give us and find out that it's a lie. You're better off telling the truth now."

The woman appeared to be considering her options — whether to fess up now or keep going with the ruse. Apparently, she decided on door number one, and her shoulders slumped.

"Okay, I was not getting my hair done that night."

"We pretty much established what you *weren't* doing. We want to know what you *were* doing."

She looked down at the floor, then raised her eyes but refused to meet Rileigh's gaze.

"I'm, I'm seeing someone," she said. Then she held up her hand. "Oh, it's not like it sounds. It's not some sordid fling or anything like that. It's," she let out a breath, "Paul and I have been having troubles for the last year or so and…"

"Define having troubles," Rileigh said.

"We haven't been getting along at all. We squabble and fight." She looked down at the floor again. "This is embarrassing to say in front of a man, but Paul just hasn't been interested in me that way, you know, like he used to be."

Rileigh thought it was probably difficult to work up romantic feelings for a woman you squabbled with all the time but she didn't say that.

"So where were you that night?"

"Like I said, it's not some sordid like one-night stand or anything like that. It's—"

"I'm not passing judgment on the morality of your sex life," Mitch said. "I'm only interested in finding out where you were at the time your stepdaughter went missing."

"His name is Reginald Daniels. I met him at a street fair in Nashville. He's an artist, a glassblower. Do you know how incredibly difficult that is, glassblowing? He has a shop in Gatlinburg called the Birds of the Air, where he makes beautiful glass sculptures of birds. He specializes in birds. Other glassblowers make whatever is commercial, whatever will sell, but not Reggie. He's an artist. He makes what he sees with his heart's eye."

She smiled. "That's what he calls it when he's out in the woods bird watching. He watches the colorful creatures with his heart's eye and he sees them differently, and that's what he makes. They don't look like birds the conventional way you and I see. They're heart's eye recreations of reality."

Rileigh wanted to ask if they looked like fire hydrants or electric toothbrushes or aardvarks, but didn't. "Where did you meet Reggie last night?"

"Well, since he has a studio here, he has a small apartment above it. His home is in Nashville, but he uses the apartment for when he has to work late."

Rileigh thought of the guest room in Gus' house where he had put Agent Devereaux after he tended to his wounds, and she suspected that the room above the Birds of the Air art gallery where Reggie Daniels shacked up with his girlfriend was probably a considerably nicer and more romantic spot than the storeroom with a bed in it that Gus had in his coroner's office.

"And what time did you meet Reggie there?" Mitch asked.

"We arranged to meet at that little French restaurant, you know, the one in Gatlinburg on Conover Street? It's usually crowded with tourists, but if you wait until later in the evening, you can get a table. So we met there and had dinner. It was wonderful. I had—"

"Mrs. Schofield, I'm not interested in the menu at a French restaurant in Gatlinburg. I want to know what time you arrived and what time you left."

She let out a sigh. "I know you think it's crass and sordid, but it's not, it's really not."

Nobody's affairs are ever crass and sordid. It's everybody else's affairs that are crass and sordid.

"We had dinner reservations for six," she continued, "and we took our time eating, had a lovey Bordeaux…" She saw the look on Mitch's face and didn't complete the sentence. "And then we went to his place, the apartment above his art studio."

"And how long did you stay there?"

"It didn't seem like I was there for long at all, but then I looked at the clock and realized I'd said I'd be home by nine, and not even counting the drive back here from Gatlinburg, I knew I was going to be terribly late."

Rileigh considered the distance and thought about driving the mountain roads at what must have been breakneck speeds to make it back to Shagbark when she said she would.

"All right, I will need this man's contact information."

"Oh no, you can't talk to him!" she cried.

"Oh yes, I can," Mitch said.

"No, no. His wife doesn't know about us. And she can't find out, she just can't, it would be the end of everything."

"I'm sure it would cause significant problems in their relationship," Mitch said.

"It's worse than that. She, his wife, is from a very wealthy family, and they're his patrons. They're the reason he gets to spend all day every day in the woods watching the birds, making beautiful art. But if she found out…"

The gravy train would quickly derail.

"Nobody knows about us," she finished.

"Hillary knows you're having an affair," Rileigh said. Tabitha didn't look surprised, just alarmed.

"How do *you* know she knows?"

"She told me," Mitch said, and Tabitha gasped.

"You knew Hillary knew about the affair, didn't you, Tabitha?" Rileigh said. "How did you find out?"

"She told me."

That must have happened sometime after the day Hillary went to Mitch's office, because she said then her stepmother didn't know she knew about her affairs.

"When did she tell you?"

"She told me that night, but she was just mad because she couldn't go to the movie. That's all. She didn't mean it. She'd never really tell Paul."

"She threatened *that night* to tell her father?"

"She wouldn't have gone through with it."

"But if she did, that would be a big problem for you," Rileigh said. "And for Reggie and his rich wife."

"She was bluffing."

"Your life would be a whole lot easier if Hillary weren't around to mess it up, wouldn't it?"

"Damn right it would. Paul and I were having problems way before Hillary came on the scene, but she made everything ten times worse. She's such a little shit, defying all kinds of discipline because her mother never made her do anything she didn't want to. So I was always on her back about something and she took so much of Paul's time. He and I used to spend evenings together after we put the littles to bed, but after Hillary showed up, that time was gone. He spent it talking to her, mostly explaining to her why she was in so much trouble for whatever the hell it was she did she wasn't supposed to. She was an absolute monster."

"So your relationship with your husband was already on the rocks."

"Not on the rocks. He came up with this glorious idea about spending time in the mountains, and I thought it was wonderful." She smiled.

"It certainly got you closer to your boyfriend in Gatlinburg."

"Well that's not, that's not why, that's not the whole... that's not *the* reason. I knew it would be good for the children and good for Paul and me to get away from the normal hustle and bustle and let the children play in the creeks in the mountains. And then Paul and I could, you know, maybe see if there was still something there worth saving. When he told me he intended to bring Hillary, I lost it. I totally exploded. I told him he was crazy. No way in hell was I going to spend all day, every day, with that angry little bitch who didn't even have school to distract her. I told him I was absolutely, categorically not going to be some kind of home-school teacher to the little shit."

"So basically you're telling us your life would be a whole lot better if it weren't for Hillary Schofield," Mitch said.

It appeared to dawn on Tabitha how all of that sounded, and she looked stricken.

"I didn't mean it that way. You don't think *I*..."

"You had motive and opportunity," Mitch said.

"You and your boyfriend could have come back here after your husband took the children to the movies. Maybe you'd been planning it for that night," Rileigh said.

"You said your life would be better off without her," Mitch added.

Tabitha sputtered some more, throwing up more denials and realizing that she had painted herself into a corner.

"Look, it's not like you see it."

"Your stepdaughter knows you're having an affair," Mitch said, "and could, at any moment, for any reason, tell your husband about it... it would sure be nice if the girl would go poof in a puff of smoke and disappear."

"No, no, it's not like that at all. It's—"

Their conversation was interrupted by Paul Schofield bringing the children back from tubing in the Pigeon River. They were wet, dripping all over the floor and shivering from the icy water, and their mother fussed over them so that she didn't have to engage with Rileigh and Mitch anymore. Paul Schofield made a beeline for Mitch.

"What do you know? What have you found out? Please tell me you found something." He sounded desperate. "Anything."

"I'm afraid we don't have any leads right now, Mr. Schofield, though we do have a few suspects."

Tabitha Schofield's head snapped up, but she said nothing to Mitch, just spoke quietly to her husband. "Talking about this is upsetting the littles." She cut her eyes to the children, all three of whom were standing in the middle of the room, dripping water into puddles, staring at their father.

"They need to get dried off. Why don't you take them

and get them into some dry clothes," she told him, and he allowed her to shoo him and the kids out of the room.

As soon as they were gone, she turned to Mitch. "Please tell me you're not going to tell my husband about Reggie. I mean, you can't. Isn't what I told you privileged information, like what you say to a lawyer and you can't—"

"What you say to a police officer, he can tell anybody he chooses," Mitch said. She looked horrified. "But no, I have no intention of telling your husband that you're screwing around on him." She looked relieved.

Outside on the porch, Rileigh said, "Well, what do you think?"

"Like I said, motive and opportunity."

"Yep, and it would be a really clever way to throw off suspicion, don't you think — admit to everything the police are going to find out anyway."

"And before they have a chance to consider you a suspect, convince them you're harmless."

Rileigh nodded and gave him a fist bump. "That woman isn't nearly as dithered and scattered as she wants us to believe she is."

Chapter Nineteen

THERE WERE, OF COURSE, SEVERAL PEOPLE IN YARMOUTH
County who would know the real story of what had
happened during the axe murders in Shagbark Manor.
However, Rileigh believed the first step, and certainly the
most accurate source, would be Thelma Rittenhouse.
Though she was older than Mama, she still had every
marble she had been issued at birth and a whole bunch of
other marbles she had picked up along the way. She was a
sweet, sharp old lady who had spent her life as a librarian.
She had never married, would probably have told anyone
who asked that she had remained single so she could have
thousands of lovers — every male character in every book
on all those shelves.

She had retired years ago and lived in a small cottage
out on Huber Lane. Rileigh called in advance and asked if
she and Mitch might come for a visit. Mama had made
brownies, and Rileigh promised to bring some.

They pulled up in front of Thelma's cottage and found
her sitting in the porch swing on the front porch, where

there were rockers and a comfortable rattan chair or two, knitting.

Mitch commented as soon as he saw her house, "That looks like a gingerbread house, like something out of a fairy tale."

"I always thought so too," Rileigh said.

The old lady rose to her feet when Mitch and Rileigh came in through the gate, and they walked up on the steps to greet her. She looked so fragile that a strong wind might blow her away, but she hugged Rileigh long and tight.

"I haven't seen you in a coon's age, sweetheart."

Her voice was soft, a whisper on a breath.

"And who is this big, tall, good-looking young man?"

"Thelma, I'd like you to meet Yarmouth County Sheriff Mitch Webster."

Thelma shook his hand. "Would you like some lemonade?"

Rileigh produced her box of brownies. "That would be good to help wash these down. They are very chocolatey."

"Oh, I love Lily Bishop's brownies! My niece made a fresh pitcher before she left. It's in the refrigerator. Help yourself. Marianne stays with me most days now. Told her I wasn't going to wear one of those 'I've Fallen and I Can't Get Up' bracelets, and the next day she was on my porch with luggage." The old lady shook her head and leaned toward Rileigh, speaking conspiratorially. "If I had it to do over again, I'd pick the bracelet."

When they were properly outfitted with tall glasses of lemonade and ice, they seated themselves back on the front porch. Thelma had remained in the swing, which protested every motion back and forth with a loud squawk — an unmuted swing, unlike the one on Rileigh's porch.

"So I understand you want to pick my brains," Thelma started, "and if there's anything I like, it's having my brains picked. After a while, it gets kind of dusty in there, and you need to go in and dig around, blow the dust off things."

"As I said on the phone," Rileigh said, "we'd like to talk to you about what happened at Shagbark Manor."

"Well, there are all kinds of written resources you could use, newspaper and magazine stories, even a couple of books with lurid titles. I can't recommend them because I haven't read them."

"I'd rather hear it from somebody who lived through the aftermath."

"Oh, I lived through the aftermath alright. You do know, don't you, that my father was the sheriff, that he was called to the scene that day?"

Rileigh was stunned.

What a wonderful surprise! "How do I not know that?"

"My mama was pregnant with me when the murders happened. We didn't have a name for it then, not like now. But when I look back, I know my father suffered from PTSD, had flashbacks for years when I was a little girl over the horror of that day. Those murders were the canvas on which my whole childhood was painted."

Rileigh had been looking for a single rose but had stumbled on a whole bush.

"Where to start…" the old woman mused. "The beginning is usually the best place, but I believe I'll drop you right into the middle of the action. And, by the way, you need to look up the details on what I tell you. Details are like frosting on a cake — they make it taste a whole lot better, but they get scraped off by time."

The old woman leaned back in the swing and began to push it slowly back and forth with her foot so that everything she said was punctuated with a squawk-squawk.

"Crawford Tillman had money, he came from money, but I don't know what it was that his parents did that made so much of it. He inherited the land, and after he married, he built that house — what a showpiece it was at the time! She was a local girl, Lenora, and they had three little girls — Jocelyn and her two sisters, whose names I have trouble remember ... Elizabeth was one, and I think the other was Regina ... no, Victoria. They were both older than Jocelyn, she was the baby. "

"Did you ever hear that people thought Crawford Tillman was odd, off, or something like that?" Mitch asked.

"He had a bad heart. Everybody knew that. Had rheumatic fever as a child, had to be real careful not to overdo. But as far as I know, nobody thought anything else was wrong with him before the bad happened. If they did, they kept it to themselves. If anything, it was Lenora Tillman who had bats in her belfry."

"What do you mean?"

"Oh, she was just kind of crazy-like, I think. I know folks thought she was way too strict on those girls, but I don't really know the specifics. Crawford Tillman was a straight-laced, upright banker." She let out a sigh. "Until he wasn't. On the first day of May, 1926, the three little girls were playing hide and seek before bedtime, and you can imagine how much fun that would be in that great big old house. Their mama was working out in the garden when Crawford came home early from an out-of-town trip.

"And nobody knows what happened after that. All anybody does know is what you can surmise by what the neighbors found when they went in the house... after. As you know, the house sits way back off the road. A couple of neighbors drove past the house when it was really late, but all the lights were still on. They thought that was odd — not just one light, but all of them. People back then didn't waste electricity like that. I think there was a gardener, or a field hand working in the hay next to the house, who knocked on the door, and when nobody answered, they went inside. And the field hand, or the gardener, or whoever it was, ran to the neighbors and said something terrible had happened at the Tillman house and the neighbors went into town to get my papa. Mama said it was early in the morning on a beautiful spring day — Papa's day off. She told him to let one of the deputies handle it, but he went anyway. She told us kids later she wished she'd tied him to the bedpost to keep him from going."

Rileigh reached out and patted the old woman's hand.

Thelma continued, "So the little girls were ready for bed, playing hide and seek in the house, and their mother was in the garden — because when they found her body, she was wearing gardening gloves. Crawford Tillman came home unexpectedly from a trip... and for some reason that Crawford Tillman carried to his grave, he went out to the woodshed and got an axe, brought it back into the house, and killed two of his daughters and his wife with it."

"Really? The killer wasn't somebody else, some stranger?"

"That's what a lot of folks believed, maybe most people. But my Papa didn't. Like I say, no one knows for sure what happened exactly. All they know is that the girls had cuts all over them, but more on their backs, like they were running away. It wasn't like the killer struck one killing blow, but he'd slashed at them. The bodies were found huddled in the corner of the upstairs hall. Jocelyn was in the middle, like maybe her sisters were trying to shield her. There was blood all up and down the stairs, and down the hallways, and in the bedrooms. The only explanation was the killer chased those poor little girls around with an axe, trying to kill them, hacking at them. And then their mother must have come running when she heard them screaming, and she tried to stop him. By then, the little girls were already all cut up, bleeding bad, and he turned on her, killed her."

She paused for a breath.

"And then he chopped Lenora Tillman into pieces. That was what Papa saw in his nightmares — pieces of that woman's body scattered all over the floor, and the dead little girls huddled in the corner. They were wearing matching pink nightgowns with lace on them, each with their initial embroidered on the front. That broke his heart."

"But Jocelyn survived, she wasn't dead," Mitch said.

"Nobody knew that at the time. She looked as dead as the other two."

"And Mr. Tillman?"

"What the neighbors and Papa found was Crawford Tillman lying at the bottom of the stairs, still in his coat and tie — even his hair wasn't mussed up. His suit and hands had blood on them, but he didn't have any wounds. Folks conjectured that when Lenora came into the house from the backyard, she and her husband fought with the killer for the axe at the foot of the stairs and Tillman had a heart attack. But that's not what my Papa thought happened. He didn't believe a stranger did it. He thought it was a family thing, that the murderer was Crawford Tillman, that Lenora tried to stop him and he killed her and cut her up before his heart failed and he died."

"Just came home from a business trip, set his suitcase down, then picked up an axe and murdered his family?" Mitch said. "Chased his kids around with an axe, chopped his wife into pieces... and *then* his heart gave out?"

The old woman shrugged. "Papa was convinced that's what happened. He knew something about Crawford and

Lenora Tillman, had seen something maybe that other people hadn't, but he never told anybody what it was."

"So how did the neighbors know that the girls had been playing hide and seek?" Rileigh asked.

"It was Jocelyn who told them. They found her with her sisters, blood all over her but she was alive, wouldn't say a word." The old woman shook her head. "Can you even imagine that? The poor little child, six years old, huddled there all night with her dead sisters — the bodies were already cold when the neighbors found them. They rushed her to the doctor and when they got the blood cleaned off her, they discovered she was unharmed. Folks figured the older two shielded their baby sister between them."

"How long did she remain catatonic?" Mitch asked.

"I'm not sure, but it was months and months. She was in a psychiatric hospital, and one day she just came out of it and was asking where her mother and her sisters were, and apparently the last thing she remembers was that she and her sisters were playing hide and seek, and that she had hidden in the window seat under the big window beside the front door. She didn't remember anything after playing hide and seek, and that happens to people some-times, something terrible happens and their minds just wipe it out."

"Let's fast forward through the generations," Mitch said. "Jocelyn Tillman grew up and…"

"Got married to Wilford, Willard, Will-something Farrington. They just had the one little girl, Sarah. I don't think Willard lived very long, but I don't remember what he died from. I just know Jocelyn raised the little girl by herself in that big old house and at some point, Josie decided to turn the place into a bed and breakfast, had all kind of work done on it, you know, to bring it up to code."

"Tell me about Jocelyn's daughter Sarah," Mitch said.

"Don't know much. She was a feisty one, real pretty, with black hair and dark eyes like her father's side of the family. She ran off with some boy when she was young, fifteen or sixteen. I don't believe she got married for a long time, and it wasn't to that young man when she did, and she kept her maiden name, Farrington, but I don't know why. She had three little girls kinda late in life. Then she and her husband got killed and left them three little girls orphans. By then, Jocelyn had got old." Thelma chuckled. "There's a lot of that going around. She was 'Grandma Josie' and she took 'em in, brought them to Shagbark Manor and raised 'em. Carly Farrington was just a little thing, probably six years old, something like that. The older two girls left soon's they was old enough to, but not Carly. She stayed. She helped her grandmother run the bed and breakfast, and when her grandmother died, she took over management of it herself."

Rileigh could tell that the re-telling of that big story had taken a lot of energy, and Thelma was clearly worn out. Rileigh could have stayed all afternoon, peppering her with questions, but she understood that they needed to leave. They thanked Thelma profusely. She made them promise to come visit her sometime. They did and Rileigh intended to keep the promise. The old woman was delightful.

Once in the car, Rileigh wondered aloud, "Do you think Grandma Josie told those three girls — Carly and her sisters — about what happened in that house? She raised them. Maybe she had more to say to them than she ever told anybody else."

"Don't know, but it's certainly worth asking the question," Mitch said.

Mitch didn't start the engine. He cleared his throat.

"There's something I've been meaning to tell you," he said.

"And what is …?"

"We got the test results back on the piece of skin we sent to the lab for DNA analysis. It came from a man named Santiago Suárez, a bag man for organized crime in Chicago. They've never recovered the body."

His words hit Rileigh like a blow to the belly.

But Mitch wasn't finished.

"And we got the results in over a week ago. I didn't tell you about it because… our date was for Saturday night, and I didn't want to give you a downer then, because you — *we* — were looking forward to it so much. But I've been feeling bad about keeping it from you. It felt like… lying to you by omission."

He paused, looked deep into her eyes.

"You need to know… I will never lie to you. Never."

Chapter Twenty

RILEIGH WAS HAPPY TO GO WITH MITCH TO POSE "THE question" to Carly Farrington — when she was growing up, did Grandma Josie tell her anything about the axe murders?

They found her in the big industrial kitchen on the back side of Shagbark Manor. Rileigh had admired it when they were searching the place looking for Hillary. She imagined that someone had simply gutted a large room, took out everything all the way back to the studs, and built new, because everything in this kitchen was modern. It had everything you would need to make meals for fifteen, twenty, maybe more people.

Carly's long hair was in a ponytail, and she was kneading dough as they entered.

She looked up when they came into the room. "I didn't expect to see you again so soon."

"We have a few more questions we'd like to ask you, if you don't mind," Mitch said.

"No, of course, I don't mind, but..." She looked a little flustered. "Would you mind asking while I finish this up? I have to get the dough ready, and making bread is not something you can stop in the middle of."

"Sure, please go on with what you're doing."

"I can't imagine what you would want to know from me that you haven't asked already. I don't know anything else."

"Actually, you know a whole lot about what we'd like to talk to you about."

"And that is?"

"Your Grandma Josie, and what she might have told you about the murders in this house when she was a little girl."

Carly froze, became a statue for a moment or two, and then went on, "What in the world do you want to know about Grandma Josie? She's been dead for almost twenty years."

"We are looking into establishing what really did happen in this house in May, 1926, when Crawford Tillman came home and tried to murder his whole family."

"Why in the world would you want to know about that?"

"Let's just say that it's the stage on which the rest of what we're looking into plays out."

"Humor us, okay?" Rileigh said and smiled. Carly didn't return the smile. Just kept working.

"So tell me about your history here," Mitch said

Carly continued kneading the dough as she spoke, not looking at Mitch and Rileigh, and it occurred to Rileigh that maybe she said she wanted to continue kneading the bread because she didn't want to look Mitch and Rileigh in the eyes.

"Well, Grandma Josie lived here and my parents and my sisters and I lived in Knoxville, and we came here to visit sometimes on the weekends. It seems like we came often, but I could be wrong. I don't have very many memories of my childhood before we came to live here after my parents were killed, and the court awarded Grandma Josie custody of the three of us."

"How old were you?"

"I was six, Kiara was sixteen, and Camille was seventeen."

"When you were a little girl, did your grandma Josie talk about what happened the night of those murders?"

"Oh, Lord, no. She wouldn't have had anything to say if she'd wanted to. She forgot it all."

"She was catatonic, right?" Rileigh said.

"As I understand it, when they found her, she was huddled in the corner with her two dead sisters, just staring into space. They tried to talk to her and she wouldn't talk to anybody. She was, of course, diagnosed as catatonic, and it probably wasn't surprising given what she had been through."

"So how long was she catatonic?"

"I don't know exactly, but it was a long time. And when she came out of it and they asked questions about what happened, she described playing hide and seek with her sisters and how she had hidden in the window seat in the foyer beside the front door. And then her father came home early from a trip and that's it. That's where her memories stopped."

"So she never talked about what happened after he came home."

"She remembered climbing into the window seat and closing the lid over her head, and the next thing she knew she was in a psychiatric hospital."

"So she didn't remember, like maybe peeking out of

her hiding place and watching what was going on?" Rileigh asked.

Carly froze again, stood absolutely still, then said simply, "No."

Then some kind of verbal dam broke, and she gushed words.

"I suppose maybe she, I mean, maybe she could have done that. I don't, I don't know. She never said anything about it. She never talked to me about it then. She never described anything except that she climbed into the window seat and closed the lid and I don't know what she may have seen after that but she didn't know either because she forgot it all. She had retrograde amnesia or whatever you want to call it, but she couldn't remember."

All of those words strung together was the most that Mitch and Rileigh had heard Carly say at one time since they'd been introduced to her. She seemed rattled and upset, so Mitch changed the subject.

"So the three of you grew up here and your sisters left and you didn't. Why not?"

"I loved it here. I'd always felt a special fondness for Shagbark Manor, and my grandmother and I were very close. We had always been very close and I just didn't want to leave after high school, so I went to work for my grandmother. She had turned the place into a bed and breakfast, and that's a lot of work, and I helped her with that."

"I happened to walk in on the argument you were having with your sisters about selling the place when I brought Hillary home the other day," Mitch said. "It appeared to me that the other two wanted to sell and they weren't happy that you didn't."

"When I was too young to know what I wanted and what I didn't want and when I was growing up, they always talked about it. 'We'll sell the place when you turn twenty-one when it and the whole estate is deeded over to us. We'll sell it. We'll sell it. We'll sell it.' I just nodded my head you know, like a good little bobblehead doll, but when it finally came to it, I realized I didn't want to sell it. When I turned twenty-one, I realized I wanted to keep it. I wanted it to stay in the family, and of course my sisters were angry about that because they said I'd agreed all along and then at the last minute I backed out, but I'd never really agreed. I just hadn't argued with them."

"Running a bed and breakfast is quite an enterprise for a twenty-one-year-old."

Carly snorted. "Oh, I'm sure my sisters thought it would fail, that I'd face plant and come crawling back, saying I was sorry. But that's not what happened. Over the years, business grew."

"My mama says it's because you were good at marketing," Rileigh said. Carly turned to her then and actually smiled.

"Well, maybe."

"Tell me what changes you made."

"It just seemed to me that the natural draw of Shagbark Manor is as a haunted house. I mean, everybody has said for years that the place is haunted, and people claim they've seen this strange thing or that strange thing, and it's all just people's imaginations, of course. But that seemed like a good hook. I advertised for people to come and spend a weekend or a week in a haunted house where they were actual, no kidding axe-murders, and when I started changing the advertising to that theme, business really picked up."

She sighed.

"And then... COVID."

Rileigh and Mitch both groaned.

"It was a nightmare if you were in the hospitality business. Everything just stopped. Nobody went anywhere. Nobody stayed overnight anywhere. Nobody took vacations. It was horrible."

"And the bills didn't stop when the customers stopped coming," Mitch said.

"You got that right. No, they did *not.*"

"How did you manage it?" Rileigh asked. "How did you keep your head above water with continuing expenses and no income?"

"A lot of places went under. I read somewhere than thirty percent of the mom and pop-owned restaurants in California went out of business. I survived. Gratefully, I had no mortgage payments to make with mounting interest payments." She sighed. "At least *then* I had no mortgage. Now… I owe a lot of money on this place. A whole lot of money. But the math worked when COVID was finally over. If I kept the place full every week, that would cover overhead and just enough that I could start paying down my debts."

She smiled. "That's why I was so thrilled when the Schofields said they wanted to rent the place for five months. He said he'd pay to be the only family in this house for five months. Meaning he would pay what I'd make if the place were full. I couldn't believe it in the beginning. It was such a such good fortune, so of course I jumped at it. And that's why they're here and no one else is. It's certainly a lot less work to only look after one family."

"Did you sign some kind of contract?"

"Bed and breakfasts don't have contracts."

"So what if they decide to leave after four weeks?"

She looked stricken. "I've been afraid of that. That's all I've thought about ever since Hillary went missing. There's a pipeline that you have to establish when you rent out places in advance. You have to book months ahead. After the Schofields told me they wanted the place for five months, I took all of that down off the website because no one else could sign up."

Then Rileigh understood. "So if they bail out on you and leave, you don't have other customers that made reservations three months ago or four months ago or five months ago."

"That's right. I don't. I just want them to stay here. I *need* them to stay."

Chapter Twenty-One

WHEN RILEIGH PULLED UP IN FRONT OF GEORGIA'S double-wide trailer on Carter's Mill Road, she noticed immediately that something was amiss. Where were the kids? Normally, there were kids playing in the yard, but there were no children visible. Georgia was home; her car was parked in the driveway. Maybe the kids had gone to see their grandparents.

Rileigh got out of the car, made her way through the obstacle course of little kid riding toys on the driveway, stepped up onto the porch, and opened the screen door. Putting her head inside, she called out, "Yo, Georgia, you here?"

"I'm not sure you want to come in," came a shout from the back of the trailer. "All the kids are sick."

Rileigh remained where she was. "Stomach bug?" If it was a stomach bug, she'd leave. She could ask what she wanted through the screen, though she'd rather do it more casually, face to face. But she'd come to see Georgia once years ago when she was on leave, and a couple of the kids had a stomach virus of the vomiting and diarrhea persuasion. Rileigh had caught it and was incapacitated for several of the precious days of her leave, unable to go more than twenty feet from the bathroom.

"No, not a stomach bug, just the usual snotty-nose malady," Georgia said as she came down the hallway to the living room. Rileigh stepped through the door then. She figured her immune system could handle a little-kid cold.

That's when she noticed the structure in the middle of the floor in the living room. Kitchen chairs had been arranged to form a square with a space in the middle, and clear plastic was draped all around the chairs and across the top, sealing the area in the middle where Mayella lay on a pillow, coughing — the distinctive seal-bark cough of the croup.

"What is that thing?" she asked, though it was pretty obvious what it had to be.

"It's a croup tent," Georgia said. "Poor Mayella always gets the croup when the boys bring home a cold. Got it so bad when she was real little, we had to take her to the emergency room and they put her in a croup tent. So as soon as she got that cough, I made one."

Rileigh went to the thing made out of plastic and chairs and examined it.

"About the only thing you can do to make the croup better is make sure the kid's breathing really moist air. It helps loosen the crap in their chests, and that's what a croup tent does. It seals the kid up, and then moistens the air." She pointed to the humidifier that had been placed in the enclosure with Mayella. "You want a cup of coffee, Rileigh?"

"No, thanks," Rileigh said, stepping from the living room into the kitchen.

Georgia was making a fresh pot anyway. "You sure? I was up all night with one or the other of them." She looked like she had been, her hair disheveled, her eyes tired. "Coffee is the only thing keeping my body vertical."

Bark, bark, bark. The distinctive croup cough sound came from the croup tent. Georgia unexpectedly smiled.

"Yesterday when I made the tent, it was so sweet... Liam wasn't too sick then, just a little cough and sneezing, but Mayella's chest was really tight, so Chigger and I made the croup tent for her. The croup's really dangerous in a child her age because the pipes in her internal plumbing are so small that they could swell shut, but when we got the tent made, she didn't want to get in it."

"Can't blame her. I wouldn't want to sit in that thing either," Rileigh said.

"So she started to cry, and that made the coughing worse, and then Liam told her, 'I'll get in there with you, come on,' and he crawled into that little space. We didn't make it big enough for two kids, but he curled up in there and cajoled Mayella to come inside with him. Then he sat in there and read her storybooks." Georgia's smile widened. "It was the sweetest thing you ever saw. No kid wants to be in a croup tent. It's damp in there and cramped, but Liam made it into a game for Mayella, and he stayed in there with her for hours till she finally went to sleep. I told him he got the Big Brother of the Year award."

"How are the other kids?" Rileigh asked.

"Well, Connor's cold is probably the worst." Connor was six. "Eli appears to be getting a sore throat from his, and I'm hoping that it's not some secondary infection, like he's got strep. And Mason feels so bad that he is just laying in his bed, all of them playing video games of one kind or another." Georgia looked up at the ceiling and held her hands up as if talking to God. "Thank you, Lord, for video games. You have saved the lives and sanity of every mother on the planet."

In truth, Georgia was rigorously strict about her children's use of electronic devices, Rileigh knew, and almost never let them near one. It was one rule she always enforced and she was definitely swimming upstream among the other moms on that one.

"I won't keep you," Rileigh said. "Obviously, you have way more fun things to do than talk to me."

"Oh, yeah, it's a laugh a minute in the Stump household these days."

"I just came by because I wanted you to ask Chigger if he'd be willing to talk to me."

"Chigger? What do you want to talk to Chigger about?"

"About a drug dealer he may know. His name is Scooby."

There was an awkward silence between them then. The fact that Georgia's husband was a drug dealer was the elephant in the middle of the room of their relationship. It was an open secret that he transported and sold marijuana, and that he was surely also growing it somewhere. After last summer when Georgia kicked Chigger out for having an affair with Tina Montgomery, she took him back on condition that he not sell hard drugs, and as far as Rileigh knew, he had lived up to that agreement. He was known throughout Yarmouth and surrounding counties as the go-to man for any kind of weed your heart might fancy — he had access to every "brand," every strain. And as always, Rileigh continued to wonder why Chigger wasn't more successful at his line of work than he was. Every drug dealer she'd ever known made a lot of money, lived on it, high and free, got hooked on whatever they were selling, and either wound up overdosed and dead or in prison. Perhaps that was the road Chigger was on until Georgia kicked him out. Rileigh knew there was a whole lot of money to be made in drug dealing, and apparently Chigger wasn't making a whole lot of it, or he would have been providing better for his wife and kids. But all of those were unspoken things between Georgia and Rileigh. Chigger was what he was, and Rileigh was not a police officer, and she was not, therefore, obligated either morally or legally to do anything about the fact that he was breaking the law. Still, it was a subject they tiptoed around, and Rileigh hadn't been looking forward to having a conversation with Chigger, but she knew that if anybody could help her find Scooby, it was Chigger Stump.

"Why are you looking for this dealer called Scooby?" Georgia said, her voice tight.

"We're working the case of the missing teenager out at Shagbark Manor, and the handyman admitted that he had hooked her up with Scooby to provide drugs, and we'd like to talk to him about that."

Georgia shrugged. "I'll talk to him tonight and see when, you know, you could get together with him."

Georgia quickly redirected the conversation.

"So you're working the case of the girl missing from Shagbark Manor?" Rileigh nodded. "I can see why somebody would be missing from that place," Georgia said, rinsing her coffee cup out in the sink as the new pot gurgled and bubbled on the counter. "It's a creepy place, and I can't imagine why anybody'd want to rent it out and stay there."

"I thought it was beautiful," Rileigh said. "We searched it up and down, went through the whole thing. It's a maze of hallways and doors."

"And secret passageways," Georgia said.

"Well, that's what the rumors say, but we certainly didn't see any."

"I did."

Rileigh looked at her quizzically. "*You* did. When?"

"You remember I told you that I went to a sleepover with Carly at Shagbark Manor when you and your mom were out of town that summer touring the national parks?"

"Yeah, you said that's when you started having nightmares, recurring nightmares. Why do you think there really are secret passageways in that place?"

"Because I saw one," she said. "Or maybe I did. I don't know."

"Tell me about it."

"Well, I should have told Mama that I was sick before she took me over there. I could feel it. You know how when you get an earache as a kid, it throbs in your jaw when it starts. I felt that before I went but I didn't say anything about it."

"That was the summer when we were nine years old."

"I kept my mouth shut because I knew Mama wouldn't let me go if I was sick, and I wanted to go. I wanted to spend the night with Carly." Georgia stopped. "Well, okay, not because I wanted to spend the night with Carly. She had the personality of a steamed turnip even then. But I did want to get a look at the inside of the place. Vacation Bible School had been outside in the yard for a whole week, and every kid there suddenly had to go to the bathroom every ten minutes as an excuse to go inside and look around."

She paused for a bit, like she was lost in thought, then continued. "Like I told you, I can't remember exactly how it came about that I was invited to a sleepover. I'm sure it was me who initiated it because I so curious about Shagbark Manor. But I was already sick for a full day before I went there and didn't say anything. So of course, the ear infection exploded on me when I got there, and then I was really sick."

Rileigh cringed in sympathy, remembering how painful an ear infection was.

"But an earache is the kind of sick you can hide, so I did. I was miserable, though, and I was running a fever, which is what the nightmares are about. A kid with a high fever could imagine anything. Eli's fever got so high once he thought there was water on the floor in his room and it was getting higher and higher. He climbed up into Liam's bunk bed above his so he wouldn't drown."

"Tell me about this secret passageway. Did you imagine it, or was it real?"

Georgia looked uncomfortable. "I've never known how much of what I remember about that time is imaginary and how much is real. But I remember the secret passageway, the door that didn't appear to be there in the wall. I think that part was real." She sat back in her chair, rubbed her tired eyes. "But the rest of it — just a little kid with a high fever in a creepy house."

"Tell me what you *think* happened."

Georgia poured herself a cup of coffee and dumped a bucket of cream into it, took a big drink, and turned back around to face Rileigh. "What do you think I imagined I saw *at Shagbark Manor*? I saw an axe murder."

Chapter Twenty-Two

RILEIGH COULDN'T BELIEVE GEORGIA HAD NEVER TOLD HER a story like that. Ordinarily, that would have been the first one out of Georgia's mouth as soon as Rileigh got home, her hands flying around in the air — she talked with her hands when she got excited.

Now, Rileigh needed a crowbar to pry it out of her. It quickly became clear she'd never talked about it because she didn't *want* to talk about it, wanted to forget the whole thing and pretend it never happened.

"Aw, come on Riles. We both have better things to do than sit here—"

"A team of Clydesdales and the Budweiser beer wagon couldn't drag me out of this chair. Spill!"

Georgia heaved a resigned sigh.

"Okay, but everything about that whole overnight is wrapped in layers of Saran Wrap in my mind, foggy and blurry. It's possible everything I tell you about never really happened. Even the things I know *did* happen are so blurred-out, they seem like dreams, too."

"Let the record show you have disavowed all responsibility for the veracity of everything that's about to fall out of your mouth."

"I think Grandma Josie was sorry she invited me. She was all in a dither because the only guest in the place had announced she was leaving early, and for some reason me being there made that complicated."

"Did your ear feel better as the night wore on?"

"Oh god no, it got worse. It already hurt bad when Mama dropped me off there. I can't believe I was so stupid that I didn't say anything, I'm sure I was already running a fever then. I spiked fevers when I had ear infections. Got up to 106 once, Mama said."

"So that's what turned your brain into a poached egg."

"Carly was excited I was there, and I tried to have fun, you know, playing with dolls — there was a whole room full of them, but Carly wasn't allowed to touch those, said they were valuable antiques. She had plenty of dolls of her own, though. Had half a dozen Barbies and every outfit and accessory ever made. I wanted to look around the house and that bored her, but then she thought of an interesting thing to show me — a secret passageway."

"Well, I'll be damned."

"It was in the music room, the room with the grand piano. She showed me a panel on the wall right beside the window seat, looked like all the rest of them, but then she got up on a chair and touched something on the top and it slid away and there was a passageway behind it. Of course, that was enough to make my ear stop hurting. I wanted to go exploring, but she said we'd get in trouble for going in it. She wasn't supposed to know it was there. She'd just seen Grandma Josie go in there once and found the thing on the wall you pushed to get it open."

"So all the stories about passageways were true!"

"Hold onto your shorts. Maybe I imagined the passageway just like I imagined all the other shit."

"Bummer. Well, maybe. Go on with the story."

"I remembered Grandma Josie from Vacation Bible School as this sweet old lady, nice and accommodating. She must have served fifty gallons of lemonade to a bunch of ungrateful little kids who left plastic cups everywhere, but I don't remember her being sweet and kind the night I stayed with Carly. I remember her being grumpy and distracted and annoyed. You know, the way you are when little kids are underfoot, you don't want them to be.

"We ate dinner — which I didn't understand since it was a bed and breakfast — with the guest who was leaving early. Now *that* woman was a sweet old lady, had the most beautiful white hair. I remember it because she had big ears and had her hair pulled back in a bun, and I remember thinking if my ears were that big, I would have left my hair down to cover them up. She wore stud earrings. At the time, I thought they were diamonds. Now, I know they must have been zirconium — they were as big as my thumb, but I remember them sparkling in her big ears. Her name was Gwynn."

"You remember her *name*?"

"Because it was Gwynn." Gwynneth was Georgia's real name, the one she'd had from birth until third grade when Rileigh had changed it to Georgia. "And her last name was something a kid would find cringeworthy. Like ... Fart or Crap or Butt. Something like that.

"Carly's bedroom had to be seen to be believed. It was huge, of course, every room in that house was huge, but it had this giant four-poster bed and then a canopy over that, it was like something out of a dollhouse. At bedtime, Grandma Josie said she didn't have time tonight to read a story, that we could sit up together in bed and tell each other stories. But instead of the usual 'if you need anything, come get me,' she told us to stay in Carly's room, not to leave it for any reason.

"And then I don't remember anything else until I woke up at some point and it was dark, and Carly was asleep, and my ear felt like someone was stabbing an ice pick through my eardrum. It hurt so bad I started crying. I must have had a high fever by then because I was cold, cuddled up in the blankets, shivering. Finally, I couldn't stand it anymore. I got out of bed, wanted to go find Grandma Josie to ask her if I could have an aspirin, but I didn't want to get in trouble. I remembered where the downstairs bathroom was, though — the other little kids and I practically wore a path on the hardwood floors from the back door to that bathroom during VBS — and there was a medicine cabinet on the wall in that bathroom where there was probably a bottle of aspirin. I knew I could only take one. Mama gave them to me when I had earaches, one adult aspirin or two of the little pink chewable ones that tasted like you were eating a piece of chalk. If there wasn't a bottle of aspirin there, I'd just have to go wake up Grandma Josie."

"So the little kid with a high fever goes staggering around that big old house in the middle of the night. That'd give anybody nightmares."

Georgia said nothing.

"That's the time that you have nightmares about, isn't it?" Rileigh pushed.

Georgia seemed reluctant to answer the question. She turned and fiddled with her coffee and then turned back around.

"Yeah, that's what the nightmares are about — what I imagined happened that night after I got out of bed and was wandering around in the dark."

"And what you imagined was…?"

"It was… it was like a…" Georgia tried a couple of times to start the sentence, then simply said, "I don't know. I genuinely don't have any idea what really happened. I've dreamed about it so often, the horrible images, that now I don't know what's something I hallucinated at the time, and what's a nightmare image I've generated since then, expanding and embellishing it every time I dream it. Because the nightmare images keep getting worse, more detailed, with more gore and blood and…"

"You don't have to sort out what they are — what's real and what's imagined and what you've made in dreams. Just tell me what the images are."

"I saw… a monster… a *thing*… a creature out of a cheap horror movie." Her voice got soft then, barely a whisper. "I stood there and watched it kill the woman who'd been sitting at the table at dinner that night. It hacked her apart with an axe at the foot of the stairs."

Rileigh froze.

"That's what your nightmares are about? No wonder you wake up screaming."

"Don't you see? It makes sense. Every kid who knew what happened in that house pictured it in their heads what it must have looked like when they heard the story. Add a high fever and stir. Of course, that's what I imagined. I was in Shagbark Manor… where Crawford Tillman had murdered his two little girls, then hacked his wife into little pieces at the foot of the stairs. The woman named Gwynn wasn't even there. She'd already left."

"How do you know she left?"

"Well, I know when she was *supposed* to leave. They talked about it at dinner. Grandma Josie didn't want her to leave early, said she needed to finish putting together her box of Goin' Home Chocolates — those really nice boxes, you know, with the mixed chocolates in them. It sounded like some kind of tradition. The chocolates were to give to her family when they got back home. I remember her saying, 'Then you can call them, tell them you're leaving Shagbark Manor and you're bringing them chocolates, special Shagbark Manor chocolates.'"

Rileigh thought about the pictures of tourists that lined the walls in the sitting room. In all them, somebody was holding a box — maybe a box of chocolates.

Georgia had fallen silent.

"Tell me what you saw."

She said the words with no emotion at all, as if she were reading off the instructions for assembling a backyard barbecue grill.

"Carly's bedroom was on the second floor. It was dark in the hall, but that big chandelier in the entryway was on and the light shone up the stairs so I could see where I was going. As I got to the stairs, I heard scuffling, so I stopped at the top and looked down. There was a... monster... wearing a pink nightgown. It was long and had lace trim on the bottom and all around the sleeves. But the *thing* was the size of a grownup, and the nightgown was a little girl's gown, worn on top of clothing like it was a coat. The gown looked filthy, old and tattered, and it was splattered with... spots, red splotches... it was blood, old dried blood, I thought. It wore a full head mask — with the skull split open and the face was white, looked like a painted doll's face, perfect except for the brains oozing down it. And it came at the woman as she was setting her suitcases at the bottom of the stairs, just came out of nowhere, and the woman looked up and opened her mouth to scream but the axe hit her in the face before she could make a sound and blood went everywhere."

"You have one good imagination, girlfriend," Rileigh said.

"The monster grabbed the woman it'd killed by the collar of her shirt and dragged her across the floor. The rug at the bottom of the stairs was light-colored and it was soaked with blood, and the body left a trail of blood on the hardwood floor. It dragged her to the wood-paneled wall under the stairs, then it touched something on the top of the lowest panel, I don't know what, and the panel flopped out onto the floor, like the door on a mailbox. Then the monster shoved the body into the space and closed the panel behind it."

Georgia shuddered.

"The way I see it in my nightmares is that the monster looks up then and sees that I saw, and it starts up the stairs with that axe to come and chop me up." Georgia had begun to tremble, her eyes fixed in a thousand-yard stare. "And I turn and run, but then I fall down. I look up and there it is, standing over me. This monster with blood splattered all over a lacy pink nightgown and an axe held up in the air. Then the axe comes *down*—"

"Hey girlfriend, chill," Rileigh said and put her hand on Georgia's arm to calm her. She had no idea the nightmares that had plagued Georgia for years were so realistic, so visceral.

"I don't remember going back to bed, I don't remember the rest of the night, but I do remember the next morning, how Mama came and got me early because I was sick, and I remember standing in the foyer, telling Grandma Josie and Carly goodbye. I had time to really look at the rug at the bottom of the stairs then. There wasn't a speck of blood or anything else on it. There was no trail of blood across the floor. None of it really happened." She paused. "But knowing that doesn't stop the nightmares."

Mayella began to cough then, sounding like a seal — *bark bark bark*. Georgia got up from the table, went to the refrigerator, and poured a small glass of orange juice, then went into the living room where the makeshift croup tent was, where Mayella was coughing. She got down on her knees and handed the little girl the orange juice under the edge of the plastic. "Here, Sweetie, drink this, you'll feel better."

"Don't want it," Mayella said, shaking her head. She coughed and barked again. "Nana."

Rileigh looked at the fruit dish on the countertop, at the pile of bananas in it. She went to it and got one, and took it to Georgia, who peeled it and handed Mayella the banana under the edge of the plastic.

Bark!

The little girl coughed one more time and then she stuck the banana into her mouth, and she was quiet.

As Rileigh was driving home, she thought about what she hadn't told Georgia. Georgia's description of the monster from her nightmares looked like the figure in the background of the tourist photos hanging on the walls in the sitting room at Shagbark and Georgia had never seen those photos.

Chapter Twenty-Three

GEORGIA TEXTED RILEIGH THE NEXT DAY, TELLING HER that Chigger would be home about six and he'd be glad to talk to her.

The text was significant. In a world where everybody on the planet texted instead of made phone calls, Rileigh and Georgia were the exception. They liked to talk to each other on the phone; they always had. So the fact that Georgia had sent her a text instead of calling made it clear this was something she did not want to talk to Rileigh about.

Rileigh showed up at Georgia's at six. Eli and Mason were playing outside, so apparently their colds were better, and Chigger's beat-up old pickup truck was parked in the driveway. Rileigh got out and, of course, Mason took one look at her, squealed "Wiley!" and came running, threw himself at her, grabbed her around the legs, and said, "I wuv you, Aunt Wiley."

Rileigh leaned over and kissed the little boy on the forehead. "I love you too, Mason." Eli came and gave her a more sedate hug. All the kids always hugged her when they saw her. Sure, this was a hugging culture where everybody hugged everybody — to say hello, to say goodbye. Hugs were as good as "aloha" — could mean just about anything. Still, she loved it that the kids *wanted* to hug her.

She went up on the porch, opened the screen, and stuck her head in. "It's me, Georgia," she called, and Georgia called back from somewhere in the trailer. "Chigger's out in the garage working on his car."

That, too, was significant, that Georgia hadn't come to greet Rileigh. This whole thing was deeply awkward.

Rileigh noticed that the croup tent was no longer set up in the living room, so apparently Mayella was better too.

Rileigh went out to the garage. The door was open, and she could see Chigger inside with his head under the hood of some old car. Chigger didn't have the money to get into cars the way he would have liked, but if he could have, he would have restored antiques. He was a master mechanic, could take any machine and make it run. No, could take any *combustion engine* and make it run. Cars with computer operating systems were above his pay grade.

Rileigh didn't know the first thing about cars, couldn't keep the little insignias straight, had to read the words Ford or Chevrolet on the car to know what it was. But Chigger knew them all, and the one he was working on was old, not old enough to be a classic car but at least old enough to have the kind of engine an amateur like Chigger could work on. Newer cars had so much electronic equipment on them you had to have a degree from MIT to be able to change a tire.

"Lo, Chigger," she called as she came into the garage. Liam was standing beside his father, peering into the guts of the engine while Chigger explained what he was doing.

"You go play with Eli," Chigger told him.

"I don't want to play with Eli. I want to help you with a car."

"I got to talk to Aunt Rileigh about something. You go play with Eli, and I'll call you when we're finished." Liam was glum, but he did as he was told and gave Rileigh a quick hug as he passed.

Chigger stood, picked up a rag, and began to wipe the oil off his hands.

"Georgia said you wanted to talk to me." He was uncomfortable and awkward, stiff and unsmiling. Rileigh didn't like this any better than he did. To talk to Chigger about a drugdealer was to acknowledge that elephant in the room, and talking to Chigger was always difficult for Rileigh because she'd never liked the man.

She'd had dealings with him when they were eighteen, and Georgia got in trouble, and Chigger helped Rileigh get her out of it. All having to do with drugs. She'd formed her dislike for him then and hadn't liked it one bit when Georgia told her that she was marrying Chigger. Rileigh was stationed at Fort Campbell at the time, and if she could have gotten in a car and driven home and duct-taped Georgia to a chair to stop her from marrying him, she would have, but she'd tried the duct-tape-Georgia-to-a-chair routine to keep her from going out with a different drug dealer when they were kids, and that had not ended well.

Rileigh took a deep breath and conjured up in her mind the scene of Chigger rushing into Walmart after Georgia had called him and told him that Mason had been kidnapped. She had watched Chigger's family lean on him, and Chigger had manned up. She was proud of him. He'd convinced Eli that Mason's disappearance was not his fault, was strong for Georgia and the other kids, and

Rileigh had rearranged her opinion of him at that time, and she sought now to see him in that light.

"Promise it won't take much of your time," she said.

"I got all the time in the world. I been working on this car for three weeks. Lester got it this far and it died, and I got it running again. But the engine's still missing."

Lester was Lester Massey. He and his brother Ben lived on Rabbit Run Road on Pigeon Ridge, and and Rileigh'd gone there to talk to Chigger the previous summer about the death of Tina Montgomery. That was a sore subject, given that he'd admitted he'd been having an affair with the girl and was the father of her unborn child. That was why Georgia had kicked him out. Rileigh hurried on, lest the name conjure up images of that time, which would make the conversation today even more awkward, if such a thing were possible.

"I don't know if Georgia told you, but there's a sixteen-year-old girl missing from Shagbark Manor. She and her parents are staying there this summer, and she disappeared. I found drugs in her room. Mitch and I got the handyman to admit to hooking the girl up with somebody to sell her drugs. He said the dealer's name was Scooby, and that's unfamiliar to me. I thought maybe you might know him. Do you?"

Chigger spat in the dirt. "Yeah, I know Scooby. Everybody knows Scooby. Least everybody in my circle of friends does. That man is bad news."

"Tell me about him."

She could tell that talking about this made Chigger very uncomfortable. She was not the police, was not officially law enforcement at all, but she was obviously working with the sheriff on a case — again — and she knew that it felt like ratting out a fellow druggie to the law for Chigger to talk about Scooby.

"He's not from around here, is he?"

"No, Scooby's from Carter County, I think."

"What's his real name?"

"I don't know. Everybody just calls him Scooby."

"Have you ever had dealings with him?"

"In a manner of speaking," Chigger said, pausing. "Okay. I had a customer once who wanted z-bars and some snow stones." Those were street names for Xanax and cocaine. "I told him I didn't do that no more, I'm strictly weed, and he wanted to know who did, so I gave him a couple of names, and one of them was Scooby's. About a week later, Scooby comes up to me when I was outside the I Gotta Spare bowling alley"—he paused—"talking to some friends."

Translate that: making a drug deal.

"And he went off on me."

"Went off on you how?"

"The guy's a meth-head now, was totally wasted and strong as a bull. He grabbed me, threw me up against the wall like I was a rag doll, pulled a knife on me."

"What for?"

"He said I had set him up. He said that fellow I had sent to him to buy drugs had stiffed him."

"And he blamed *you* for that?"

"I think the guy made it sound like him and me was close, BFFs or something. My friends grabbed Scooby and tried to pull him off, three of them, and they couldn't hold him. He was crazy, reached up and ripped my tee off me, grabbed my neck and just tore down. He was out-of-control wild. He threatened me, waved that knife in my face, and said if I ever sent him another customer who didn't pay up, he'd take the money out of my hide."

"Didn't that strike you as odd that he blamed you for not getting paid?"

"Hell yeah, it struck me as odd. It'd have struck anybody as odd. That ain't the way it works. You got a customer, you deal with your customer. It's between you and him. You don't drag somebody else into it if the guy don't pay you. Scooby wasn't thinking right. Meth-heads fry their brains, and they're like to do *anything*."

"So where could I find Scooby?"

"You don't want to find Scooby. That is one *dangerous* dude."

"I still have to talk to him."

Actually, she needed to talk to him now more than ever. Hillary knew her family wouldn't be at home that night — a perfect time to make a buy. What if he showed up and Hillary didn't pay him for the drugs he brought her, or did some other little thing to piss him off? A violent meth-head — and there's an axe hanging above the mantel! — could explain a room full of broken dolls and blood splattered everywhere. And the missing body. He could have thrown her body over his shoulder and carried her away.

"I can tell you where he used to hang out, but he ain't easy to find."

"Where was that, and why is that, and where do you think he could be now?"

"He used to hang out behind Turtle's Liquor Store up there on the bypass, him and his buddies, but last I heard the staties was all over that and he had to find some other place to roost. But the thing is … you don't *find* Scooby — don't nobody find Scooby. He finds *you*. He's like a shadow, a puff of smoke. You put it out there what you want and he'll decide when, where, and *if* he'll make the deal. I do know he don't live where he used to."

"How do you know that?"

"I was in the hardware store buying some socket wrenches yesterday, and Herbert Talbot was talking about him to Joe Tungate. Said he'd been renting a trailer house of his, somewhere on Carter Creek, and owed him a couple of back months' rent. He went to collect. Scooby was gone. He didn't have much shit, but all of it had been moved out."

"And that was when?"

"Sunday."

Scooby had bailed the morning after Hillary Schofield went missing. Where was he now? Somewhere still in the county? Or was he long gone?

"That's all I need to know. Thanks."

Rileigh turned to go back to her car parked in the driveway, but Chigger spoke to her, and she turned back around.

"So you're working on some case about that teenager who went missing from Old Shaggy. Is that right?"

"That's right," she said.

"Georgia has been having them nightmares again," he said.

"Yeah, she told me she dreamed about something that happened Shagbark Manor when she was a little girl."

"Wasn't no dream. It was a nightmare. Full-on night terror. She wakes up screaming in the middle of the night."

"She's done this before?"

"Hell yeah. Every now and then she just, it comes back over her. Usually it's when something brings Shagbark Manor to her mind. Somebody mentions it or she has to drive by there or something."

Rileigh remembered that Georgia had told her the bad dreams had started when she had met the Schofield children at Vacation Bible School. Sage and Sam and Liza. Sage and Sam were the same ages as Eli, and Liza was the same age as Connor, so they were in the same classes.

"Georgia told me she started having those nightmares because she met some children who're staying there now."

"Is there anything you could do, you know, to help Georgia with them nightmares, maybe find out, prove to her that all that haunted house shit, all them stories, ain't real? Maybe that'd help her stop having them dreams."

He paused, shook his head. "It's... *pitiful.*"

Chigger was momentarily vulnerable and her opinion of him shifted yet again. It was clear he really did love Georgia.

"She wakes up screaming, absolutely terrified, scares the shit out of the kids. She's trembling all over, broke out in a cold sweat, face white. It's like she's got PTSD. It's that *real* to her. If there's anything you can do..."

His voice trailed off and he was silent. Then he turned and stuck his head back under the hood of the car, and Rileigh left.

Chapter Twenty-Four

MITCH SAT BACK IN HIS CHAIR AND RUBBED HIS EYES, knowing that he was only making them more red.

He had come up against dead ends with every angle he had tried. He had just gotten off the phone with the last of six of Hillary Schofield's friends in Nashville, checking to see if they had seen her or had heard from her. It was a solid no all the way, although one of them, whose name was Hermione, had filled his ear full of Hillary's complaints about having to stay there. And another of the friends, Joanna, had told him Hillary confided in her that she had seen strange things there and didn't know what to make of them.

"What kind of strange things?" Mitch had asked.

"She said she saw lights and shimmering shapes and heard crying like a little girl crying and, you know, the basic stuff that you see and hear in a haunted house. But the thing was, Hillary thought it all was real. I tried to tell her that she was nuts, that that kind of thing didn't really happen, but she was convinced it was real and was pissed because her father and The Bitch wouldn't believe her."

"Did she tell you that she had plans to run away?"

"No."

"How would she run away?"

"I guess she could backpack up in the mountains, but that's not really how Hillary rolls. And if she had, she would have called me. We've been BFFs forever."

"Do you know if Hillary used drugs?"

"No," the girl said, "Of course not."

"I'm not asking because I'm trying to bust her or you. I'm asking because I'm trying to find her."

"Like I said, I don't know what you're talking about. Hillary never used drugs."

Riiiiight.

He had spoken to every one of the teenagers, boys and girls, on the list that Hillary's parents had provided, and none of them had heard a word from Hilary since she disappeared or had any idea that she was planning to run away.

The forensics guy from Gatlinburg was certainly not as responsive as Gus would have been under the same circumstances, but he did get back to Mitch with sobering news. The blood samples taken from the crime scene were indeed Hillary Schofield's blood.

Mitch couldn't estimate how much blood there actually was at that crime scene. Blood had a way of looking like there was way more of it than there was, but even so, he had trouble believing that the girl could have lost that much blood and still be up walking around. If she was dead, that changed this from a missing person's investigation to a murder investigation, though he had no body.

He had run a background check on Richard David Stevenson and found that he'd been mostly truthful about his criminal record — property crimes committed ten or fifteen years ago — theft by unlawful taking over $100 vehicular, receiving stolen property vehicular, the kind of crimes you were charged with if your chop shop got busted.

Mitch was about to move on when it occurred to him that he'd just made a rookie mistake. He had believed a liar. If a man lies and says his name is Spriggs when it isn't, why would you then believe him when he says it's Stevenson? And Mitch had done just that, dutifully checked the criminal history on Richard David Stevenson.

He had put the fingerprint off Rileigh's phone in an evidence bag but had never run it. Pulling a file from a drawer, he reached inside, took out the print, and called Deputy Mullins into his office to run the print. When Mullins returned, he said the print had immediately popped NCIC, the national law enforcement database. It belonged to a man named Richard David *Sturgis*. Guess he didn't want to have to get new monogrammed towels.

Sturgis had a decidedly different criminal record than Spriggs/Stevenson. He, too, had been repeatedly busted for crimes related to running a chop shop. But in addition to those arrests, he had been busted for more than property crimes — specifically, sex crimes.

Sturgis had been charged twice with sexual assault, once for second degree rape, four times for sexual abuse, along with miscellaneous crimes of violence like assault and carjacking. He had never been *convicted* of a sex crime, always pleaded to a lesser charge and got off. But those charges were not far back in the man's rear-view mirror. The last charge had been just three years ago. Mitch had picked up on the fact that Carly had been very defensive of the man when he and Rileigh had told her he'd lied to her on his job application. Maybe there was something going on between the two of them, as unlikely as that seemed.

But there had to be a reason Carly seemed so unconcerned about his lie.

The fake identity, complete with driver's license, gave Mitch probable cause to arrest Sturgis, aka Stevenson, aka Spriggs. He'd haul his ass in and have a come-to-Jesus conversation with him about his criminal record. A pretty sixteen-year-old girl was missing, and the man who'd been mowing the grass under her bedroom window had been busted on numerous occasions for sex crimes.

Sturgis was now elevated to the same level of suspicion as Scooby the drug dealer. Rileigh had reported what Chigger had said about him, that he was a volatile meth-head, a hand grenade with a loose pin. He had officers scouring the county, looking under every rock, but they hadn't located him yet. Hillary Schofield had associated with some very unsafe people and never known she was in danger.

There was also a list of other employees of the bed and breakfast, and he had different deputies checking them out. Most of them were locals, though, and women. The level of violence suggested by the blood splatter everywhere was more the MO of a male than a female assailant. There were three housekeepers and three maids who came in for various shifts, plus a cook and a gardener.

And that was it. He was doing everything he could, had checked out or was checking out every person who had access to Hillary Schofield since she came to Yarmouth County. And none of them had any *obvious* motive to have harmed her.

What was he missing?

He set to drumming his fingers on his desk, recalling what Thelma Rittenhouse had said about the original murders. How Crawford Tillman had come home from a trip one day and hacked his family apart. He'd had no *obvious* motive either. And he thought about Lily's comments about how there had been people mysteriously disappearing from Shagbark bed and breakfast for years. It was part of the mystique of the haunted house that people who went there vanished. But he'd run a quick check of the sheriff's department's records, and they showed no missing person reports from anybody at Shagbark Manor.

Stella brought him in a cup of coffee and set it on his desk. He looked at her quizzically. "I didn't ask for a cup of coffee."

"No, but you need one. I can tell when you sit in here and drum your fingers and dig your thumbs into your eyes that you're not sleeping, obsessing over this case, and if you haven't been sleeping, you need coffee."

Stella turned to leave.

"Hold up a minute, Stella. How long have you worked here?"

"Longer than anybody else in the building. I went to work here right out of high school, then I was a dispatcher for a while, and I worked for Mum." She shook her head sadly. Mum was former Sheriff Jedidiah Mumford. No one who knew him had any idea why he had decided to commit suicide. They could find no *obvious* motive. Mitch knew the motive all right. He and Rileigh had discovered that Mum had killed Rileigh's father years ago and faked his suicide, because her father and Mum and a lot of other men had been involved in kiddie porn. Then Mum had come very near killing both Rileigh and Jillian, and when he'd known he was going to be outed, he'd killed himself. Nobody knew those secrets except a select few, and there was no reason to tell them as long as Rileigh's mother was alive and believed her husband who had "killed himself" was a saint.

"I've got a question for you. What do you know about Shagbark Manor?"

"Old Shaggy? Well what do you want to know?"

"Whatever you can tell me. I hear all the time that it's haunted, but I don't understand why. What specifically has led people to believe that?"

"Any place where a father chases his daughters around with an axe and hacks them and their mother to death is likely to be considered a haunted building. You'd think those kinds of disturbed spirits would be the kind that'd come back and haunt a place. And people have been vanishing out of there for thirty or forty years."

"About the vanishings. Who vanished? What people?"

"I really don't know."

"But if you've worked here at the sheriff's department all this time, you would have been processing the papers or at least been aware of all the missing persons reports."

"The deal is that the folks who went missing were tourists, and…"

"The reports would have been filed in wherever they came from."

"Apparently nobody at Shagbark Manor reported anybody missing, but word just got out around town."

"Can you tell me about any of those people?"

"They were tourists."

"Did you know any of them?"

"No… they were tourists."

"So you don't remember any names you heard—"

"I do remember one — not the tourist, but I remember we got a call from someplace in Texas, up, you know, in the Panhandle, I think. What I remember about it was that it was the local sheriff who said somebody's mother had spent the weekend at Shagbark Manor and never came home."

"I'd be interested to see that report."

"It'll take me a while to find it. Like I said, it was a long time ago. What I remember about it was that the family said she'd already left Shagbark Manor before she went missing, but this sheriff was just crossing his T's and dotting his I's."

"Go find that report for me, will you please?"

"No problem, Sheriff."

Sheila returned to his office forty-five minutes later and laid papers on his desk. "This is a printout of that report."

Mitch lifted the top page of the report. It was sparse. It listed the Bailey County Sheriff as the inquiring agency seeking information about Mrs. Edna Snuff, seventy-five, who had come to the mountains on vacation, stayed in Shagbark Manor, started home, and never got there.

The date on the report was 2012. Twelve years ago. He decided to give it a shot and picked up the phone and dialed the number listed.

"Bailey County Sheriff's Department," said a perky voice with a Texas accent.

"My name is Sheriff Mitchell Webster, Yarmouth County, Tennessee, and I'm looking into an old missing person's case. The person was from Bailey County, Texas, and all I have is the report that your Sheriff's Department inquired about her."

"Whoa, that's not much."

"I can make it even more difficult than that," Mitch said. "It was in 2012."

"That was before I went to work here. Well, give me the person's name, and I'll see if I can find anything out."

"Her name was Edna Snuff."

"Snuff? The Snuff family is very prominent in Bailey County, and the circuit judge is Edna's son. You might want to give him a call."

She gave him the number and he called. The judge was in court, but the bailiff said that when the court went into recess, he'd have the judge give Sheriff Webster a call.

About an hour later, Mitch's phone rang and the gruff voice on the other end said, "This is Judge Harold Snuff. I understand you want to talk to me about my mother."

"I'm looking into missing persons reports, looking for people who went missing from the bed and breakfast where your mother stayed."

He let out a sigh. "I was in law school when it happened. Mama was supposed to go off with a couple of friends to the mountains, but for some reason or another they bailed on her, and she went anyway. I remember she called me, said she loved the place where she was staying. It was something like Shag."

"Shagbark Manor."

"Yes, that was it, but I don't know how her disappearance could be in any way related to that place because she'd already left. She was on her way home when she disappeared."

"How do you know that?"

"Because she said so. She called and said she had a surprise for me when she got home, told me she'd call me that night from Texarkana. A few minutes later, she texted to say she was driving away from the haunted house. When she didn't call that night, we called her, but her phone was turned off. We filed missing persons reports in Texarkana. Hired private investigators to look into what might have happened to her along the way. I mean, that's a long drive for a woman by herself."

"What about her car? "

"We never saw Mama or her vehicle again after she drove out of here on her way to Tennessee. Why are you looking into this?"

"I'm working a case on a teenager who went missing from Shagbark Manor, and I'm looking for a pattern of people disappearing from the place, trying to chase down any leads of people who were reported missing."

"Well, you wouldn't have found a missing persons report in Tennessee, because it was filed in Arkansas."

"But the Bailey County Sheriff's department called here. That's how I got your number."

"Well, if you turn up anything, anything at all, will you give me a call? It's been a burden on my family for twelve years. What happened to Mama? She was one of those larger-than-life little old ladies who might have looked her age, which was seventy-five, but who never acted it. Who could — and did — do everything she'd ever been able to do. Who said in one of her phone calls from Tennessee that she'd gone white water rafting and had the time of her life. You can imagine she left a big hole in our family. I would dearly like to know what happened to her."

"If I find out anything, I'll let you know."

Mitch hung up the phone and sat thoughtful at his desk. So a woman, an old woman, who had been staying by herself in Shagbark Manor, left there and never made it home. How did that in any way relate to a teenage girl who went missing from there and had her blood splattered all over the floor?

Chapter Twenty-Five

Rileigh went along with Mitch the next morning to Shagbark Manor to bust Rick Sturgis. He'd leave him with Rileigh and let him stew in handcuffs in the backseat of his cruiser while Mitch informed Paul Schofield about the result of the tests run on the blood samples found on the floor and stairs. Carly Farrington needed to know the truth about Sturgis, and he wanted to ask her about the missing Edna Snuff. She had vanished during the time when Carly had been helping her grandmother run the bed and breakfast. He wanted to know what she remembered about the woman.

They saw no sign of Sturgis outside in front of the bed and breakfast when they drove up the driveway. They went inside to find out if he was working today, but didn't have to go looking for Paul Schofield. The man saw him and Rileigh in the foyer from the top of the stairs and thundered down the stairs to talk to them.

"What do you know? What did you come here to tell me?"

"Actually I came here to talk to the handyman."

"He's not here. I saw his pickup going down the driveway toward the road half an hour ago. Now what do you know about Hillary?"

Mitch would dispatch a unit to pick Sturgis up at his house.

"I do know something, Mr. Schofield, but I'm afraid it's not good news. Forensics says that the blood found at the crime scene was your daughter's blood."

The man took a step back as if Mitch had clocked him in the jaw. He shook his head, as if to dislodge the very thought, then suddenly got right up in Mitch's face.

"Fine. Maybe it was her blood, but that doesn't mean she's dead. It doesn't. It does not mean my daughter is dead. Hillary is just fine. We're going to find her. *You're* going to find her. Tell me you're going to find her."

The man was only barely holding it together, and it took Mitch and Rileigh both to calm him down.

Carly was in the backyard wearing garden gloves, down on her hands and knees, planting a rosebush.

She used the back of her hand to rub her hair out of her face when she looked up at him and Rileigh, and he thought again how much she reminded him of Hillary Schofield — it was that white-blonde hair — though Carly's was natural and Hillary's had come from a bottle.

"We'd like to ask you some questions about a woman who stayed here at Shagbark Manor about twelve years ago," Rileigh said. Carly had stopped what she was doing when they approached, and she sat back on her heels.

"Seriously? Twelve years ago? Do you know how many people stay here?"

"No, I don't," Mitch said. "Tell me."

"Well, I don't know exactly."

"That's something I'd be interested to find out," Mitch

said. "How many people have stayed here since this place became a bed and breakfast?"

"Oh, hundreds. Probably thousands," she said.

"Do you keep track of all of them?" Rileigh asked.

She drew herself up. "Well, we know who they were when they checked in."

"You still have those old records?" Mitch asked.

"Oh, no, not the old records," she said. Mitch looked disappointed. But then she continued. "I mean, not the paper records, the registration forms. But I have everything digitized, and I made an effort to go backwards and put that information in, but there was a flood before my sisters and I came to live here. The records were stored in the basement, and they are all ruined. But I have digital records dating back thirty years. If you need for me to, I can go back into the system and look this person up, but it would be a stretch for me to actually remember her unless she was particularly memorable for some reason."

"She's memorable because she went missing on her way home from Shagbark Manor."

"Really? Well, I don't know how that would make her memorable to me if she went missing after she left."

Rileigh had pointed out to him, yet again, when he told her he had found a real, flesh and blood, went-missing tourist that tourists were a safe target because if they went missing, their disappearance would first be reported back home. If it was determined that they had already left Tennessee and were on their way home when they disappeared, there would be no record of any kind in Yarmouth County.

"Her name was Edna Snuff," Mitch said and thought he caught a twitch at the corner of Carly's eye.

"And she stayed here... when did you say?" She was getting to her feet and taking off her muddy gloves.

"It would have been summertime in 2012."

"Well, let's go into the office and see what we can find." Carly led Mitch and Rileigh back into the house, where they could smell the aroma of pot roast in the oven that would be served to the Schofield family for lunch or dinner today, though he doubted any of them had much of an appetite.

Carly went into the office, which had managed to retain the style and character of the big old house and yet was totally functional as a modern office. She sat down behind a big oak desk and palmed her mouse and began clicking away. Mitch saw various sheets appear on the big monitor, lists of names and dates She typed Edna Snuff into the search box and hit return. The woman's name popped up immediately.

"Well, here's what I know about her," Carley said and indicated what had come up on her computer. There wasn't much. Her name, her age, her driver's license number, her home address, how long she stayed, when she came, when she left, and how much she paid for her room.

"I talked to this woman's son this morning. He's a district judge in Texas."

"What did he tell you?"

"He said that his mother had called him right before she left here on her way home, said she'd be bringing him a surprise. She sent a text after that saying she'd left here and would call him again that night from Texarkana, but she never did. So somewhere between Black Bear Forge and Texarkana, this woman disappeared. Do you know what the surprise could have been?"

Carley smiled. "Yes, I do. Or I imagine that this is what he's talking about. When our guests leave, we give them a going-away gift, a box of handmade chocolates — it's for whoever they left behind. We suggest that they let their loved ones know they're bringing home a surprise for them."

From the look on her face, the answer seemed to tick some box in Rileigh's mind.

Mitch stood staring at Edna Snuff's information on the computer screen. "I don't suppose you remember this woman. You would have been here then, wouldn't you? In 2012?"

"I would have been here. But no, I'm sorry. I don't remember her."

"Her son said she was one of those larger-than-life people. Memorable."

Carley thought and then looked at him sadly. "I'm sorry. I don't remember her."

Mitch had a thought and discarded it as soon as he had it and then picked it back up and examined it.

"So you have information about every person who has ever stayed here."

"*Had* information, back as far as Grandma Josie started keeping track, which she did shortly after she opened the place forty-four years ago. But since the flood, the earliest entry I still have is"—she scrolled down the list to the first name—"a family named Winslow on May 9, 1994."

"I'd like to take a look at those records," Mitch said.

Carly looked surprised. "Why?"

"Well, a teenager went missing from here. And I want to see if I can find anybody else who ever did."

"Well, you don't have to look through the records to find that out. I can tell you. No, nobody ever went missing from here. I certainly would have remembered it if was like Hillary. All that blood." She visibly cringed.

"Oh, I'm sure you would remember. But I'd like to have the names so I can search through missing persons reports in their hometowns."

"Do you have any idea how many names you're talking about here?"

"No, because you never got around to answering that question."

"Because I never totaled them all up."

She picked up a legal pad and a pen and started figuring, jotting down numbers.

"Okay, during the season, which is May, early May to early November, depending on the weather, let's say in a month there were..." She thought, then wrote down a number and said immediately that it was a bad guess.

"It's hard to estimate because when Grandma Josie was running the place, there were far fewer than there are now. Our clientele has grown considerably, thirty, maybe forty percent."

"Just a ballpark," Mitch said. Carly went back to figuring, speaking as she jotted down numbers.

"Guests stay for varying periods of time. Some of them would have been simple overnights. Most of them were weekends, Friday to Monday. Some were longer, some were a whole week. Grandma Josie kept the total number of people at one time to ten when she was running the place."

"That's a small number," Rileigh said, "for such a huge place with all these bedrooms."

"Remember, I told you the number wasn't based on how many beds we have and how many people we could sleep. This isn't like a vacation rental. The number was based on how many people Mama could take care of. And ten was about as much as she could handle. When I took over, I hired some staff, so it wasn't all on me. Grandma Josie did everything herself. The garden, the laundry, the cooking and cleaning, everything. I hired people so I could scale the operation. I calculated back from overhead how many guests I had to have to keep the lights on. Any more than that was profit. That overhead has ballooned on me because of COVID. Now, I'm paying off the debts from when there were no guests, but I still had to keep the place warm enough that the pipes didn't freeze."

"It's a close enough estimation," Mitch said. "Run the numbers on what you have just to give me a ballpark." Carly did the math and sat back.

"This is such a bad number... it's an *estimate*. We've been in business for forty-four years, but I subtracted the fourteen early years for which the records were destroyed and two years for COVID when we were empty or virtually empty. The total comes to seven thousand six hundred and one guests. So you see, there's no way you can track them all down and make sure they all got home safe."

"Yep, that's a lot of people," Mitch said. "If you would send me that file, I'd appreciate it. And those calculations, too."

Carly ripped the page out of her pad of paper and handed it to Mitch.

"Good hunting," she said.

He had saved the information about Sturgis until the end, when Carly was relaxed, had dropped her guard.

"You need to know that your handyman lied about his identity."

She froze.

"I know. You told me that already."

"What you don't know is that the *second* ID he gave us when we talked to him was also a fake. He isn't Rick Spriggs or Rick Stevenson. His name is Richard David Sturgis, and he has a criminal record for crimes against women — sex crimes."

The color drained out of Carly Farrington's face so fast Mitch could see the blue veins throbbing in her temples.

She might have known before they told her that Spriggs was not his real name, might even have known he had a criminal background as a thief. But she definitely didn't know he was a sexual predator. You couldn't fake that level of surprise and alarm.

"What?" she gasped. She covered her mouth and shook her head. "No... I had no idea... I never would have... I just needed him..."

"Needed him? For what?"

She caught herself then, grabbed hold.

"Needed... his service ... as a handyman."

She wasn't lying about needing him, but she was definitely lying about what she needed him for.

He and Rileigh talked about it on the way back to town and Rileigh agreed — Carly Farrington didn't know about his real criminal history, but she might have known about the fake one. And she'd been okay with that.

"What could she possibly have needed him for?" Rileigh mused. Neither of them could figure a plausible reason.

Mitch changed the subject to a niggling itch that had been in his mind as soon as he met Carly Farrington and what it might mean.

"Every time I see her, I am surprised by how much she looks like Hillary Schofield," he said.

"I've noticed, too. It's the hair, mostly."

"What if that *matters?*"

"Matters?

"It's a far-out theory, but I'm convinced now we need to look into it." He took a breath. "What if Hillary Schofield wasn't the intended victim? What if the killer was gunning for Carly Farrington... and got the wrong girl?"

Rileigh was surprised, but she rolled with it.

"Okay, that's definitely far out. So what if Carly Farrington was supposed to get hacked apart instead of Hillary Schofield, who had a motive to kill her?"

Her face lit up with the answer.

"Her sisters!"

"You win the kewpie doll!"

"They both would be better off if Carly vanished in a puff of smoke. But come on… she's their sister. They'd have recognized that Hillary Schofield wasn't Carly."

"You're right. They would have. But what if neither of them was the actual killer? What if they hired somebody? The pattern of that blood splatter was so violent that it looks like a man did it."

"Well, you've sure opened up a whole new can of worms."

"We need to go have a talk with those ladies."

"And while we're at it, we could find out if their grand-mother ever told either of them about the night her father killed her mother and sisters."

Chapter Twenty-Six

CARLY'S SISTER, CAMILLE, OWNED A BUSINESS IN Knoxville. Rileigh and Mitch drove there to talk to her. Mitch told her that he needed her help to watch for the female things she always noticed, but that was a ruse, and they both knew it. He wanted her help because he wanted her company. The circumstances that had put them together in the beginning no longer existed, but they pretended like they still did. Mitch had been forced to ask for Rileigh's help — and he hadn't wanted to — in the first murder case he investigated after he was named interim sheriff when Sheriff Jedediah T. Mumford took time off to have double knee replacement surgery. The case was the murder of a young woman named Tina Montgomery, who'd worked as a waitress in the Rusty Nail Tavern in Gatlinburg. She had been murdered and her tongue had been cut out, and something similar has happened when Rileigh's sister Jillian disappeared almost three decades ago.

They eventually found the murderer, Rileigh's Aunt Daisy, as a matter of fact, but the only reason Mitch had gotten anywhere at all was because of Rileigh's help. He was the new guy. The guy from away-from-here. The man nobody knew. And the small, insular community of Black Bear Forge, Tennessee wasn't likely to open up to an outsider. Rileigh had been his ticket to the dance. She had been the local face on the crimes, and he had taken her with him in the investigations that followed so the locals would cooperate.

Now, Mitch didn't need a go-between to pave his way in the county with the locals. Oh, he was still from Away From Here and Rileigh knew what he didn't, which was that he would carry that baggage with him to the grave. But they trusted him now. They'd seen him in action for all these months. Watched how he conducted his affairs. If they were paying attention, they were impressed by how much better a sheriff Mitch was than Jedediah T. Mumford had ever been.

Though he no longer needed her help to get the job done, it did grease the skids, gave him an excuse to spend time with her, and Rileigh was absolutely down with that.

Camille Vindiola ran a business called Trendy Threads in Knoxville. She designed clothing, had a small workforce who turned those drawings into actual garments, and a distribution system to send them out to various boutiques in Knoxville and Nashville.

The offices were all chrome and glass and square corners and modern architecture. A woman dressed as stylishly as Camille greeted them and showed them into her office.

Mitch introduced her to Rileigh, and she smiled and offered a limp handshake that said it all. It was a woman thing. When a woman offered you a limp handshake, it was for one of two reasons. Either she offered everybody that same dead-fish-on-a-stick, or she wanted to dismiss you.

The intended put-down was clear — you were not worthy of the effort it took to shake hands firmly. Rileigh suspected that with Camille Vindiola, it was door number two.

As a strong woman accustomed to elbowing aside other strong women, Camille directed all of her attention and responses to Mitch, which was fine with Rileigh because it left her free to study the woman's body language and see what it might be saying that her words were not.

Mitch had said she reminded him of a tropical fish, and Rileigh could certainly see why. Her blue and green and blue-green hair was cut in a style that swished the colors along like stripes blended, like seawater over a coral reef.

Mitch introduced himself and Rileigh but got only that far.

"My assistant said you want to talk to me about Shagbark Manor, some missing teenager there," Camille said. "You're wasting your time and mine. I have nothing to do with the running of Shagbark Manor. My sister Carly is in charge there."

"I just have a few questions."

"The only contact I had with that girl was when you arrived and brought her back from your office. She put on quite a show, claiming she saw a dead body in a pool of blood at the foot of the stairs — but then it was gone." Camille chuckled. "Moving a dead body *and* a puddle of blood — that'd be a neat trick to pull off. I stood and watched for a minute or two before I left, but I never said a word to her, never had any interaction with her at all. So how could I possibly know anything about her disappearance?"

"Actually, I'm interested in talking to you about the

Shagbark Manor estate that you and your two sisters inherited when Carly turned twenty-one."

"What do you want to know about it, and why is that in any way relevant?"

"If you don't mind, just answer the question, please. So you and your sister Kiara want to sell the place and Carly does not. Is that right?"

"And you know that how? Because you were eavesdropping on our conversation the other day."

"I came into Carly's office in the middle of your argument about it."

"Okay, fine. Yes, that's accurate. Carly squirmed out of the deal she made with us years ago. She betrayed both of us. Both of us were counting on the sale of that place." Camille gestured to her small shop of workers. "It would have been an infusion of capital that would have been rocket fuel for this business, and for Kiara's bar. And it would have set Carly up for life in some kind of profession that didn't involve—"

"Making pancakes for strangers for breakfast?" Mitch finished for her, and she looked at him, surprised.

"That's exactly right. She could have done anything she wanted. She could have gone to school. She could have started a business. She could have traveled, seen more of the world than a backward little town in the Tennessee mountains. But instead she dug her heels in and refused to honor the agreement we made."

"If she failed to honor a legal agreement, why didn't you file a lawsuit?"

"Oh, it wasn't a *legal* agreement. My bad. I'll never make that mistake again. Everything signed and documented from now on. But... we were sisters. It's just what we all knew would happen, had talked about it and planned for it for years. The estate was tied up in a trust and we couldn't sell it all until Carly turned twenty-one. We knew that as soon as she did, we'd sell the monstrous rat trap and make some money off of it."

"But Carly backed out?"

"She said she wanted to run it as a bed and breakfast just like Grandma Josie had done!" The woman spewed out some colorful expletives, then continued. "Carly was twenty-one years old. She knew nothing about business, but she was bound and determined. So after we got over the initial shock and anger, Kiara and I decided to let her try. We knew she'd bomb, wouldn't be able to pull it off, and then she'd have to honor the original agreement."

"But that's not what happened?"

"Somehow, she made a go of it. I don't know how. That place is a total money suck. It's going to need all kinds of repairs, hundreds of thousands of dollars' worth. Have you seen the HVAC unit? It's a relic, huge air-return fans to blow... it's on its last leg, and the shingles on that roof — the next big storm will..." She sighed. "But Carly managed to make ends meet — at least I assume she has, because if any creditors had filed liens on the place, I'd have been notified. I know she's barely scratching by, though, month to month, trying to keep her head above water."

"So what happened that prompted you and you sister to go talk to Carly about it again?"

"Nothing happened!"

Rileigh noted she answered the question too fast and too forcefully.

"There was no reason. Kiara and I were just together and decided we'd give it another shot, hoped maybe the little shit had come to her senses by now."

"It didn't have anything to do with the buyer who'd made an offer on the place?"

She looked like he'd slapped her.

"No, it did *not*.

"Who was it?"

"That is proprietary financial information, and I will not discuss it with you." She locked her jaw, looking like she thought he might try to pry it out of her with a crowbar.

"So nothing had changed?"

"No! And nothing changed with her either. She's still bound and determined to live in her fairy tale house and live her fairy tale life."

"I was wondering about when you and your sister went to live at Shagbark Manor — how old were you?"

"I was sixteen. Kiara was fifteen, and Carly was six. Our parents had just been killed, so we were shellshocked. Grandma Josie was our only option. We didn't have any other relatives."

"Had you spent a lot of time with your grandmother as a child?"

"Good god, no! My mother and her mother did *not* get along, but then my mother didn't get along with anybody, spent all her time on a shrink's couch counting the tiles in the ceiling. Mom cut off all contact with her mother when we were little. It's possible Carly had never even met Grandma Josie."

"Do you know what happened between your mother and her mother?"

"Not a clue. Look, how is this in any way relevant to the disappearance of that kid from Shagbark Manor?"

Rileigh spoke for the first time. "We were wondering if your grandmother talked to you much about what happened to her when she was a little girl."

"She didn't talk to me or Kiara at all, except to say hello and goodbye."

"What do you mean?"

"We were fifteen and sixteen years old, and Grandma Josie was a cantankerous old biddy we didn't even know. Living at Shagbark Manor was like moving in with the Munsters."

"Given the circumstances of Hillary's disappearance, the blood at the foot of the stairs and all, we're interested in finding out what happened to your grandmother and great-grandmother the day of the axe murders. Did your grandmother ever mention it?"

"Not to us she didn't, but like I said, she didn't talk to us. She spent every speck of her time and lavished all her attention on Carly. You know why, don't you?"

"How about you tell me."

"Did you even look at that life-size family portrait in the living room? Carly was like a doppelgänger for Grandma Josie when she was a little girl. Like a clone — same face, and that hair! I felt sorry for the poor kid — moves in with an ugly old witch who turns her into a life-sized baby doll like those dolls in the room on the third floor."

Rileigh recalled the room full of dolls of all sizes and shapes, baby dolls and dolls with long hair, older dolls that said "Mama" when you picked them up. They were the ones that had been destroyed the night Hillary disappeared.

"You mention those dolls… you do know, don't you, that they were all shattered the night Hillary vanished?"

"No, I didn't, but I'm glad somebody finally got rid of them! I hated those dolls — we weren't allowed to get near them. Grandma Josie turned Carly into a doll like that. She let Carly's hair grow out, braided it and tied the braids with pink and blue satin bows so she looked like the dolls she'd played with when she was a little girl."

"So your grandmother ignored you and your sister and doted on Carly?" Rileigh asked.

The woman sneered. "Don't go there. It wasn't like that. We weren't pining away for our grandmother's affection. We didn't give a shit about the old biddy. We felt sorry for Carly, though. Grandma Josie didn't even want to put Carly in school. I think the county forced her to. If Grandma Josie told anybody about the day her father went on an axe rampage, it was Carly, not Kiara and me. She gave us nothing, and all she got from us was pimples and teenage angst. We got out of there as soon as we could."

"So there was nothing that prompted you and your sister to go see Carly and try to talk her into selling again?"

"How many times do I have to say it? No, there was nothing that... nothing happened. We went. We talked to her. She said no. End of story. And while we were there, we never said a word to that kid who went missing."

Camille probably didn't realize she'd been pacing back and forth in front of them as she spoke, but she stopped then, gave Rileigh a condescending look, and focused her gaze on Mitch.

"Are you done? Because I am. I have work to do." She motioned to the woman they'd spoken to earlier. "She'll show you out."

"Where were you the night Hillary Schofield went missing?" Mitch asked.

The question was a drop of water in hot grease. Camille exploded.

"What?" she screamed. "You want to know where I was, like I'm some kind of suspect or something? Well you can go to hell! Straight. To. Hell. Do not pass go, do not collect two hundred dollars! Now get the hell out of my office. You have any more questions for me, direct them to my lawyer."

Then she turned around, and in a swirl of tropical fish pastel colors, she marched away.

They turned to go.

"Obviously, she didn't want to answer that question," Mitch said.

"I wonder why not. What's she hiding?"

Chapter Twenty-Seven

GIVEN THAT THE TRIP TO KNOXVILLE OFFERED THE opportunity, Rileigh was delighted when Mitch took advantage of it and suggested they go to lunch.

There was a little Italian restaurant off of Bank Street that Rileigh had passed a time or two and always wanted to give it a try.

"I bet it has ambiance," she said. The place was called Mama Mia's.

Just as Rileigh had suspected, Mama Mia's was a place with atmosphere. Candles on the tables, low lighting, and soft music in the background, even at lunchtime.

They were taken to a table in a back corner, and Rileigh didn't know if Mitch had asked for that, or if that had just been luck of the draw. They sat and ordered. It was a place that offered all-you-can-eat salad and soup, plus an entrée. Rileigh got Zuppa Tuscana. Mitch passed on the soup and said, "No onions in the salad," and then the waiter left their table.

Mitch wasted no time. "So, I'm wondering how you'd feel about going out to dinner again. Maybe next week."

"I'd like that a lot."

"We have to figure out some way to go out on a date without being interrupted," Mitch said. "And the only way that's going to work is if we get away entirely."

"Are you suggesting we leave town… and stay gone?"

"I'm thinking we go to Nashville."

"And stay the night?"

"If we go back to Yarmouth County, as God made little green apples, something, some crisis will come up, and I'll get a call or somebody will come banging on my door. And I'm tired of that. I want to…" Mitch reached over and placed his hand on hers, just a light touch because they were, after all, in professional mode, not personal mode, and the line had been drawn between them. But with that one light touch, he communicated a lot.

"I want time, just us, with no interruptions. How does that sound?"

Rileigh smiled so wide she feared the ends of her smile might meet in the back of her head and the top of her head would drop off. At least, that's what Georgia told her when they were little kids.

Mitch purposefully took his hand away, and they stepped back into professional mode, at least in what they said to each other. But he looked at her sometimes, putting butterflies in her belly and making it hard for her to think. And she believed that those looks were a window into who he was and what he was really thinking, and she suspected that if he were half as discerning as she believed him to be, he was seeing the same looks in her eyes.

They left Mama Mia's and went to a bar on the other side of town called Booze and Giggles, where they found Kiara Farrington behind the bar.

She looked up when they came in. The place was

almost empty. Only the hardcores showed up in a dark bar at three o'clock in the afternoon. They stepped up to the bar, and she offered no smile.

"So, what is the sheriff of Yarmouth County — at least that's what your badge says — doing so far from home?"

"You're Kiara Farrington, aren't you?" Mitch said as he sat down on a stool. She nodded.

"We'd like to have a few minutes of your time, if you don't mind," he said.

"Time for what?"

"We'd like to talk to you about your sister and about Shagbark Manor. A teenage girl went missing from there. We found blood—"

Kiara interrupted him. "Yes, I know all about it. I always know what's going on there. The kid went missing, and there was blood all over the floor at the foot of the stairs and axe marks on the wood. Am I right?"

"You are."

"So, why in the world would you drive all the way to Knoxville to talk to *me* about it? My only connection to Shagbark Manor is that I own a one-third interest in the property. I wasn't there when she disappeared. I never had a conversation with the girl. Why do you want to talk to me?"

"A couple of reasons," Mitch said. "One of them being that I walked in on an argument between you three sisters about the sale of the property the day I brought Hillary Schofield home."

"Yeah, we noticed you listening in on our conversation. And?"

"So, obviously, there's animosity among the three of you."

"Not among the *three* of us. Camille and I want to sell, and Carly doesn't. It's really that simple. What does that have anything to do with the disappearance of this teenage girl?"

"Just checking out all the possibilities for motives."

"Motives? Why is me wanting to sell the building a motive for me to... what... kidnap that girl?"

Rileigh and Mitch looked at each other and then back at Kiara. "There has been speculation that perhaps the teenager was not the intended victim of the abduction."

"Then who was?"

"You can't have failed to notice how much Hillary Schofield looks like your sister Carly."

"Yeah, I did see that, only Carly's hair is real, and that other girl's was obviously bleached out. I only saw her that one time, but I thought she looked more like Carly than either Camille or I do. So, what does..."

Rileigh saw it dawn on Kiara where the conversation was going.

"So you think that maybe somebody went there to kidnap Carly? And wound up taking the kid by mistake?"

"I'm looking at any and all possibilities," Mitch said. "That kid vanished in a puff of smoke, and I have no suspects and no evidence."

"So you're grasping at straws. And you came to talk to me because... Let me walk myself through this in my head. You came to talk to me because you think I was mad enough at my sister for not selling to want to kidnapper or kill her. Only I... *accidentally* kidnapped that teenager who looks like my sister by mistake. How far-fetched can you get? You think I wouldn't recognize my own sister?"

Rileigh noticed that Mitch didn't put forward the idea that they had had, that perhaps one or the other of the sisters had hired someone to get rid of Carly and the hired help didn't recognize Hillary.

Rileigh figured if Mitch didn't tell Kiara that, he didn't

want her to know. So Rileigh picked up the ball and ran in a different direction with it.

"There are similarities between this girl's disappearance and what happened in that house a hundred years ago. What appears to be axe attack on someone at the foot of the stairs is right where Grandma Josie's parents were both found dead. Did your Grandma Josie ever talk to you about what happened to her?"

"She never said a word to me. She never said a word to anybody, as far as I know. What I was told was that when they found her, she was catatonic, and when she came out of it, she didn't remember what happened."

"Do you think she told your mother?"

Kiara barked out a laugh. "My mother was so screwed up — God only knows what Grandma Josie talked to her about. If she discussed the axe murders, my mother never told me. But it wouldn't surprise me to find out they did. *Something* screwed my mother up."

"Did you go to visit your Grandma Josie at Shagbark Manor?

"One time. We were there one time before we got hauled away by the Department of Social Services and dropped bag and baggage on the doorstep, and when we moved in, we might as well not have been there. At least with Camille and I, she ignored us. It was like we didn't exist. The only human being she saw was Carly. She treated Carly like a little princess."

"The argument that I witnessed between you and Carly was about the fact that you and Camille wanted to sell and she didn't."

"Yeah, Camille called me a couple of days before and said, 'Let's go see if we can talk some sense into Carly.' I laughed at her. I said, 'Why in the world would she have changed her mind?' But Camille said it was really important to her, that she really needed for Carly to change her mind, and maybe now was the time. So I went. You saw the argument, you saw how successful the effort was."

"So, it was your sister Camille's idea, she suggested that you go down there?"

"Yeah, and when I didn't want to, she pretty much twisted my arm."

That wasn't what Camille had told Mitch and Rileigh. Nobody lies unless they're hiding something.

It was clear from the look on Camille's face when she saw them return that she was not happy to have another conversation with Rileigh and Mitch. She decided to play indignant and when Mitch approached, she held up her hand, "Look, I've already talked to you once today and that's enough. I don't know anything that would help you in any way, and I have a business to run."

"A business that's got some issues, right?" Rileigh said. She threw that out there as a Hail Mary. Kiara had stressed how much Camille wanted Carly to sell. So maybe she needed the money because she was having financial problems. It was worth throwing the ball up in the air and see if it would go through the hoop.

Camille looked like she had been slapped. "What are you talking about?"

Rileigh pressed her advantage. "I was just saying that the way I understand it, your company has hit some rough water."

Mitch looked a question at Rileigh but didn't ask it out loud. The question was: where the hell did you hear that?

"Well, I don't know where you ... that information is totally in error. Totally wrong."

"You know we can check," Rileigh said. She was enjoying this. The woman had been so haughty and condescending to the female of the Rileigh-Mitch duo that it was entertaining to give her back some of what she had dished out.

"You can check what?"

"Give me fifteen minutes and a phone, and I'll have your financial records laid out in front of me. Your tax returns, your..."

Camille held up her hand. "Okay, fine, so I've got some creditors who are giving me problems. What does that have to do with anything?"

"I'd say it has something to do with why *you* suggested to your sister that the two of you go try to talk Carly into selling again."

That caught her unaware. "Why would you think it was my idea?"

"Because your sister said it was. She said you called her, pressured her into trying again to get Carly to sell. So why didn't you tell us that when we were here before? Why did you say there was no particular reason why you just happened to be yelling at Carly about selling the day Mitch witnessed your argument?"

"Because it isn't any of your business. None of this is your business. You don't have any right to come in here and question me as if I were a common criminal." She turned on Mitch. "You are out of your jurisdiction, Sheriff Webster. You have no authority here in Knoxville."

Since Rileigh's first ruse had worked, she threw out another one. It's a common misconception, probably from all the inaccurate television cop shows, that there is some obligation on the part of law enforcement officers to be honest and truthful. That couldn't be further from the truth. A cop could say anything he wanted. There was no law or regulation requiring him to stick to the facts. In fact, it had been Rileigh's experience over the years that the officers who made the most arrests were the ones who were good at concocting some kind of tale that convinced suspects they knew more than they did.

So Rileigh Bishop ran the sail up the mast and set out across the sea of deception.

"He's out of his jurisdiction, but I'm not out of mine. I'm a federal officer." Camille's face turned white. "I am Rileigh Bishop, senior special agent with the Federal Bureau of Investigation operating out of Nashville."

She gave a mental nod to Agent Devereux when she said it.

If Camille had demanded to see identification, Rileigh would have been shit out of luck. She could have come up with some excuse why she didn't have it on her, but the act would be way more effective if Camille didn't ask.

Camille didn't ask.

"So I will ask you again, Ms. Farrington, why didn't you tell us that it was your idea to go talk to your sister about selling Shagbark Manor? What were you hiding?"

"I wasn't hiding anything."

"Buzz," Rileigh said loudly. "Wrong answer alarm. Try again."

Finally, the woman sat back on the edge of her desk and sighed.

"Okay. It was my idea. I called Kiara and suggested we go talk to Carly again about selling."

"Why? You just woke up that morning and thought, 'Gee, it sure would be nice if my sister would agree to sell that property today'? What was the hook?"

"I told Carly that I might have a buyer... but it was more than that. I got an *offer* on the place."

That upped the ante considerably.

"Really? A good offer?"

"No, not a good offer, a *great* offer. I was under a non-disclosure clause, so I couldn't offer specifics. But it's a great offer, and if we can nail it down in the next twenty-one days—"

"Why the time frame?"

"Carmichael Realty has a lot of irons in the fire. They move fast. They pick up their chips and go somewhere else if they run into snags along the way."

"Carmichael Realty." Rileigh rolled that name around in her mind, trying to place where she'd heard it before. "So, who is Carmichael Realty?"

"Oh, you've seen their signs all over everywhere, particularly all over Gatlinburg. They're putting up an apartment complex on Hardy Boulevard."

"Where on Hardy Boulevard?"

"They're gonna bulldoze that old wax museum. And there's a condominium development out on Busher Ridge."

Right, Rileigh remembered. Carmichael Realty. She'd heard gossip that the firm could be predatory.

"And the offer that they have made to you is only good for three weeks, right?"

"Yep, three weeks."

"So you have to talk your sister into selling in *three weeks.*"

"And you're set to lose a lot of money, or at least potential money, if your sister sticks to her guns on this," Mitch pointed out.

"Yes, I am. And so is Kiara, and so is Carly. It is a wonderful offer. And that stupid little bitch is crazy for turning it down."

"So if there was anything you could do to convince Carly to sell, you'd do it, right?" Rileigh suggested.

That hit a nerve. Camille stiffened and collected herself.

"Look, if you're going to ask me any more questions, I want my lawyer."

"You're not accused of anything."

"Well, if I'm not accused of anything, and I don't need a lawyer, then I don't have to answer any more questions, and I'm not going to. Please leave."

Mitch and Rileigh complied, walking back out of the chrome and glass office into the area where two office workers had been pretending to be busy with the copy machine so that they could eavesdrop on what was going on in Camille's office.

Mitch waited until they got to the car to point out the obvious.

"If there was anything that Camille could do to get Carly to agree to a sale, she'd do it," he said.

"Right. And if tanking the bed and breakfast by getting Carly's five-month tenants to move out would get Camille what she wants, she'd be all over it."

"That's a little extreme. Kidnapping a teenager and faking some kind of awful crime scene? Maybe even murder?"

"If Carmichael Realty is what I've heard it is... I need to do some digging, but the word on the street is that they play dirty. *Extremely* dirty. It's not out of the realm of possibility that the prospective buyer decided to take matters into his own hands."

"This case gets more convoluted by the minute."

Chapter Twenty-Eight

On the way back to Yarmouth County from Knoxville, Rileigh asked Mitch, "So, where do we go from here?"

"In terms of suspects, we have several lines in the water. Mullins texted me that Sturgis wasn't at his house, and none of his neighbors have seen him today."

"Goody. So he's in the wind."

"He and Scooby are high on my suspect list, and Sturgis moves into first place because he ran."

"Maybe Scooby ran, too. You're not having any luck locating him."

"At least he's local. Sturgis is from who knows where."

"As far as motives go, Sturgis might have tried something with Carly, and she threatened to turn him in. He knows enough about the place to know that lots of blood and axe marks would send the investigation in some other direction. And Scooby? A volatile meth-head, a bad drug deal, and an axe hanging above the mantel. Add water and stir."

"I've got Rawlings digging into the background of

Tabitha's squeeze, Reginald Daniels. If he has a rich wife who's bankrolling him, he'd be even more invested than Tabitha in shutting Hillary up. If he pops with any kind of record — doesn't have to be assault, I'll settle for shoplifting — he goes to the head of the class and we can start checking out that alibi. Did they actually go out to eat in a cute French restaurant that night, or were they engaged in some other activity altogether?"

"And if your alternative universe scenario is true — that Hillary was not the intended victim — then we have the lovely Farrington sisters and Carmichael Realty."

"That one grew legs and started walking after we talked to Camille Farrington," Mitch said.

"I think we have to find out whether it's rumor, urban myth, or reality that people have disappeared from Shagbark Manor often over the years. We know of two — the lady Mama met years ago and the mother of that Texas judge." Rileigh paused. "Three if you count the one Georgia remembered from that sleepover at Carly's."

"I thought you said she thinks she imagined the whole thing."

"I did. And she does. But… the jury's still out on that one."

"Carly said she'd send us the full roster of every man, woman, and child who has stayed at Shagbark Manor since right after the earth cooled off. I'm not sure how much good it's going to do us, though."

"Why?"

"There are too many names on it. No way to check them all out."

"I think maybe we can find ways to narrow down the list."

"I'm listening."

"So… we have three possible victims. We're looking for

a serial killer/copycat killer with a certain MO, who's operating by his own self-imposed set of rules for how he does
his job."

"Check."

"All the victims were women. That just about cuts the
list in half."

"Whack! Keep cutting."

They got to Rileigh's house then and tabled the discussion. When they got out of the car, they walked up the
sidewalk to the porch, where Mama sat, smiling.

"I'm sure you've never met him personally," she said,
"but I know you've heard of him." She turned to the
person who wasn't sitting beside her and said, "How do
you want to be addressed? Mr. Dali Lama? Mr. Dali? Or
Mr. Lama?"

Rileigh almost choked. She coughed and tried to
strangle her laughter.

Mitch drew himself up tall.

"I'm very pleased to meet you, Mr. Lama, sir," he said
to the person who wasn't sitting there.

"So am I," Rileigh said.

"Sit down and chat with us," Mama offered.

"Thanks, Mama, but we need to go inside and do some
work on the computer."

Rileigh hauled her laptop computer out onto the
dining room table and called up the information that Carly
Farrington had sent to them. It was a list of seven thousand six hundred and one names. Though Rileigh was no
computer whiz, she did have a data entry program on her
computer that allowed her to enter information and then
apply various filters to it to show only what the filter
allowed. She entered Carly's list into the program.

"Let's narrow the list down to only women. Take out
all the men and children."

Rileigh touched a key, and the list rearranged itself. And when it did, there were only 2,626 names. Roughly 35% of the people who had stayed at Shagbark Manor over the years had been female adults.

"Alrighty, let's put another filter on it," she said.

"Single occupancy. These women came by themselves."

Rileigh added that filter, and the list of 2,626 names shrank to 1,312. Roughly half.

"How can we narrow it down any more than that?"

"Well, Georgia said that the big-eared woman who should have put her hair down over her ears had a white bun. Mama said the woman she met in the funnel shop had a white bun, and that Texas sheriff's mother was seventy-five."

"So at what age does a woman's hair turn white?" Mitch asked.

Rileigh cocked her head to the side and lifted an eyebrow. "In my case, never."

"Let me rephrase that: at what age do women who choose not to color their hair go white?"

"I'd say at least over sixty."

Rileigh applied that filter, and the list shrank to 395 from 1,312.

"Okay then, 395 of those occupancies were female, over the age of sixty and checked in by themselves."

"And this is a filter that just seems common sense to me," Rileigh said. "If you were picking out victims that you didn't want to be missed, then you would need to pick out those it would take more than a few hours for them to drive home. You'd want as long a period of time as you could get before they'd be missed. And the farther away it is, the less likely it is that anybody will look here."

"How far away?"

"Golly, I'd say at least three hundred miles."

"Make it five hundred," Mitch said.

Rileigh punched in the filter, and that filter reduced the list down to eighty names.

"So now we have a mildly manageable list of eighty names. Older women who came here by themselves and drove home more than five hundred miles. How do we reduce it further?"

"I don't think we do," Mitch said. "I think eighty names is as small as it gets. Now what?"

"I suggest we call them."

Mitch looked surprised. "Call all of these people?"

"Well, be grateful for small favors. When we got here, it were more than seventy-five hundred names. Now it's eighty. That's manageable. And we have the home phone numbers they gave when they checked in."

"So you're going to call these phone numbers and say what?" Mitch asked.

"I'll figure that out as I go along."

"We just ask to speak to the women and see what they say?"

"We could get lucky. Maybe they'll say, 'I'm sorry, she can't come to the phone right now. She went to the Smoky Mountains twenty years ago and never came home.'"

Mitch rolled his eyes. "Don't hold your breath. Are you sure you want to take on this task?"

"Take on what task?" said a voice from the doorway. Mitch and Rileigh turned to see Jillian standing there.

"The task of finding out if people really have been going missing from Shagbark Manor for years, or if it's a myth."

"And you're going to find that out how?"

"Well, we have a much-narrowed-down list of eighty possible victims who have stayed there over the years —

women over sixty who checked in alone and drove longer than eight hours to get here."

"And you're proposing to call all of the names on that list?" Jillian asked, with her right eyebrow lifted. Rileigh realized that she and her sister both tended to lift an eyebrow when they were suspicious of something.

"Yup," Rileigh said.

"That's a task for somebody who's got way too much time on their hands," Jillian said. Then she shrugged. "I definitely qualify. Need some help?"

Rileigh went to her sister and hugged her.

Maybe with two of them, they could actually come up with something.

Mama brought them sandwiches for supper while they worked. Each took forty names from the list. Rileigh set up shop at the dining room table and Jillian worked at the kitchen table. As Rileigh listened to Jillian's chatty voice making calls in the other room, she thought the two of them had missed their true calling. They should have been telemarketers.

Each call was a separate adventure. The numbers they were calling were those that had been recorded on the register when the people checked in to Shagbark bed and breakfast. But that could have been years ago. Maybe the numbers had been disconnected since then. Maybe the number was from a cell phone that had been lost and replaced. Maybe somebody else now had that number.

Rileigh tried to be as honest as she possibly could. She said she was trying to locate the person whose name was on the registration form because they had stayed at Shagbark bed and breakfast in Yarmouth County, Tennessee, on whatever date. Then she shut up and waited to see what they'd say.

She went down her the list, taking the names one at a

time. Jillian had said she planned to pick names at random, but going down the list ensured that Rileigh would call the most recent numbers first, and she thought she was most likely to be successful with people who had stayed at the bed and breakfast recently.

The difficulty of the task was compounded by the fact that they were looking for single individuals, not families and all of the women were old. Maybe they had died, maybe they no longer lived by themselves.

The first person Rileigh called was Henrietta Thorne, who had checked into the bed and breakfast on August 2, 2022, and checked out on August 5.

The voice on the other end of the line said, "I'm Henrietta Thorne. What can I do for you?"

Well that answered Rileigh's question, so she exited the conversation as quickly and politely as she could.

"I won't disturb you any further," she said. "I'm just making sure that the bed and breakfast records of guests was accurate. Thank you." She hung up.

She chased down one woman through three different relatives before finding her and discovering that she probably had about as many marbles as Mama, maybe fewer.

She'd been working for about an hour when she ended a call and looked up to see Jillian standing in the doorway. She looked like a little kid who needed to go to the bathroom, almost jumping up and down.

"I found one! I found one!" she cried out.

"Who did you find?"

"Her name was Harriet Risma. She was seventy-two years old. She checked into Shagbark on June 15th, 2023 and checked back out on June 19th. I talked to her daughter, who got upset as soon as I mentioned her mother's name, said I couldn't talk to her because nobody knew where she was. She had disappeared."

"What did you say then?"

"I asked what happened to her and she said nobody knew, that she had gone on a vacation to the Smoky Mountains and she never came home."

"What else did she say?"

"You didn't tell me what to do if I actually found somebody, so I just blurted out, 'When was the last time you heard from her?' And the woman said that her mother had called and said she was bringing home a surprise."

"Bringing home a surprise," Rileigh repeated, her breath shallow.

"And then her mother told her she had left where she'd been staying and would call back later, but she never did."

Rileigh looked at her watch and decided immediately not to call Mitch and give him the good news. He had not been sleeping well, and the last thing she wanted to do was wake him up. There was no hurry. These dead old ladies would be just as dead tomorrow.

Sitting back down, she started working her own list, moving from one name to the next, chronologically. She reached for her cup of coffee as she moved down to the next name on the list and she froze with her coffee in her hand, suspended in the air precariously over her laptop.

The name leapt out at her. She didn't know why she hadn't noticed it before because it appeared to be in bold-face type. And italic. And maybe painted purple.

The first name was Gwen.

The last name was Pugh.

Pugh... what a little kid says when they smell something bad.

She looked at the date. July 12, 1999. That would have been when Rileigh and Georgia — and Carly Farrington — were nine years old.

Chapter Twenty-Nine

Mitch had said Carly Farrington had been dumbfounded when he called her that morning to tell her that they had identified some missing tourists from the list she'd given him and he wanted to talk to her about them.

She greeted them when they arrived with a fresh made pitcher of lemonade — which was not nearly as good as Mama's — and seemed eager to help.

Rileigh studied her as she poured glasses for each of them. She seemed to be an unnaturally calm woman. Rileigh had seen her upset, but when she wasn't, there was a peacefulness about her, an economy of movement, no fidgeting.

After she set the glasses in front of them, she sat down on the other side of the table and folded her hands on it. She sat perfectly still but expectant, like bees that had just settled in the hive, humming.

"The first one I found was in 2023," Rileigh said. "Her name was Harriet Risma."

Carly's face lit up. "I remember Harriet Risma. What happened to her?"

"She disappeared. Never made it home after she stayed here."

"Oh no." She shook her head. "She left. I helped her carry her bags out to her car. Gave her the special chocolates myself and gave her a hug. She was a nice old lady."

"Tell me about the special chocolates again," Rileigh said.

"As I said, it's a tradition my grandmother started. When guests leave, we give them a box of freshly made chocolates for them to take to whoever they left behind at home."

"You're sure she left?"

"Yes."

"Do you remember watching her drive away?"

Carly thought.

"No. But I do remember setting up the picture."

"Picture?" Mitch asked.

"You can see them on the wall in the blank room. We take pictures in front of the staircase with the chocolates. I remember setting up the tripod for my iPhone."

"There's something in the background of all those pictures," Rileigh said. "What is—?"

Carly smiled. "Photoshop."

Was there such a thing as Photoshop thirty years ago? Rileigh didn't know, so she quietly Googled it while Carly and Mitch kept talking. *Photoshop was developed in 1987 and sold to Adobe Systems Incorporated in 1988, as a subset of the design software Adobe Illustrator.* So, if you knew thirty years ago how to use Adobe Illustrator, you could have Photoshopped a creature into the background of a picture.

"The second woman was in 2021," Mitch was saying when Rileigh tuned back in. "Her name was Helen Bigby from Anaheim, California. She checked in on July the 3rd, and according to your records, checked out three days later on July the 6th. But according to her family, she didn't come home."

"That's so awful," Carly said, "They sound so similar. They leave and then they don't make it home. But she left. I know she left."

"So you remember her."

Carly shook her head. "Not really. That was a really, really busy time. The first summer after lockdown, when I was running around trying to get things up and operational again so that we could start entertaining guests. I don't remember her. In 2021, I employed no maids. I would have cleaned her room. I would have known if she'd hung around for some reason."

"If she was from Anaheim, California, she had a long drive ahead of her," Rileigh said. "Probably left pretty early in the morning."

"Yes, probably."

"And you gave her the bye-bye chocolates, right?"

"I suppose. I told you I don't remember her, but we gave them to everybody. So if she was here and she checked out, we gave her the bye-bye chocolates."

"The other woman we know about was here when you were a little girl. Georgia Stump told me about her. She checked out when Georgia was here for a sleepover."

"Georgia Stump spent the night here... *with me?*" Carly was incredulous.

"She did. The two of you would have been nine years old. She said she remembered sitting at the dinner table with the woman, that she had big ears," Rileigh said.

Carly looked confused.

"Georgia said that she'd wondered at the time why the woman didn't cover her ears up with her long hair." Carly had started shaking her head halfway through what Rileigh was saying. "It took a while to track her down, several phone calls. The closest we could pin down what happened to her was that she had disappeared in the summer of 1999."

"I absolutely don't remember a sleepover with Georgia McGinnis... uh, Stump. With her or any other little girl. Is she sure it was *me?*"

Rileigh nodded.

"Maybe one of my sisters remembers. I could ask — no, 1999. They were gone by then."

"We talked to both of your sisters yesterday."

"Whatever for?"

Mitch didn't answer, just said, "I interrupted the argument you were having with them the day I brought Hillary home from my office. It looked like it was about to turn violent."

"I'm sorry that my sisters have issues that selling this place would solve. But this place is where I live. It's what I do. I don't know why they would think I'd sacrifice my home for them when we barely know each other."

"Meaning?"

"Kiara was nine and Camille was ten when I was born. They were teenagers by the time our parents died and we moved here. And then they left. Camille went off to beauty school as soon as she turned eighteen, and Camille left at seventeen and ran off with some guy."

"But surely they came back to visit."

"Oh, you mean like family holidays?" Carly rolled her eyes. "Grandma Josie was *not* a baking cookies for Santa kind of grandmother."

"So you never saw them again?"

"Oh, sure. I saw them now and then, but it's not like we were close. Not like we had the kind of bond that would mean so much to me I'd sell off everything I care about and my livelihood just to pull one of them out of a jam."

"So you were pretty much raised here by yourself by Grandma Josie," Mitch said

"Yes. It was like being an only child."

"Your sisters painted a pretty bleak picture of what your life was like, said you looked so much like your grandmother when she was a child that she treated you like you really were her, dressed you up like a doll, hovered over you."

She bleated a bark of mirthless laughter.

"You make it sound so... sinister. It was nothing at all like that. My grandmother put ribbons in my hair and dressed me in pretty dresses, treated me as tenderly as a china doll — what's not to like about that? I adored all the attention."

"Tell us about living in this big, old house... *alone*... spending all day every day with—" Rileigh almost said "with a little girl who survived an axe murder." But she didn't. Instead just ended with, "with Jocelyn Farrington."

A strange thing happened to Carly's face then. Her whole countenance went totally blank. Like somebody had taken her batteries out. She stared at nothing, catatonic... for one, two, three seconds... and then tuned right back in. A look from Mitch told Rileigh he'd seen it, too. Maybe Carly had a form of epilepsy, the kind that causes numerous brief seizures.

Because that's what it looked like: a seizure.

"I had a normal childhood. I grew up. I played with my friends. I went to school. What do you want to know about it?"

She sounded... different, somehow, but Rileigh couldn't put her finger on exactly how.

"Did any bad things happen while you were growing up?"

"No."

"Not even maybe that time when... I don't know, you got hurt or scared of something?"

"No, nothing."

"Did your grandmother tell you about what happened the day her mother and sisters were murdered with an axe?"

"No!" Carly said as if she'd been jabbed with a cattle prod. "She never said a word about that. Not a word. She didn't talk about that. She wouldn't have talked about that. She *couldn't* have talked about it because she didn't remember. Just playing hide and seek and then... nothing. Nothing else. Nothing at all. Not a thing. She was hiding and she couldn't remember anything after."

That whole spiel came out on one long breath. After her monosyllabic responses to previous questions, it was jarring.

"So you don't know any more about what happened on that May afternoon in 1926 than anybody else. Is that what you're telling me?"

"How would I know? Unless Grandma Josie told me, and she never said a word."

Rileigh had begun to feel creeped out for no reason she could put her finger on. She wanted to drag the conversation back to solid footing, reality.

"There's one more, but we don't have a time frame on it. Sometime between 2011 and 2014. We don't know her name, but Mama ran into her one day in the funnel cake store in Gatlinburg, struck up a conversation — my mother never met a stranger — and wanted to get together, but the woman said she was staying here at Shagbark Manor and leaving the next day. Mama thought nothing else about it until she was in the funnel cake store about six months later and a couple came in showing a picture around and asking if anybody'd seen her. Mama looked at the picture and it was the woman she'd met months before, the one staying here."

"I remember those people," Carly said. "It was a young man and a young woman. They came here with pictures of their mother and said she had left here and never made it home. They said they'd been looking for her for weeks, had stopped at various places along the way where they thought she would have stopped. Rest stops and convenience stores. Places like that."

"And you recognized her?"

"Yes. I recognized her."

"And did you see her drive away?"

"No, I didn't."

"Did you give her the bye-bye chocolates?"

"I'm sure Grandma Josie did. She gave them to everybody. "

Rileigh shook her head. "Well, that couple never got their box of chocolates. The families of those other women didn't get theirs either."

"Look, I'm really sorry about all of these people. But I don't know how I can be held responsible for what happens to somebody after they check out. They get in their car and they drive away. I have no say over where they go or what they do or who they see. Anything in the world could happen to them."

"Doesn't it strike you as an odd coincidence that it's older ladies — white hair in a bun — who leave here and don't make it home?"

Mitch added softly, "I don't believe in coincidences."

"But what do all those women have to do with the teenager who disappeared from here?" Carly asked. "And we all know she did. She's gone and there's blood all over everywhere and her parents and everyone else are afraid she's dead. How will finding out what happened to these women help you find her?"

Mitch had no answer for her.

Chapter Thirty

MITCH AND RILEIGH HAD MADE IT ALL THE WAY OUT TO HIS cruiser when Paul Schofield came thundering down the steps. Rileigh thought he looked like he'd aged ten years. There were dark circles under his eyes. His hair was disheveled. He appeared to have slept in the clothes he was wearing.

"I need to talk to you, Sheriff," he said.

"I'm glad to talk to your sir, but I don't have anything concrete to report. I have some leads, though."

"Something's going on," Schofield said. "Those things that Hillary said she saw, told us she saw, and we wouldn't believe her." The last words sounded like a strangled sob. "We told her she was crazy, we——" He stopped himself. "Well, she wasn't crazy. Some of the same things are happening now, and we've seen them."

"What are you talking about, Mr. Schofield?"

"I'm talking about… about words — 'You Die' written in blood on the wall."

"Written in blood?" Rileigh asked.

"That's what Hillary said she saw. She told me she saw

231

it. She begged me to believe her, and I told her she was seeing things, nuts. Her mother... Tabby... told her she was making it up just so she could go home, but it was true, it was all true. I saw it myself."

"Did you report what you saw to Carly?" Mitch asked. "Did you take her and show her?"

"I went and got her and dragged her up the stairs to the wall where the blood was... and it wasn't there anymore."

Mitch let out a sigh. "Mr. Schofield, you've been under an awful lot of stress lately, and—"

"See! You're doing the same thing to me I did to Hillary. I blew her off. But I'm not losing my mind. I'm telling you what I saw. The littles are so freaked out they don't want to go upstairs to bed."

"Freaked out by what?" Rileigh asked. "Something specific?"

"Liza calls it a shiny thing. Sam and Sage say there are lights at the end of the hall that look like shapes, and the lights come at them, and they run away screaming."

"And all of this has happened since Hillary left?"

"The littles have been freaked out since that night. They haven't wanted to sleep by themselves. Liza started wetting the bed. Tabby is a wreck because the littles are so upset. I never should have brought them into the house that night. Why did I bring them into the house?"

"Don't beat yourself up," Mitch told him. "You didn't know that there was blood all over the floor!"

"I shouldn't have let them see that. They're having nightmares and they're seeing things, too."

"Seeing things like what?"

"Well, the lights, but not just seeing things. They say they hear moaning like somebody's hurt, and whispers when they're in their beds at night."

"What do the whispers say?"

"They don't know, they couldn't tell. Mumbling and other sounds, weird music... and smells."

Mitch was sure Paul Schofield didn't realize he was pacing back and forth in front of Mitch's cruiser. The man was undone.

"What smells, Mr. Schofield?"

"When you go into the library, you smell roses, but there are no roses in there. And in the parlor on the second floor at the end of the hall, there is rose smell, too, but it changes, like it... it's like the roses wilted and it smells rotten."

"Did you smell that, the rotten flowers?"

"Liza said she did, and she came running for me. She dragged me into the room, and I smelled it too as soon as I got in there, like flowers that were left in a vase in water and the water got stagnant, and the petals fall off and the stems rot."

"Did you see any flowers?"

"There weren't any flowers in that room. There wasn't anybody smoking a cigar in the dining room either, any more than there was a skunk under the covers in Liza's bed."

"The children told you those things?"

"Some of them — some of them, we saw ourselves. Tabby wanted to come down here with me to talk to you, back me up, but you can't leave the littles alone for a minute or they freak out."

"Mr. Schofield, it's none of my business, but I can't imagine that it's healthy for your children to live in this environment. They're just little kids, and their imaginations run away with them."

"It wasn't my imagination when I got up this morning and the mirror in my bathroom was cracked. But when I took Tabby to show her, it was fine. Tabby said that she hears mournful singing and sounds like little kids crying and..."

Paul Schofield stopped, forced himself to get a grip, and stood up straighter.

"Sheriff Webster, you have to find my daughter. Do *something*."

"Mr. Schofield, I'm doing everything I can. We have some leads, but no solid evidence."

"Please. My whole family is falling apart."

"Like I said, this isn't any of my business, but if I were you, I would take my wife and three small children and get them out of this environment for a while. I know you said you closed up your house in Nashville, and maybe going home isn't an option. I just think you need to get your children away from here for a few days."

Mitch stopped and thought for a moment, then cast a glance at Rileigh as if to get her tacit agreement on what he was about to say.

"I tell you what, Mr. Schofield. What if — how about you take your wife and children away for the weekend, and I will stay here in this house while you're gone. I'll see if I can figure out the source of all these unexplainable events. How does that sound?"

"Sure," he said. "Anything's better than the way it is now." He stopped then and looked deep into Mitch's eyes, speaking quietly. "Hillary's gone, isn't she? I don't mean just missing, I mean *gone*." There was such profound sadness in the man's voice and tone, it broke Mitch's heart.

"We don't know that, sir."

"Maybe you don't. But I do. She's gone. I brought her here for us to bond as father and daughter and now she's gone and I'm never going to see her again. I know that, and you know that." He stifled a sob. "I just wish we knew what happened to her."

"I'm sorry, Mr. Schofield. I'm doing the best I can."

The man shook his head sadly. "I'll go tell Tabby to pack up the kids and we'll go somewhere. Anywhere but here."

Mitch and Rileigh got into his cruiser.

"You know when you were a little kid, your friends used to dare you to spend the night in a haunted house?" Mitch said.

Rileigh nodded.

"Consider yourself dared."

"Looks like I don't have any choice. I've never turned down a dare."

Chapter Thirty-One

A BIG DROP OF RAIN SPLATTERED ON THE WINDSHIELD OF Mitch's cruiser as he and Rileigh drove the winding road up to Shagbark. Rileigh burst out laughing.

"What did I miss?"

"It's going to rain," Rileigh said, gesturing toward the sky, and as if on command, more raindrops began to pelt the windshield, the hood, and the top of the car, making rat-tat-tat sounds like machine guns.

"And that's humorous because…?"

"Because it just fits. What else would you expect? "

"I'm not tracking."

"We are about to go spend the night in a haunted house," Rileigh said, enunciating each word as if she were talking to a three-year-old.

"Yes."

"And how does every really bad ghost story begin?"

Then Mitch got it. "It was a dark and stormy night," he said.

"So here's the storm. I hope this one doesn't turn into

something like the raging gales in gothic novels," Rileigh said. "Or the electricity will go out."

It was Mitch's turn to laugh. "Well, of course the electricity will go out. That's just part of the experience."

When Mitch told Carly Farrington he and Rileigh would be staying the night at Shagbark Manor, she insisted on preparing dinner for them. By the time they got to the manor, it was raining hard, and Rileigh ran from the car to the front porch, with Mitch close on her heels.

"Obviously you weren't a Boy Scout," Rileigh said.

"And that's obvious to you because I was not prepared with umbrellas."

"I carry an umbrella with me everywhere I go," Rileigh said. "Back floorboard of the car."

"I shall try to learn from this experience," Mitch said. They swiped as much of the water off their clothes as they could before they stepped into the spacious, well-lit foyer of the bed and breakfast. Rileigh recalled then how gothic and imposing and intimidating the house had seemed the night they were called to investigate the disappearance of Hillary Schofield.

It seemed that way again. Daylight mitigated its creepiness. Nighttime highlighted it. There were deep shadows in all the corners, and Rileigh thought again that it was probably intentional that there were dim bulbs in all the lights to increase the coziness... or the creepiness, one or the other.

Rileigh and Mitch crossed the foyer toward the hallway leading to the kitchen and followed the smell of something delicious down the corridor.

"Is that fresh-baked bread I'm smelling?" Mitch asked when they stepped into the kitchen.

Carly Farrington turned around with a shy smile. "I don't mean to brag, but I think you would be hard-pressed to find any bread in the county that's better than mine. It'll be out of the oven in just a few minutes. Why don't the two of you go have a seat in the dining room, and I'll be serving dinner in just a little while."

Rileigh and Mitch did as they were instructed. The huge formal dining room loomed around them. The backs of the chairs were probably six feet tall. Mitch set on one end of the huge table and Rileigh sat to his right. They looked down the long expanse of table at all the empty spaces.

Rileigh said, "I can't imagine how much work it would be to take care of as many guests as this dining room will seat."

"Well, she said she had hired help, and apparently she has done a good job, because she scaled what her grandmother could not."

Out of the corner of Rileigh's eye, she saw something and turned toward it, but there was nothing. "Did you see…?"

"Did I see what?"

"Nothing. Nothing."

Carly arrived with big glasses of cold iced tea for both of them. "I've made vegetable soup tonight, with the vegetables fresh from the farmers' market this afternoon." She was dressed in the black dress of a proper British maid, her long hair pulled up, not in a fashionable messy bun but a sedate bun with no stray hairs. Carly slipped through the swinging door back into the kitchen, and Rileigh smiled at Mitch.

Over his shoulder, she saw something again. "What is that?"

But it was gone.

"What do you think you're seeing?" Mitch asked.

"I don't know. It's like shimmering lights, maybe? I

don't know. I only see them out of the corner of my eye, and then when I turn to look at them, they're not there."

There was a sudden clap of thunder like the roar of a battery of cannons. The crack sound made Rileigh jump, and the rumble that followed seemed to shake the window-panes in the old house.

Rileigh smiled. "Like I said. It was a dark and stormy night."

Carly brought in bowls of fresh vegetable soup and set them in front of Mitch and Rileigh. The aroma filled the room.

"Are there like blinking lights of some kind in this room? I keep seeing lights or flashes," Rileigh said.

Carly stood very still, pensive, as if she were deciding what she was going to say. "The pot roast will keep," she said as she pulled out a chair on the other side of the table from Rileigh and sat down. "There's something that you need to know."

Both Mitch and Rileigh leaned in. "I don't play tricks on my guests. I wouldn't do a thing like that, but… but I do sort of enhance the atmosphere."

"Define 'enhance the atmosphere.'"

"Music," she said. "I have speakers where you can't see them in several rooms, and I have recorded music that plays sometimes."

"Recorded music of what?"

"Well, of a violin and of a harp and a flute." She paused when they didn't immediately get the reference. "Those were the three instruments the Tillman girls could play."

"What else do you do to enhance the atmosphere?" Mitch asked

"Well, you've noticed the lights. The lights sometimes

flicker, or appear to flicker on their own. It's a timer, that flickering... to add to the atmosphere."

"Anything else?" Rileigh asked.

"I don't know if you noticed, but in the library, you can always smell roses. Roses were Lenora Tillman's favorite flower, and supposedly she had vases of fresh roses in every room."

"I didn't see any roses in the library when I was in there," Rileigh said.

"You can buy scents, flowers and things, to put into a diffuser. One of the most popular smells is roses, and I have one of those devices in that room, and it's wired to a switch in another room." She paused and drew herself up. "That way, I can be in another room and produce the smell of roses in the library."

"Is that all?" Mitch asked and she nodded her head and let out a sigh.

"I know it's a deception, but it's harmless, and people expect to come here and hear strange sounds and see strange things. That's why they chose to come to a haunted house... where the original owners were killed by an axe murderer. They come here because they hope it's haunted, and I just help their imaginations along. That's all."

Carly rose from the table. "I'll bring in your dinner now."

"What about wilted flowers?" Mitch asked.

"What?"

"Paul Schofield said he smelled wilted flowers. Was that your doing?"

"He's gotten more and more upset, and I don't blame him, really I don't, but he dragged me upstairs to show me where he thought he saw writing in blood on the wall. There was nothing. Wilted flowers? Where would you buy the scent of wilted flowers to put in a diffuser?"

After Carly finished serving them their meals and had left them alone, Mitch asked Rileigh. "Do you think that some of the strange things Hillary said she saw were orchestrated by Carly?"

"I think the strange things that Hillary saw were the result of an overactive imagination and a desire to convince her father either to send her back to her mother or for the whole family to leave."

"So you're saying you don't think she saw what she said she did?"

"How could she?"

"Drugs."

"Ah, yes, drugs," Mitch said. "We keep coming up with a handful of nothing trying to locate Scooby."

"Chigger said he was like smoke."

Rileigh cut into her roast beef and took a bite. "Oh my goodness, this is as good as Mama's," she said. "You don't even need a knife. You can cut it with a fork."

"I suppose that one of the prerequisites of running a successful bed and breakfast is good food," Mitch said. Rileigh took a long drink of sweet tea and noticed a flickering light at the corner of her vision, but she didn't try to locate it.

"We need to remember to tell Carly to turn off all the special effects tonight," Mitch said. "I want the sanitized version, not the orchestrated one."

"And what exactly do you think the experience is going to be like?"

"I have no idea. There are people telling me they see messages written in blood on the wall, dead bodies at the foot of the stairs, pentagrams chalked on the floor. And my plan is to see if any of those phenomena happen to you and me tonight."

There was another loud clap of thunder that seemed to shake the windows, and the rumble went on and on.

"Cinematically speaking," Rileigh said, "looks like this is going to be a pretty good storm."

"Let's just hope it doesn't knock out the electricity," Mitch said. But then he patted his pocket. "I thought to bring a small flashlight."

Rileigh laughed out loud. "I did too, just in case."

"You're the one who should have been a Boy Scout."

Chapter Thirty-Two

CARLY CLEANED UP THE LAST OF THE DISHES, INCLUDING the saucer that contain half a piece of key lime pie, because Rileigh was so full, she couldn't finish it.

They thanked Carly for dinner, and she said she would be in her apartment on the third floor if they needed anything.

She chucked. "I'd say give me a holler if you need anything, but…" She gestured at the cavernous room with its high ceiling. "Good luck with that. That's to guard my own privacy. The only way to get to my apartment is up the back stairs, which open into the kitchen. So…"

"We're pretty much on our own," Mitch said.

"No more so than the other guests here."

Alone now in the dining room, Rileigh asked Mitch, "Do you have a particular plan of attack?"

"Oh yes, detailed and tactical. I use the basic wander around method."

"Use it often, do you?"

"It's very effective.

"Actually, I just want to go into the spaces where

anyone said they saw ghostly things and see if we see the same."

There was a rumble of thunder outside, and for a moment, Rileigh thought that perhaps that meant the storm was abating, because it hadn't been as loud as the others. But on top of that rumble of thunder came a gigantic crack and boom.

And the lights went out.

"Perfect," Rileigh said, "just perfect. It's going to be a neat trick to see ghostly apparitions in the dark."

"But you have to admit it is appropriate. Dark and stormy night. We had the stormy part. Now we've got the dark part."

He gestured to the glow of red above the doorways. "It's not completely dark."

Tennessee building codes required that any place that offered public accommodations had to have exit signs and exit lights, and those had come on when the electricity went off.

Both Rileigh and Mitch took out their small flashlights and shone them around on the walls and the floor. Mitch told her that he regretted not bringing the gigantic flashlight he always carried in his cruiser. It would certainly have lit things up, but he wasn't keen on going out in that raging storm to get it now. The lights from the combined glow of their two small flashlights was enough to dispel the darkness immediately around them, but left a cocoon of black out beyond where the flashlight beams reached, and it was easy to imagine what might be lurking there in the darkness.

They made their way from the dining room to the foyer and stopped at the bottom of the grand staircase. Mitch shone his light up the stairs all the way to the landing above and then back down again.

"The wildlife that is native to this particular habitat include a dead body and a pool of blood at the foot of the stairs." They shone their lights to the foot of the stairs.

"No body," Rileigh said.

"Check."

"Didn't Hillary and her father both say they saw writing on the wall beside the landing?"

"Yeah, but that's on the second floor. Let's make a circuit of the first floor first, and then we'll venture into that habitat."

So the two crossed the foyer together, listening to the rain hammer the outside of the windows, went into the sitting room and shone their lights around.

"I don't remember any specific things that Hillary said occurred in this room," Mitch said. "But there were several life forms native to the whole ecosystem like—"

And before he could say another word, they heard a sound like a low moan. Like someone was in great pain in the next room, so that you could barely hear them.

"Didn't Carly say she would turn off all her special effects?"

"She did indeed."

"So let's go investigate the moan."

The sound came again as they approached the door to the parlor.

When Rileigh took the knob and turned it, the door opened with a great creaking sound.

"Seriously!" None of the hinges in the house had sounded like they needed WD40 before.

Stepping into the pitch-black parlor, they shone the lights all around. There were comfortable, old-fashioned overstuffed chairs, beautiful lamps that were not lit right now, and a settee, a couch, and a love seat.

Rileigh stood beside Mitch, shining her light to the

right as he shone his to the left. As the cocoon of silence in the room settled around them, it was actually enhanced by the distant sound of rain falling outside, a little like your eyes adjusting to the dark of a room so that you can see better, her hearing seemed to have become more acute it the quiet.

As it did, she became very aware of Mitch's presence next to her.

The human body takes up space in the world. Rileigh had always envisioned it like water being displaced when you put something into it. She'd felt she'd never put it into words before, but she'd always had a sense that some people just appeared to displace more space than they actually did. This was probably the source of the phrase "larger than life," but that seemed more about personality than about the physical presence. Mitch was one of those people. She had noticed it when she'd first spent time with him months ago.

She had followed him, which had pissed him off, out to the dope shack to look for Tina Montgomery, the young woman whose mother had laid three one-hundred-dollar bills on Rileigh's kitchen table and begged her to find her daughter because she didn't believe that new "away-from-here" sheriff could do it.

He had gotten out of his cruiser that day, angry that she was there.

"You going to tell me why you followed me out here?" he'd started.

"You are looking for Tina Montgomery. I'm looking for Tina Montgomery. You got a tip on where she might be, and it's a free country. If I happen to want to drive out Shady Creek Road on this fine Tuesday morning, there's no law against it."

"Can you say obstruction of justice?"

"I'm not obstructing anything. You can't obstruct from behind. All I did was follow you here."

She'd sensed it then, that day. The *bigness* of him, the more of him in space than the size of his body should have required.

She felt that sense wash over her now. He suddenly felt much nearer than just a person she was standing beside. His arm brushed hers. He turned toward her, shining his flashlight around behind where they were standing.

"The flashlight beams certainly contribute to the creepiness factor," he said and she said nothing. He turned his face down to hers. She could see his features in the ambient light from their flashlights. The planes and hollows of his face were outlined with shadow, making them even more pronounced. The firm jaw, the high fore-head. She couldn't see his eyes, though, but she could imagine them, could imagine the look in them.

They stood facing each other, both of them holding flashlights pointing in opposite directions. Time did one of those flip-flop things, unhooked from reality, leaving her and Mitch suspended alone in some place where time didn't count, in that space between seconds, hanging there in suspense like a paused second hand on a clock yearning to move on.

He began to lean his face down toward hers, and she looked up into his eyes, but couldn't see the look in them. It didn't matter though, because she had registered the tension that had suddenly shocked his body. She imagined that she could hear his heart kick into another gear and begin to beat faster, but that was surely her imagination. She couldn't possibly have heard his heart beating when hers was hammering away like a lunatic woodpecker.

Closer.

Closer.

She closed her eyes and lifted her face up, and her lips waited for the feel of his on hers. His lips were soft and warm, and the kiss was gentle.

Ahhhh.

Maybe she made the sound. Maybe he did.

She leaned into him, and he put his arms around her, and she found hers slipping around him. The kiss deepened. His lips became more insistent and she felt a passion like none she'd ever felt before suddenly rise up in her. She pressed her mouth against his, hungry, wanting more and more.

The kiss went on and on and grew more intense with every second. His arms around her crushed her to him, and when his tongue touched her lips, she opened her mouth and greedily took it in. This was the stuff of fantasy.

She lost herself in desire for more and more of him. They stood together in that space between the seconds on a clock, and then she was lying on the love seat. She didn't remember how that had come to be, but knew he must have eased her down onto it as if she was weightless.

Mmmm.

She made the sound when she felt the weight of him on top of her. She arched her body up into him, bit down on his lip—

Thump.

Rileigh didn't know what the sound was, but it froze both of them. It came from that cocoon of darkness that surrounded them. Then she saw light.

She looked up past Mitch's shoulder and saw a glow of light that appeared to be coming from the center of the room. Mitch had his weight on his elbows. He lifted his body, turning toward the light. Then they both saw it. It was, by Hillary Schofield's definition, a no-kidding-for-real ghost, an apparition, a light that shimmered, but it had features, the features of a man, frozen in a rictus of rage and hatred that was terrifying to behold.

The apparition remained where it was as Mitch got to his feet.

"Who are you and what do you want?" he demanded and the ghost vanished. Simply went poof and was gone.

Mitch and Rileigh were both startled.

"Did you just see what I saw?" she asked.

"Of course I saw what you saw. A light with a face. It was right over there. There was something here in this room only seconds ago. It left out one of two doors." He pointed to the right and left at the doors that led from the library into the hallway on one side and into a sitting room on the other.

"You go that way. I'll go this way."

Rileigh didn't hesitate, moving instantly the direction he pointed, feeling for the security of her revolver in her holster at her waist.

Chapter Thirty-Three

MITCH TURNED AND BOLTED OUT THE DOOR TOWARD THE hallway. Rileigh took two steps toward the door of the library and stopped. Maybe the apparition had never left this room. Maybe it was hiding somewhere in here. There were certainly plenty of places where it could have done that.

She showed her flashlight in a circle 360 degrees around her and saw nothing. Then in her mind, she divided the room into quadrants — the same way she had divided that meadow into quadrants months ago to search for Tina Montgomery — and searched each one of them carefully. Behind the chairs and the settee, the loveseat, the couch. She looked around behind tables and chests.

The apparition had just gone poof — vanished. She thought perhaps it had escaped through a secret passageway, but she dismissed the thought immediately. She'd heard rumors all her life about secret passageways at the old haunted house. They had asked Carly and her sisters about that, and all three of them said it was myth and tall tales.

She remembered specifically what Carly had said when Mitch asked her: "Are there passageways, tunnels behind the walls?'"

Carly had paused and answered just as specifically, "No, Sheriff. There are no tunnels behind the walls in Shagbark Manor."

Rileigh had hoped that by now Mitch would have returned, because if the man hadn't been hiding in that room, Rileigh had definitely given him plenty of time to disappear from the rooms beyond. So she hurried back out into the foyer and then down another hallway altogether. She remembered it from when they searched the house. How it seemed to be an opening to where the wild things are, because rooms then opened off rooms opened off rooms with no hallway connecting them, just one room to the next to the next, and each of those rooms had more than one door, and each of those doors led to a different room. As Rileigh tried to make her way through, it quickly became a maze, and without Carly to direct her, Rileigh became disoriented and wasn't certain how she got into the room where she now stood or how to get back to the parlor where she and Mitch...

The thought of him blossomed huge in her mind, and she realized without taking the time to analyze it that there had been a shift, a seismic shift in their relationship. They were on a case, they were in police officer mode, and yet he had kissed her.

"And the walls came a' tumblin' down," she said aloud softly and smiled. She banished the thought. That was for later, to ponder and *enjoy* later.

Rileigh was embarrassed that she'd gotten lost so quickly and that there was no chance in the world she was going to find the apparition that had appeared in the center of the room, and finally acknowledged, though she did not want to, that she was lost.

Breadcrumbs, she thought.

She remembered the children's story that Jillian had read to her, huddled under the sheets with a flashlight when she was a little girl. The one about the wicked witch who ate children. The little girl and boy in the story had been forbidden to set foot in the woods because they were so dangerous. When they decided to disobey, the little girl was afraid they would get lost, and so the little boy left a trail of breadcrumbs to find their way back to their home. The problem was, of course, that when they turned around to go home, the breadcrumbs weren't there anymore thanks to the birds and the little critters who lived on the forest floor. The story was confused in Rileigh's head now and she couldn't remember how it was that they wound up in the cages in the house with the witch who planned to keep them and fatten them up before she ate them, or how the children had escaped. She did remember that the little girl suggested they drop rocks the next time they went into the woods — why would they go back if there was a witch there who wanted to *eat* them? — and they'd found their way back home safely.

But Rileigh had neglected to drop either breadcrumbs or rocks, and she had no idea where she was in that huge house. Should she just call out to Mitch, yell and keep yelling until he came to the sound of her voice? No, the rooms were so large, the walls so thick, the ceilings so high, the doors always closed between rooms, that he wouldn't hear her. She just needed to turn around and find her way back the way she had come. She turned 180 degrees, knew which door she had come into this room through, and went back through it to the previous room. But that's when it got vague. Going through that room, she'd been daydreaming about Mitch kissing her, didn't have her head in the game as her soccer coach had once admonished, and she wasn't completely certain which door she had used to come into that room. She decided it was the one on the right and started toward it when she saw there was also a third door she hadn't even noticed, inset in the wall, a smaller door. She would have remembered if she'd come in through a smaller door, but out of curiosity she went to it and opened it. It was a coat closet with boxes and coats on hangers and boots sitting on the floor. And no ghost.

She closed the closet door behind her, then turned and headed in the direction of the door she was mostly certain she had entered through. So it was that she wandered from one room to the next, hoping that in every doorway she would see a light in the next room, meaning that there was someone in that room, that that's where Mitch had gone. It didn't work that way though, and she moved on and on, thinking that if she had been a little girl growing up in this house, she would have had the time of her life playing hide and seek with Georgia.

Chapter Thirty-Four

MITCH RACED OUT OF THE DOOR THAT LED BACK INTO THE library, his flashlight lighting the way. His heart was thundering in his chest — and not from the sudden exertion — but he forced himself to center his thoughts on the prey at hand.

The apparition had to have left through one of the doors into the room. How else could it get out? It was not a spirit that just slid through a crack in the wall and was gone or went poof and vanished like a genie in a bottle. It was a real live human being, and if he got lucky, maybe he could catch the son of a bitch.

He ran through the library, shining his light around on all the walls to make sure he wasn't bypassing the meddling stranger in his haste. He blew through the room and flew out into the foyer and caught sight of something, just a flicker of movement going through the doorway into the hall that led to the kitchen. Mitch raced as fast as he could across the foyer and into the hallway, and again saw something ahead of him. He doubled his speed and heard actual footsteps in front of him. The hallway opened into the dining room, and when it did, Mitch leapt, diving like a tackle going after a running back about to make it into the end zone. He heard a grunt as he connected with the real live body of a real live human being, and the two of them went crashing to the floor.

Mitch landed on top of the guy and realized that he was wearing something, some kind of fabric draped over him, almost like a little kid who had decided to be a ghost on Halloween and had borrowed one of Mama's sheets, cut holes for the eyes and mouth in it. This fabric was far superior to a white cotton sheet. It was filmy, and it glistened where light struck it, but so thick that you could only see a vague outline of the figure beneath it.

Rolling off the man, Mitch grabbed the fabric, then yanked it up and looked into the eyes of a terrified stranger.

"What are you doing here?" Mitch demanded.

"I just, I, I—"

Mitch quickly got from his knees to his feet, reached down, grabbed the man by the collar, and hauled him upward. Then he shined his light square into the man's face, blinding him.

The man was in his early thirties with close-cropped black hair and a neatly trimmed beard. He stared at Mitch in abject terror and quaked. "What do you want from me? Who are you?"

"I'm Yarmouth County Sheriff Mitchell Webster, and you are in deep shit, pal. Now tell me what the hell you're doing here."

There was a crash outside and another rumble of thunder, and the lights blinked on briefly, giving Mitch a quick view of the gossamer fabric the man had pulled over himself that now lay in a pile at his feet.

The lights flickered then and went back off, but Mitch

knew that they had remained on long enough for the guy to see his uniform, and he appeared to be properly impressed.

"Look, I didn't mean any harm. What did you tackle me for?"

"*I* will ask the questions, and *you* will answer them. Who are you and what the hell are you doing here?"

"Look, I don't have to answer any—"

Mitch had the man by the collar, and he shoved him a few feet from where they had landed to the wall and slammed his head into it. He got right up in the young man's face.

"I don't have time for your bullshit. I'm conducting a murder investigation, and you, son, just became my prime suspect. You had best start talking and start talking now."

"*Murder?* What murder?"

In truth, it wasn't a murder investigation, just a missing person, but Mitch agreed with Hillary Schofield's father in his heart. With that much blood on the floor, Mitch did not expect to find the young woman alive. And besides, a murder investigation sounded way more intimidating than a missing person's investigation. So he ran with it.

"Her name is Hillary Schofield, and she disappeared out of this house, and I want to know what you had to do with it.

"I didn't have anything to do with it," he said. "I don't have any idea what you're talking about."

"Maybe you would be a little more forthcoming if I arrested you and hauled you in." He lifted the young man away from the wall and then slammed the back of his head back into it. "Talk now or I see handcuffs, a mugshot, and a jail cell in your future."

"I don't know anything about some murdered girl. I've just been hired to do a job, and I've been doing that job.

It's not illegal. I haven't done anything illegal. I'm not a criminal. I wouldn't hurt anybody."

"What's your name?"

"Scott Higgins."

"And what specifically is the job you were hired to do?" Mitch had such a tight grip on the man's collar that it was hard for him to talk, but Mitch didn't let go.

"Look, I work for a company called Ghosts R Us out of Nashville. I could show you my business card."

"I don't want to see your damn business card. Keep talking."

"Ghosts R Us is a company that... the man who founded it used to have a television show. Maybe you saw it. Spirits and Spooks. It was a reality show where my boss, B.J. Grainger, went from one purported haunted house to another and took instruments with him and mostly outed people who were pulling some kind of hoax. He developed a reputation at being very good at smoking out conmen."

"What does that have to do with what you're doing here?"

"What it has to do with it is B.J. was running out of clients. If you owned a haunted house, would you want B.J. Grainger to come investigate it on his TV show? Show you up as a fraud? There's a finite number of haunted houses in the country, and he had worked his way through a considerable number of them. The network dropped the show after two seasons. So B.J. and his business partners—"

"Who are his business partners?"

"Me and another man named Stan Hilliard and our college roommate Carl Benson. So, when the show got cancelled, we sat around and tried to figure out what we could do next. And that's when Carl came up with the idea of flipping the script, changing the whole concept."

"Change it how?"

"Look, could you let go of my throat? I'm not gonna go running off anywhere. You're choking me."

Mitch eased off on the pressure but kept the man's body pinned up against the wall.

"So, tell me about this change of concept."

"Carl suggested that instead of outing hoaxes, showing up people who were trying to con the public, why didn't we go over to the dark side? Maybe there was a bigger market for haunting a house than there was for revealing hoaxes and we certainly knew how. Over time, B.J. had figured out just about every scheme and con that people used to make it appear a place was haunted. The electronic devices they planted, the ghostly videos, the sounds and smells. Things like handwriting on the wall that people used to trick others into believing a place was haunted. So we started advertising ourselves as a business that could haunt your house."

Mitch relaxed his grip a little more.

"It didn't take off right away. We had a customer here and there. Somebody who wanted to scare their guests at a dinner party. Stuff like that. But after we came up with the name, Ghosts R Us and the name got out there, we started do some serious business."

"Who were your customers?"

"People who wanted it to appear that a house was haunted."

"And who might those people be?"

"My customers' names are confidential," he said with a burst of confidence.

"All I need is a court order, and I can find out every-thing about your business up to and including whether or not you provide Charmin bathroom tissue to your employees. And if you make me go to the trouble to of getting a court order—"

The man held up his hand. "Okay, okay. Just, just let me go."

Mitch slowly released his grip on the man's shirt but still stood too close to him, in front, invading his space.

"Answer my question."

"Have you ever heard of Snowden mansion in Colorado?"

"No, I have not."

"How about the Swamp Shack in Florida?"

"Nope."

"There's a big manor house in Vermont called Waverly and another one in Vermont called the Bingham House. All of those places have engaged our services to make it appear that they are haunted."

"To what end?"

"Different ends, different people. One of them just enjoyed the idea of living in a place his friends all thought was haunted. But mostly it was for business reasons."

"Like?"

"Like scaring off the people who have agreed to buy a house because you no longer want to sell."

"What was the reason you were hired to haunt this place?"

"Look, I don't take care of the bookings. If you want to know the specifics, you're gonna have to talk to B.J or Carl. All I know is that the point was to scare the people who were here into leaving."

"And you don't know why?"

"I never talked to the customer."

"Who was the customer?"

"I don't know. I just told you, I don't take care of bookings. B.J. does. All I know is what I overheard, that it was some real estate company that wanted to buy the place."

"So tell me what it is you have done."

"The standard things that you always do."

"Like what?"

"Like writing in blood on the walls."

"How do you pull that off?"

"It's a projected image. Sounds of people crying. Ghostly images — a violin floating in the air, a dress that dances. Bad smells."

"Was one of the tricks you pulled a dead body lying at the foot of the stairs in a puddle of blood?"

"Yeah, that was one of them."

"How did you pull *that* off?" Mitch said. "Hillary, a girl staying here, told me she saw the body, a man with a knife in his chest. She immediately brought her father to see and it was gone. I get the body, but how can you clean up a puddle of blood that fast?"

"I don't know about you," the man said, "but when I was in middle school, I never went anywhere without fake vomit in my pocket — looked absolutely real, chunks of hot dog in it — to throw down somewhere and gross the girls out. You can buy a puddle of blood, too. It's the same thing."

"So tell me about the blood that you left splattered on the staircase after you kidnapped Hillary Schofield."

"Man, you have totally lost your mind. I don't have any idea what you're talking about. I didn't kidnap anybody."

"So you're telling me that it was not some trick of yours — cutting chunks out of the stairs with an axe?"

"That's exactly what I'm telling you. I've never done anything like that, would never do anything like that. It's just simple tricks. Sleight of hand. Magic."

"And you don't know specifically who hired you — a name?"

"I don't have any idea. Just let me go. What crime have I committed?"

He landed one there and knew it, and that gave him energy, so he kept going.

"Tell me that. What crime have I committed? What is it you're gonna arrest me for? I didn't do a damn thing but maybe scare somebody, and as far as I know, that is not currently against the law."

"How about assault on a police officer?"

"I didn't assault you. You tackled me!"

He had Mitch there.

"You are a suspect in a murder investigation."

"Then arrest me. I want a lawyer."

The guy had Mitch there, too. It wasn't a crime to frighten someone, and beyond that, he had absolutely no evidence that this man had been involved somehow in the disappearance of Hillary Schofield. Mitch backed up a step and gave the guy some room.

"You said you had a business card. Let's see it."

The man stuck his hands in his pocket and came out with a card. It was black and embossed in bold gold letters on the front was Ghosts R Us. Beneath it were ghostly words that appeared and disappeared depending on how the light struck the card :"Who you gonna call?" His name and a phone number were on the back.

"I'll be wanting to talk to you again, Mr. Higgins."

"Fine, my phone number's there." But the man was gaining confidence and getting angry at the same time. "The next time we talk, I want a lawyer." The man brushed past Mitch, bumping into him intentionally, and walked back down the hallway.

"Wait a minute, Mitch called after him. "I have one

more question. How did you get out of the dining room so fast?"

"There's an opening in the wall."

"A secret passageway?"

"No, just a panel that opens into the next room. There are doors like that in several rooms, makes haunting a lot easier."

"Show me."

Chapter Thirty-Five

RILEIGH STOPPED IN HER TRACKS. *GEORGIA.*

She remembered the story that Georgia had told her about spending the night at Carly's house and getting sick and imagining that she saw somebody with an axe kill somebody else at the foot of the stairs. She'd said she saw the axe murderer drag the corpse across the floor, touch the wall paneling, and a panel had opened up near the floor. The axe murderer had shoved the body into the opening and closed the panel behind it. Had Georgia actually seen that secret compartment in the wall? Which of course begged the question if she'd seen that, had she seen the rest of it? How much of it was a fever-induced hallucination in a small child?

But what else Georgia had told Rileigh was that the secret *passageways* were not a myth either, because Carly had *shown* her one.

It was in the room with the grand piano.

Rileigh swept the room with her flashlight and paused to better illuminate the puddle of darkness she'd noticed earlier in the corner. It was what she thought — a grand piano. Like in most of the rooms, the walls in this room were panels of wood shined to perfection with molding of all kinds around the edges. Boxes within boxes, connecting to the molding on the floor and the crown molding around the ceiling.

Rileigh knew it was a totally lost cause, but she went to the panel where Georgia had said Carly had been able to open a passageway entrance. She'd said the panel was on the right side of the window seat in the room with the grand piano. Rileigh used her flashlight to find her way to the window seat, then looked out at the rain hammering the glass on the outside, the water streaming down the glass making little worms of shadow on the floor. Georgia had said Carly had moved a chair and climbed up on it to reach the top of the piece of paneling. Rileigh didn't need a chair. She felt around for some kind of catch or switch or lever or something on the panel beside the window seat, but there was nothing. She felt all the way around it, ran her fingers along all the casements, all the panels, the floor-boards, the window sill, and the casing around the window. Nothing. It was as Georgia had figured out — everything she thought had happened to her in her overnight with Carly Farrington had been a blur of fever-induced delusion.

But she hadn't imagined the woman. Gwen Pugh had been real.

Rileigh concentrated. Georgia had said that the panel was on the right side of the window seat. Hadn't she? Or had she even said which side? Had she just said, "*right* beside the window seat?" and that's when Rileigh heard "right"?

Rileigh moved to the other side of the window and shone her light over the panel there. She began running her fingers along the edges of the molding, the window casing, the windowsill, the fancy woodwork, and the panel next to the casing.

She felt something with her finger. It was like a small splinter sticking out of the seam between the panel and the one above it. She tried to push the splinter to the right. Nothing. She tried to move the splinter to the left ... and suddenly a panel moved to the side, and behind it was a passageway.

"Holy shit, Batman."

She couldn't help herself, started calling out. "Mitch! Mitch!" She had to show him *this!* "I'm in the music room with the grand piano, Mitch!"

When she stopped calling, the silence rushed back in around her. He couldn't hear her... and she damned well wasn't going to wait until he showed up to go explore this. Who knew where this passage might lead to? She might get lucky and come out into the room where Mitch had gone. Oh how she would love to pop out of the wall and surprise him.

Rileigh stepped into the space. It was tight, but wouldn't have been for a little girl. Both her shoulders brushed against the wall; it was just wide enough to get down without turning sideways, and of course it had a musty, unused smell. She took two steps into the passageway and heard a thump behind her, turned around, and the panel that had moved to allow her entrance had just moved back.

She turned around and tried to find the catch on this side of the panel, ran her fingers along all the edges up and down, the ceiling, the floor. Nothing. She could find no way to open the panel from the inside. Perhaps there just wasn't one.

Well, she could stand there and bang her fists on the panel and eventually somebody, Mitch or Carly or someone, would hear her banging and hollering and would come to find her, but it made more sense to just see where this passageway led, because it led *somewhere*. Now she was going to have to find out where.

She walked slowly along the passageway. The ceiling was only about eight feet tall, which felt small after the twelve- and fourteen-foot ceilings in the rooms. And of course, there were no lights, so she shone her flashlight down the dim corridor and continued.

Then up ahead, she could see that passageway connected with another passageway.

Well, shit!

How was she supposed to know which way to go? How would she find her way back to the music room if there were multiple connecting passages? Now more than ever, she longed for a pocketful of rocks. Hell, she'd settle for breadcrumbs.

She got to the connecting passageway, shone her light down it, but the darkness extended out beyond the light.

Turn or stay the course?

Stay the course.

She passed one more connecting passageway, and that passage was larger than this one, but she'd decided to stay the course, so she plunged ahead. In the light of her flashlight, she could see a corner coming up where the passageway she was in took a right-angle turn. She began to smell an odd smell that she couldn't place. It was unpleasant, but she wasn't certain what it was. The closer she got to the corner, the worse the smell was. Both Paul Schofield and his daughter said they'd smelled a bad smell. Was this just that, piped in to disturb and frighten her? No. If somebody got this far, a little bad smell wasn't likely to deter them.

When she got to the corner, she shone her light down

the passage and peeked around the corner to see what might be there. What she saw, she couldn't understand. There was something in the passageway about forty feet away. She didn't know what it was. It was as big as she was. Something wrapped in plastic, taking up most of the area in the passageway. Well, whatever it was, Rileigh was going to have to move it if she was going to get down the passageway. Either that or backtrack to one of the connecting tunnels. No, she'd stay the course.

She approached, and as she did, the smell became more and more familiar. When she was only a few feet away from it, she stopped and examined it with her flashlight. The light reflected off something near the bottom, something that glowed in the plastic. She got down on her knees and looked more closely. What she saw was a shoe. One of those shoes that had reflective tape that glowed in the light.

Fluorescent stripes.

She got slowly to her feet, raising the light up along the thing in plastic as she rose. She reached up and touched the plastic at the top, and what she saw horrified her. The plastic smashed up against a *face*. A horror face with skin hanging down off it, bloated.

What was wrapped in plastic was a decomposing body. And she knew whose body — Hillary Schofield wore running shoes with reflective tape on the sides.

She couldn't help jumping back when she touched it, grossed out by the realization of what this was. She stepped back away from the body, not wanting to stay near it, but she was going to have to do more than get near it. She was going to have to move it out of her way in order to continue down the passageway. Gross. The only way to continue down the passageway was to move the body out of the way.

She put the flashlight in her teeth so that she could see what she was doing and reached out with both hands, took hold of the body in the plastic, and tried to scoot it sideways. But all she managed to do was knock it over, and it fell with a disgusting, muffled squishy sound into the floor of the passageway.

Rileigh swallowed her gorge. She could get past it now. Stepping over and in some places on and around it, she eased her way past the dead teenager, her mind swirling with the implications of the discovery. Hillary Schofield was indeed dead, and given the decomposition of the corpse, she had been dead since she'd disappeared. Hillary had been murdered at the foot of the stairs the night they found the pool of blood there, and her body had been wrapped in plastic and stuck in a hidden passageway behind the walls ever since.

Rileigh concentrated on where she was putting her foot, trying not to step on the body, but there was no way. She took a couple of steps and then jumped past where the body was lying on the floor.

The fact that it was in a secret passageway certainly narrowed down the list of suspects. Who knew about the passageways in the house? Certainly Carly did, and surely so did Carly's older sisters — but they'd all lied about it. Both of her sisters had a motive to drive the Schofield family out of the house. But killing Hillary Schofield was certainly an extreme measure.

Perhaps the sisters hadn't intended to kill Hillary at all. Perhaps one or both of the sisters had hired a killer and he had killed Hillary Schofield by mistake, when the real target was Carly Farrington.

If one of the sisters had committed the crime, that would explain the axe murder at the foot of the stairs. The most terrifying method of murder they could have used —

certainly a murder that would have driven the Schofields away.

Rileigh could think of no one else who would know about the secret passageways other than the three girls who had grown up in the house.

Or maybe not. What about the handyman? Carly had been unexplainably defensive about him, and she'd said she "needed" him. Needed him for what? Maybe the most obvious answer to that question was the correct one. Carly was sleeping with him — which meant she might have revealed all her secrets.

If he'd known about the passageway, certainly dumping Hillary's body here was more convenient than having to carry it out of the house and being careful not to drip blood. Rileigh supposed it was even possible Carly didn't know what he'd done.

But conjectures about who the killer was and what the motive had been were for later. Right now, Rileigh had to find a way out of this passageway and find Mitch to show him the gruesome discovery she had made. She turned her back on the corpse and started carefully down the passageway, swinging the light back and forth to light the way.

Chapter Thirty-Six

RILEIGH CREPT SLOWLY ALONG THE PASSAGEWAY BEYOND the horror of the decomposing Hillary Schofield on the floor. The passage was so narrow in some places that she had to turn sideways and could barely get through. In other places, it was wide enough she could have walked together with somebody. She was sure that the variations in the width of the tunnel had to do with the rooms it was going past. She had gotten so turned around, she had absolutely no idea what direction she was going, but the direction no longer mattered. She would come to a door eventually, back out into the menacing old house where the monster stories were true. At least they had been for a sixteen-year-old kid who saw the Boogieman, who had killed her.

As soon as she found an exit from this spaghetti warren, she would yell at the top of her lungs for Mitch and keep yelling until she found him. Why hadn't she thought to bring a whistle? A loud whistle could come in handy sometimes. Just ask the woman in *Titanic*, floating on a piece of wood after her boyfriend froze to death.

When she came to a particularly narrow place in the tunnel, she felt a wave of fear and nausea slide through her belly and had to talk herself off her own ledge. Every now and then the claustrophobia that she had developed after a serial killer tried to bury her alive reared its ugly head. Sometimes just getting in a car would cause a flashback and a knee-jerk fear, and certainly these narrow passageways were enough to send anybody into a claustrophobic meltdown. They weren't nearly as tight and constricting as the little-kid gerbil tunnels on the Smoky Mountain Queen. She had totally lost it there, had screamed and kicked and cried, batshit hysterical, until the voice of the essential Rileigh calmed her, pointing out that she was throwing a temper tantrum and there was no real danger. The clawing sense of claustrophobia that was itching in her belly now wasn't quite the same circumstance, because there'd been no real danger in the plastic little-kid tunnels she had been sealed in. This was a secret passageway where she had discovered the decomposing body of a murder victim. Whoever killed that person frequented these tunnels.

The wave of fear that washed over her almost prompted her to draw her gun, a Glock G43X. It was loaded ten plus one, which meant that she'd loaded the single stack magazine and chambered the first round, then removed the magazine and replaced the round she'd chambered.

She discarded that notion because she already had one hand occupied holding the flashlight and she didn't want to fill both her hands so that she had no use of either one. There was danger here, yes, but not imminent danger. Not yet anyway.

Around the next bend, the light in her flashlight began to flicker, and that sent a jolt of fear through her as well.

The only thing worse than being trapped in here with a decomposing body worse would be being stuck in here in the dark. She shook the flashlight and the beam that had been growing pale grew bright again, and she breathed a sigh of relief. Inching her way down the tunnel carefully, she examined all the walls with the flashlight. She didn't want to pass by some opening panel and not notice it. She tried to gauge how far she had come, but it was impossible and would serve no purpose. The tunnel wound around and around in circles, and she might not have covered more than thirty-five or forty yards in forward progress.

It seemed incongruent to her that she could hear the sound of the storm outside through the walls on the outside of the house and through the thick interior walls, but she suspected the sound was being piped in through the multitude of chimneys that fed the array of fireplaces. Seemed like every single room had a fireplace.

When she heard a sound behind her, she ignored it, telling herself it was just her imagination. But the second time she heard it, there was no ignoring it. It was a sound that didn't belong here — not the sound of footsteps, but something else. She heard it again, then turned and shone her light down the passageway that she had just traveled. Nothing. How could somebody be coming up behind her unless they had come in through an opening she missed? Or had they come in the same one she had and then had to step over the dead body on the floor behind her? Neither of those were particularly comforting scenarios.

The sound was an odd sound and she couldn't place it, but it was getting closer. She stopped all movement, held her breath, and listened. And when she heard the sound again, she knew what it was. It was the sound of a giggle, a little girl's giggle. It sounded like Mayella might have been in the passageway behind her, and that somebody had given the little girl a banana.

She heard it again, but this time it didn't seem to be behind her anymore. It seemed to be in front. How could that be? How could the giggle have changed positions? Or was it an echo? This place was sealed up. Was it some kind of sound chamber?

The giggle was much closer now, but it was ahead of her in the passageway, not behind. The twisting and turning of the passageway made it impossible to see more than a few yards in front before the passageway turned again. She stopped again, stayed silent, and held her breath. No giggle. She could feel the sweat forming on her forehead, heard her heart hammering in her chest. She grabbed hold of her emotions and pulled her sidearm, holding it out in front of her with the flashlight shining along the barrel. She continued down the tunnel, feeling the reassurance that having a gun in her hand always gave her. She went around another bend, and the giggle was much closer. In fact, she thought she could see a dim light shining in the tunnel around the next bend. Whoever or whoever was giggling had obviously brought light with them.

She reached the bend and spun into it, gun ready, flashlight shining on the tunnel beyond. What she saw made no sense. Her mind rebelled. That couldn't be. What she saw was obviously Carly Farrington, except her hair lay in big fat braids on her shoulders, tied with blue satin ribbons, and what was she was wearing? It was hard to tell. It appeared to be an old-fashioned nightgown, high neck and long sleeves, with something embroidered on the front. It was ridiculously too small for her, but she had stretched it around her on top of her clothes.

The look on her face was the placid, innocent look of a little girl.

"Carly, is that you? Can you show me the way out of here?"

Little-girl Carly didn't answer, just moved so she could pull out what she had been holding behind her.

It was an axe — the axe that hung on a hook over the mantel, the murder axe. Rileigh could see the brown of dried blood on the handle and on the blade.

"Carly, drop the axe!" Rileigh commanded in a stern voice.

Carly giggled and took a step toward Rileigh, lifting the axe as she did.

"Don't make me shoot you, Carly. I will. Drop that axe."

Rileigh backed up a step, hoping the apparition would do as she had ordered. She flat out did not want to have to shoot Carly Farrington, but she absolutely would.

Little-girl Carly took a half step toward her, almost like a basketball player faking right when he meant to go left.

In response, Rileigh took another step back, and when she did, the little-girl Carly's face burst into a beatific smile, and the giggle escaped her lips.

"You fall down," she said. It wasn't Carly's voice at all. It was the voice of a small child. "Fall down and go boom."

Suddenly, the floor beneath Rileigh collapsed out from under her. Frantically twisting herself sideways, she tried to grab hold of something, but merely banged into the side of the opening before she found herself falling through darkness into more darkness.

Chapter Thirty-Seven

GASPING, STRUGGLING TO GET HER WIND BACK, RILEIGH felt something crawling on her arm and she swatted at it. The movement shot a bolt of shattering pain down her right side, from her shoulder to her hip.

The world was spinning.

She didn't know if there were bugs, big crawling ones, in Mammoth Cave. Blind cave crickets, maybe, but crawly bugs? Her head swam, made her feel like she was on a ship in a rolling sea, rather than lying flat on... on what... where?

The tour guide had just seated everyone comfortably on the floor to show them what the cave looked like in its natural state — totally inside-a-lump-of-coal dark! No light. Black.

Mammoth Cave.

No, she wasn't in Mammoth Cave. She was somewhere else, somewhere as dark as that.

She moved her body again and was rewarded by a pain in her left side that almost made her cry out. She knew that pain. Rileigh had broken ribs before, and there was no other agony quite like it, nothing quite as staggering and immobilizing. Even breathing hurt. She'd hit her side on something when she'd fallen, had at the very least cracked a rib, though it felt a lot more like it was broken.

She was lying on something solid but not hard. She'd fallen there and it had knocked the breath out of her. Carefully sucking in a breath, then another, her head cleared.

No, not Mammoth Cave — she was in the basement of Shagbark Manor. Understanding welled up with fear in her chest, making it even harder to breathe. Something else crawled across her face and she swatted it away in disgust, pain stabbing in her side. She lay still, panting, trying to think how she could sit up. She had hit feet first and collapsed, but it wasn't a clean collapse like in parachute training. She had landed sideways, with her legs stuck under her,

She tried to get her bearings, but it was hard to do in a place that was absolutely pitch dark, as profoundly dark as Mammoth Cave had been that day years ago.

Something else crawled up her blouse, and she resisted the urge to swat it, grabbing it instead. Though she couldn't look at it, she felt it. Nothing exotic, a simple cockroach... with lots of friends.

She slowly moved herself up into a sitting position, felt around on the surface where she had landed. It was firm but not hard. She pushed at it with her fingers, and there was some give. It felt almost like a bag of sand, and maybe it was. She figured out in her mind's eye that she was lying on a stack of bags of some kind filled with some soft substance, sand, or maybe flour, sugar, or cornmeal. That would make sense here in the basement of the bed and breakfast where Carly had to prepare meals for dozens and dozens of people. She probably bought supplies in bulk and stored them here in the basement, in a part of the basement Carly had *not* revealed the night they'd searched in vain for Hillary Schofield, whose body now lay wrapped in plastic in the tunnel behind where Rileigh had fallen though the floor. She had wondered that night why the basement had been so small, taking up so little space in the footprint of the big house. She was now in the rest of the basement, and that space could be enormous.

Finally sitting upright, Rileigh tried to straighten her legs out, and that's when she discovered that she'd screwed up that ankle again, the one she'd hurt when she dumped a dirt bike coming down the mountainside. Dammit! That sprain had just healed enough for her to wear the beautiful green spike heeled shoes that went with the dress Mitch said made her eyes look like emeralds.

Mitch!

The thought of him hurt in her chest almost as much as the rib hurt in her side. Where was he, and how was she going to get out of this basement and find him?

Her thoughts were ping-ponging, going from one thing to another. She needed to concentrate. Focus. First things first — she needed to find her flashlight first and then her gun. Preferably in that order. The sack she had landed on was stacked beside other stacks of sacks, so the flashlight and gun could have fallen down into the cracks between them and be very difficult to find. She rolled carefully and painfully over onto her hands and knees and began running her hand around the edges of the sack she had landed on searching for anything hard.

She felt around all the edges, jammed her hand down as far as she could go on first one side and then another. Then she moved to the sack beside the one she'd landed on and began digging around on the edges of it, then her fingers touched something metal. She scrabbled to dig it out from where it had lodged between the sacks. It was her flashlight! Now she could find her gun.

She pushed the switch on the top of the flashlight.

Nothing!

No, no, no.

She hit the switch again. Still nothing. She banged the flashlight into the palm of her hand trying to make it work again, as she had done before. She flipped the on-off switch back and forth. Nothing. Then a beam of light flashed from the bulb and went instantly out. Rileigh began to turn on the flashlight carefully, inching the switch carefully from off to on. A dim light flashed out again and went out. Eventually, she was able to find the sweet spot on the switch that turned on a pale, dim light and she settled for that, using it to examine her surroundings. The light was so dim it didn't illuminate anything farther than a couple of feet around her, but at least she could use it to find her gun. She spent an indeterminate amount of time trying to do just that and found nothing. The gun had either fallen into a crack between the sacks so deep she couldn't feel it, or it had hit the sack and bounced somewhere out there into the darkness.

The beam on the flashlight appeared to be getting dimmer. She could use up all the juice looking for her gun, but a better use of what little light was left was to find a way out of this place. She had to find an outside wall in the basement, feel her way along it until she found a door. In other words, she needed to climb down off the sack of flour to the floor and get moving, then point herself in one direction and keep going that way until she hit a wall.

The agony that any movement provoked was something she'd just have to grit her teeth and bear.

She slid down off the sack to the floor, landed on her right ankle, and grunted in pain, only remaining upright by grabbing hold of the sacks. She shifted her weight to her other foot and surveyed her surroundings. There were stacks of cans in front of her. In the dim light, she could read kidney beans on one can, but there was no telling what other cans were stored there. She made her way along beside the bags, bent over with her arm against her injured side, limping on her bad ankle, until she came out at the end of the row and pointed her flashlight out into absolute blackness.

She couldn't see far, but there appeared to be garbage scattered everywhere. Junk of every kind and size, all of it swarming with cockroaches that were attracted to warm places with water and something to eat. She heard a faint sound then, a whump, and suddenly she could feel air moving around her. The fan had turned on.

It didn't remain on for long, and as soon as it clicked off, she became aware of a smell, and realized she'd been smelling it all along but had just dismissed it because it was the same lingering aroma that had been in the tunnel she had fallen down out of and she'd already identified the source of that — a moldering corpse. Why would the whole basement smell like that?

Rileigh was moving slowly forward and began to make out something. Her light was reflecting off shimmering, shiny things, but she couldn't tell what they were. Something that reflected light. She moved toward the nearest one on the floor but couldn't figure out what it was. It was slightly bigger than a bread box and black — something wrapped in the thick, opaque plastic used for drop cloths. That's all she could see through the plastic wrapped around and around it. She knelt carefully down, holding onto a post and shooing a cockroach off the plastic.

Sucking in a gasp, she leapt up, stumbled on her bum ankle, and almost dropped the flashlight.

The thing wrapped in plastic was a dog. Its skull was pressed up against the side of the plastic. Then she allowed her eye to travel from the body of the dog... to the corpse of its owner.

Only a few feet away lay a shiny object the size of the one she'd found upstairs in the passageway. Rileigh touched the plastic wrapped around the corpse and it squished under her hand, and she could see the horror of a decaying human face through the opaque plastic.

Beside the dead body was a dust-covered suitcase propped against a pile of indeterminate garbage, one of those overnight bags that had a special compartment where you could put your passport so it was easy for you to grab when you needed it. Rileigh reached out trembling hands and unzipped the passport compartment, then slid her fingers inside and withdrew a blue plastic folder with the seal of the United States government on the outside. Opening it, she shone the light on the picture of a pleasant looking, round-faced old woman with white hair and no smile, because they wouldn't let you smile in a passport picture, and beneath it was the name Harriet Risma. She flipped through the passport briefly and found that Harriet had visited England, Ireland, Scotland, Norway, Germany, and there was a combination stamp for Tanzania and Zanzibar. This was a well-traveled old lady who had gone on a trip to the Smoky Mountains and never returned home.

Rileigh slid the passport back into the zipper pocket of the piece of luggage and stood up, shining her light in a circle, searching desperately for a wall. Her view was mostly blocked by a concrete pillar, one of the pillars that held up the ceiling of the basement, and when she stepped out around it, she could see the glimmer of shiny objects as far as the light of her feeble flashlight would shine. She didn't have to wonder what they were. In stunned horror, Rileigh limped to the nearest plastic wrapped corpse that had been here long enough that the decay had left nothing behind but a skeleton. She could see the eye socket holes and the holes of the nose.

Rileigh staggered on — what else could she do? — in fascinated horror looking at the shiny objects that appeared all around her. There was luggage all around and personal items, purses and wallets she was sure had belonged to the dead bodies, people someone had murdered and then wrapped up in plastic and placed here.

That was it. That was the hold the handyman had over Carly. Their cars! He ran a chop shop and helped her get rid of the murder victims' cars so they were as untraceable as their owners.

On the floor in front of her was a set of golf clubs that she had to maneuver around, careful not to trip over the bag.

Her light found a hat box beside a shiny cylinder of plastic. The hat box lid was ajar, and she shoved it aside, revealing an ordinary woman's wide-brimmed hat with a red feather in it... but something was sitting on the top a hat. It looked like... a building. She looked closer, saw the twin spires and recognized the building — Churchill Downs. This was a derby hat. Over the years, the tradition of fancier and fancier hats had morphed into a tradition of joke hats, each unique and strange. Rileigh let out a shaky sigh. This poor old lady was someone on her way to or from the Kentucky Derby, and she had never made it home.

Rileigh realized her light was still growing dimmer. She couldn't use what was left of the battery to examine the bodies that had been stored in this house of horrors under

Shagbark Manor. She had to use it to guide her to a wall so she could travel along the wall and find a door.

Hunched over, every movement causing agony in her side and ankle, she moved forward as fast as she could go. Ignoring the shiny objects she could see sparkling in the darkness around her, she watched the dim light fade. Dimmer and dimmer. Any second now, it would go out and leave her in absolute darkness. She couldn't think of anything worse than being locked in a basement with moldering corpses in the dark... until she heard the sound. The *giggle*.

Then she knew there was something worse. It was being locked in a basement with dead bodies... and the crazy axe murderer who had killed them.

Chapter Thirty-Eight

RILEIGH HELD HER BREATH AND HEARD THE SOUND AGAIN: the little girl's giggle. She stood frozen, not knowing what to do.

She could see no light around her anywhere, but Carly probably knew this basement well enough to find her way around in it without any light, and Rileigh's light did not illuminate enough area around her for her to see Carly and her axe coming.

But... as long as she held the flashlight, she was directing Carly to her own position. She heard the giggle again; it was closer. Carly and her axe were coming, and Rileigh was lit up like an Olympic torch.

Though she didn't want to, it was the smart thing to do — Rileigh put her flashlight down on top of a nearby box and then she moved away into the darkness. With the little bit of ambient light she had, she looked around frantically for a weapon of some kind, anything. Her eyes fell on the golf bag, and she grabbed a club out of it. A putter was the best weapon she could find.

Easing farther away into the shadows, Rileigh backed

up until she found a stack of cardboard boxes filled with canned goods, and she moved around behind it, held the putter in her hand, and waited for Carly.

She heard a giggle nearby now, very nearby.

The silence spread out around her as thick and intimidating as the darkness, broken only by the scuttering sounds of cockroaches scrambling all over everything. She could feel one climbing up her leg inside her jeans, but she didn't dare move. She listened for the sound of breathing in the darkness beyond her, the putter raised high. As soon as Carly stepped from the darkness into the pale glow of the flashlight beam Rileigh had left on the box, Rileigh would slam the putter down on her head.

The giggling now was very close by, but she couldn't get a direction on it. Behind her? In front of her? She thought she saw a shape approaching to her left, just a darker blotch in the blackness. Maybe she was imagining it, but she watched that blotch, waited for a giggle to come from it, grinding her teeth, her heart hammering so hard she was sure that Carly could hear it.

The blotch began to form itself out of the black. Rileigh thought she saw the light reflect off something shiny within the blotch. She heard a giggle then and knew she was right; it came from that spot of darkness. She lifted her putter up higher, biting her lip to keep from groaning at the stab of pain the movement caused. She'd let Carly take two more steps and then slam it down on the top of her head. Now she was sure she could see the light reflecting off the shiny blade of the axe as the blob in the darkness resolved itself into the shape of a person.

One more step. Rileigh steeled herself for the agony that would slice through her side when she leapt forward — onto her sprained ankle.

Suddenly there was brightness all around her, like a

flashbulb in her face. Everything was illuminated, not just like a light turned on in a room, but like the headlights of an approaching 18-wheeler shining right in her eyes. She squinted, tried to get her bearings, and heard the giggle.

"You didn't say you wanted to play hide and seek," came a voice from the direction of the giggle. "I like hide and seek. It's my favorite game."

Squinting into the blazing light of an electric lantern, Rileigh could see the form behind it: the woman with her hair in braids. But she wasn't holding an axe. The light had been reflecting off the barrel of Rileigh's Glock.

Well, that answered the question of what happened to her gun. She'd dropped it on the floor of the passageway as she'd fallen. Now Carly had it, and Rileigh was unarmed.

Carly set the lantern down on a box and stepped up beside it, an odd smile on her face. In the glow of the lantern, Rileigh got a good look at her. Her hair was indeed hanging down in twin braids on her shoulders, tied with blue ribbons in big bows. She was dressed in a t-shirt and jeans, but on top of her clothing, she had stretched that little girl's lacy pink nightgown with the letter J embroidered on the front. It was filthy and worn, had spots all over it, and Rileigh didn't like to think what those spots might be.

"Do *you* like hide and seek?" Carly asked in the little girl voice.

"Well… uh… sure I do," Rileigh replied, trying to lower the putter casually.

"If you want to play hide and seek, what are you doing with that stick? You were going to hit me with that stick, weren't you?"

"No, why would I do a thing like that?" Rileigh was

fumbling and scrambling, trying to figure out what Carly was going to do next.

Replaying in her head were the words of her firearms instructor: "It is almost impossible to deliver a fatal wound to a moving target." She could jump Carly, but she wouldn't be able to do much zigging and zagging in her current condition. If she didn't get shot, she'd still have to fight Carly for the gun — and she feared the crazy person in front of her would be granted the strength genuine madness sometimes imparted.

"This isn't just a stick. It's a golf club." Rileigh held up the putter. "Do you like to play golf?"

Carly cocked her head to the side. "I don't think I ever played golf."

"Oh it's easy, I can show you."

"No, I don't want to play golf with you. You're a bad person."

"What makes you say that?"

"You're just like the others."

"What others, Carly?"

"Stop calling me Carly. She's that whiny idiot who doesn't know anything about anything. I'm the only reason Carly's still alive. I've protected her, kept them from coming for her, and kept all the Mama people from hurting her, too."

"Mama people?"

"The people with Mama's ghost inside them, the ones who want to kill us."

"If you don't want me to call you Carly, what should I call you?"

The little girl snuffed, "I got away that day. I *survived.*"

Not *she* survived — *I* survived. First person.

"So, why do you have to protect Carly from… the spirits and the Mama people?"

"They want to kill her."

"Kill Carly?"

"They're really after *me*," she said and rolled her eyes with the disdain of a little girl for a person too stupid to understand. "They want to kill *me*, but I'm hiding inside Carly, and they know that, so they try to kill her. The moment Grandma Josie saw Carly, she knew it was *me* — JoJo — that I had come back."

Carly Farrington believed the whole house was full of ghosts, and that the ghost of her dead great-grandmother lived inside her.

"Grandma Josie didn't really forget what happened that day, and she made sure I wouldn't, either. So she'd put me in a pink nightgown at night like little JoJo wore, and she'd tell me the story, walk me around the house, show me where it happened and describe every detail."

No wonder Carly was crazy!

"So all the other ghosts are after *you*, they want to kill you… JoJo. Is that right?"

Carly nodded.

"Why?"

"Because they know it was *me*. That *I* did it."

"It was you who did what?"

"It was me. I killed Mama and Papa."

If ever there was a conversation stopper, that was it.

Chapter Thirty-Nine

JoJo Farrington is hiding in the window seat in her pink nightgown. She hears her older sisters screaming, running from Mama, who's slashing at them with an axe.

JoJo doesn't know what it was that finally broke. But when Mama said she was going to put them in the dark, buggy place again, Victoria pleaded with her not to do it. Elizabeth just stood there, though, her jaw clinched tight shut. She hadn't meant to knock over the glass of milk. It was an accident, but that didn't matter. JoJo looked at her mother with begging eyes, knowing that no matter what she said, Mama would still lock the three of them in the dark place where the bugs would crawl all over them.

"No," Elizabeth says. She's the oldest, ten.

Mama turns around slowly to look at her.

"What did you say?"

"No. I won't. I won't go down there again!"

JoJo is so stunned, she gawks in amazement.

Mama's eyes blaze with a fury JoJo has never seen in them before.

Then Victoria speaks. Just eight, she's not as bold as Elizabeth, but trying to be strong, too.

"Me neither, Mama. I won't go down there." Then suddenly she adds a desperate, "You can't make me!"

She turns and bolts from the room, with Elizabeth on her heels.

JoJo stands frozen. She watches her mother's face darken and distort with a hideous rage. Her mother suddenly turns and slaps JoJo out of her way, knocks her to the floor as she marches down the hall and down the stairs.

JoJo runs to find her older sisters. They're in the playroom, with Elizabeth pacing back and forth. Elizabeth looks up when she runs into the room.

"You two don't have to do this. It's on me. I spilled the milk and I disobeyed. You don't have to go along."

Victoria throws her arms around her older sister.

"I'll stick," she chokes out.

Elizabeth turns to JoJo.

"JoJo, honey, you need to run. Run fast and hide."

"Maybe Papa will come home and make her stop," JoJo says.

Victoria sneers. "If Papa was gonna make her stop, he would have made her stop a long time ago."

All of the girls turn to the door when they hear it open behind them, and standing in the doorway is Mama. Only maybe it's not Mama. It's Mama with a look on her face unlike any they've never seen. They've seen her angry. It's a daily, sometimes hourly occurrence. It takes nothing to make Mama mad. If you accidentally track mud into the house, she flies into a raging fit. But this look is different somehow.

JoJo is suddenly more terrified than she's ever been when her eyes slide from her mother's face to what her mother is holding. It's the axe. Mama went out into the backyard where the handyman had been chopping wood, then had put on his gloves and got the axe.

"You don't tell me no," Mama roars in a voice that doesn't even sound human. "You will never tell me no again."

Mama lifts the axe into the air and slams it down toward Elizabeth. Elizabeth leaps out of the way, but not before the axe tears a giant cut into her back. She screams and runs for the door. Mama is lifting the axe again, looking at Victoria. Victoria stands frozen, holding onto the handle of the big wooden rocking horse. The axe comes down hard. JoJo's eyes can't be telling the truth, because this is too awful to be true. The axe slams down on Victoria's arm— and cuts off her hand. Blood squirts everywhere, and suddenly JoJo is moving as fast as a baby rabbit. She dodges around Mama and runs out the door. She can hear Victoria screaming, and Elizabeth is some-where else in the house, wailing. She dashes down the steps three and four at a time and dives into the window seat beside the front door and listens, terrified, as her sisters scream and her mother chases them around upstairs, trying to kill them with an axe. It can't be real. It can't.

"It's bleeding, it's bleeding!" Victoria cries, but her voice is weak and wobbly.

"Mama, stop!" Elizabeth screams.

Right in the middle of it all, the front door opens and in strides Papa. Papa is supposed to be gone. He's on a business trip. He's not supposed to be home for three days. What is he doing here? He sets his suitcase down and JoJo starts to rise up out of the window seat to run to him, screaming that Mama is trying to kill her sisters. But before she has a chance, she hears Mama yelling upstairs. "I'll teach you to say no to me!" There's a loud thump, and then she hears silence.

Papa calls from the bottom of the stairs. "Lenora? Lenora, are you up there? What's wrong? What's going on?" JoJo hears his steps going toward the stairs and she opens the window seat just a crack, just enough so she can turn her head sideways and look out with one eye.

Mama is standing at the top of the stairs, panting. She's wearing a white dress splattered with big splotches of blood. And there's a bloody axe in her hand.

Papa staggers back a step at the sight. "Lenora, what in the world... Lenora?"

Mama lifts her chin and cries out in a loud voice, "Jo-ce-lyn, where aaaare you?"

She starts down the stairs. Mama is looking for JoJo to chop her up with the axe, just like she did Elizabeth and Victoria. She'll find her, too, because JoJo always hides in the window seat by the front door.

Mama is coming to kill her. She whimpers, makes some kind of little animal sound.

"Lenora, what in the name of God is going on?"

"They'll never defy me again."

"What are you doing with that axe?"

"I killed them!" There is such horrible triumph in her voice. "Elizabeth and Victoria. I'm going to kill JoJo, too."

Mama gets to the bottom of the stairs, intent on dragging JoJo out of the window seat and killing her, but Papa is in her way. She tries to push him aside and he grabs the axe. Then JoJo's parents begin to scuffle. Mama tries to pull away, but for a moment he holds onto the axe. Then he lets go, throwing Mama off balance. The axe turns sideways in her hand and swings downward, hitting her in the front, high up on her leg. She looks down in surprise and her white skirt is suddenly soaked with blood, a horrible gush of red that spews everywhere, and she drops the axe.

JoJo looks at Papa now, sees why he let go of the axe.

He's clutching his chest, staggering backwards. Mama drops the axe, reaches down and lifts up her skirt slowly with both hands to see the wound. JoJo gets a glimpse of her leg, her upper thigh, where a gash from the axe had laid it open to the bone, and blood is squirting out in heartbeat bursts.

Papa has a strange, panicked look on his face and starts ripping at his tie, trying to take it off. He's gasping for breath. JoJo knows what that means. For her whole life, everyone has told her that Papa has a heart condition. Papa can't get upset. Papa can't be too happy or too mad or too anything because his heart could stop, and now it's happening. She watches all the color drain out of her father's face as he collapses to the floor.

Mama doesn't collapse, she just sinks to her knees. JoJo hears the clunk when they hit the hardwood floor, still holding up her skirt, watching the blood gush out, the pool of it oozing across the floor to where Papa lies. But the stream is not as strong as it was before. It doesn't squirt as far.

And then Mama slowly turns her head toward the window seat where JoJo is hiding. Maybe she even sees JoJo peeking out through the crack. She drops from her knees to all-fours and begins to crawl toward the axe, her bloody fingers outstretched for the handle.

She intends to kill JoJo just like she did JoJo's sisters, and there's nowhere to run. JoJo sinks back into the window seat in terror as she sees Mama's fingers close around the axe handle. She grasps it and drags it with her as she crawls slowly toward the window seat.

JoJo suddenly understands what she has to do. She has to be as brave as Elizabeth was today. JoJo has to say no.

She rises up in the window seat and looks at her mother crawling slowly toward her, hauling the bloody axe with her. Like in a dream, JoJo climbs out of the window seat, lifting one leg over the side and then the other. She walks to her mother, then uses her foot to shove her mother sideways. Mama topples her onto her side and lies there panting, looking with hatred at her youngest daughter.

Then JoJo leans over and tries to take the axe out of her mother's hand. Mama won't let go. JoJo has to peel her mother's fingers off the axe handle, one at a time, never unlocking her eyes from her mother's, whose lips curl in a snarl when JoJo pulls the axe free.

Her mother says nothing, glaring defiance and hatred. JoJo raises the axe above her head. Then she smiles brightly as she slams it down into the middle of her mother's face, splits her skull open like a melon. She slams it down again. And again and again, cutting her mother's body into pieces.

And then she steps back holding the axe, her face splattered with blood, panting. She looks at Papa, lying on the floor a few feet away in a pool of her mother's blood, splattered with it. He's gasping like a fish on a dock and his eyes are closed.

Yes, his eyes are closed. His eyes are always closed.

When the girls go to him and beg him to make their mother stop forcing them into the basement with the bugs, Papa closes his eyes to their pleas and does nothing. When Elizabeth told Papa that Mama had poured scalding water on her hand, when Victoria told Papa that Mama beat her with a flyswatter — the end came off, and Mama kept hitting her with the handle — Papa did nothing.

Suddenly, his eyes pop open and he looks at JoJo in desperation. His hand paws at his pocket. He has pills made from foxglove some snake oil salesman sold him. He always carries them. They fix it when this happens. He has no air to speak, but his blue lips form a word—"Help."

Rage wells up in JoJo's chest and she lifts the axe... then lowers it. If not for Papa, JoJo would be as dead as her sisters. She stands looking down at him, drops of her mother's blood sliding down her face. He gets his hand into his pocket and pulls out the bottle of pills but is so weak now that it tumbles out of his fingers to the floor. The pills spill out into the puddle of her mother's blood around him, turning red and starting to dissolve.

"Please," his lips beg silently.

Then JoJo decides to do the same thing Papa always does. She closes her eyes.

She stands quietly as his breathing slows, listening to him struggle for air. She waits. It doesn't take long before he stops struggling and lies still.

JoJo drops the axe because it is suddenly too heavy to hold onto and walks slowly up the stairs, finds her sisters huddled together in a corner in the hallway. She kneels down onto the floor and wiggles her way in between the bodies of her two dead sisters, their pink nightgowns as drenched with blood as hers is. Then she closes her eyes again, and this time she leaves them closed.

Chapter Forty

Rileigh was stunned. "*JoJo* killed her parents?"

The woman standing beside the bright lantern in front of Rileigh had seemed not to hear the question, lost in thought. Rileigh cursed her injuries. If she had been operating on all cylinders, this was her opportunity. She could have swung her putter in a wide arc and clocked the woman in the head, but she couldn't move that fast.

The woman came back to herself then, looked around at her environment in much the same way that Jillian did after she'd had a flashback, in that quizzical "where am I? what's going on here?" way indicating that for a time, Jillian had left the building, but now she was back.

In an almost dreamy voice, Carly said, "Mama dropped the axe. I picked it up. I didn't chop up Papa, though. He saved me. I just let him die." The dreamy quality left the voice. "I survived. But they're still here, all of them. Their ghosts will never leave. So I keep Carly alive by keeping Mama and the others away."

Rileigh was reeling, trying to make sense of the words of this shattered person who believed that a ghost lived inside her — the ghost of JoJo Farrington, a little girl who'd killed her parents and then spent all night huddled in the dark between the bodies of her cold, dead sisters.

"I helped the old lady get rid of the Mama people, too," she said with pride. "When they came here with hair like Mama's, looking just like Mama, Mama's ghost climbed down inside of them, controlled them, used them to try to kill Carly." She looked out into the darkness. "Now, they're here. Where they can't hurt anybody. I helped Grandma Josie make the Goin' Home chocolates so their families would think they left."

Rileigh's face must have revealed her confusion, because Carly sighed and explained, like she was talking to a three-year-old.

"Grandma Josie got the Mama people to call home and say they were bringing a surprise. Then Grandma Josie got the mask and axe... the old lady stood *still* in front of the tripod for the picture, and... after, Grandma Josie'd call that number back, put wax paper over the mouth piece and say 'Just drove away' or something short like that, then make it sound like a disconnect. It's easy peasy now with texts."

Apparently, the ghost of JoJo was tired of bragging. When Carly looked at Rileigh, her eyes turned hard, as cold as the dead eyes of a shark cruising the sea.

"I want to play a game — candle hide and seek. Will you play with me?"

"Sure, how do you play?"

"I'll be It," said the little girl, "and you go hide." She giggled again. That sinister, awful, unnatural, giggle. *"I'll come find you."*

Carly suddenly threw the gun out into the darkness, and before Rileigh could react, Carly was holding the axe again and smiling a predatory smile. No, not Carly — JoJo's ghost.

"And I *will* find you."

Rileigh took a look around, trying to remember if she had passed anything that would have made a good hiding place, but she hadn't gotten a good look at anything she passed in the dim light of that flashlight. Surely she could find something in the bright glow of the lantern, somewhere in all the piles of junk lying around.

Click.

The room returned to utter darkness. Carly had turned off the lantern.

"Hey! Why'd you turn the light off? I have to go find a place to hide."

"I've been playing hide and seek in this basement my whole life," the little girl's voice said. "I can do it in the dark. You can, too."

Then she began to count.

"One ... Two ... Three..."

Rileigh didn't know how high she planned to count. Rileigh and Georgia had always gone to one hundred. But Carly might just go to fifty.

Or twenty-five.

Or ten. She was making the rules for this game.

Rileigh turned around, holding on to the box next to her with one hand and the putter in the other, and began to hop away as fast as she could into the darkness. The jolt at the end of every step was agonizing on her broken rib. Every time she put weight on the ankle, agony shot up her calf and into her thigh.

"1Ten." Carly paused with Rileigh only a few feet away. Rileigh wondered if it was possible to block an axe blow with a putter.

"Eleven... Twelve... Thirteen..."

Rileigh kept hopping until she heard.

"Twenty-four... Twenty-five... Twenty-six..."

She figured then that best-case scenario was at least fifty. Rileigh could get nowhere hopping. She was in constant danger of losing her balance and either injuring her sprained ankle worse or falling on her cracked rib. Sinking down to her hands and knees, she began to crawl, and only then realized that the motion made the pain in her side worse.

When Carly started the game, Rileigh had turned to go back in the direction she had come. As she scuttled away now, feeling her way along, she built a mental picture in her head of what she had seen — boxes and crates, piles of junk, moldy piles of clothes. None of them offered any great place to hide.

"Thirty-three... Thirty-four... Thirty-five..."

She had seen spaces between the stacks of boxes that appeared to be an aisle. If there was an aisle, maybe she could crawl down it and find somewhere back in there to hunker down. She scrabbled along on her hands and knees, bruising her knees on the concrete floor, her injured ankle and rib screaming, feeling around in front of her for any opening. She was simply crawling along in the dark, didn't know where she was.

Her hand felt open air off to her left, so she plunged that direction. It was a small space between cartons or boxes or something, and she pulled up into it, panting.

"Forty-eight... Forty-nine... Fifty. Ready or not, here I come!" cried the voice from not far away at all. cried the voice from not far away at all. So much for Georgia counting to a hundred.

Then to her horror, Rileigh saw a light, a glow. Not the big lantern. What was the light? It flickered, made dancing shadows on the floor. It was a candle. Now, Rileigh knew what Carly meant by candle hide and seek. The person who was It had a candle. The person who was hiding did not.

The flickering light did nothing to illuminate where Rileigh had shoved herself into a crack as the flickering light grew brighter. The light wasn't bright enough to reach down to the floor.

"Where are you?" said the little girl's voice. "I'll find you. I always win this game."

The flickering light grew brighter, reflecting now off the tops of the boxes above Rileigh's head. How far did the light extend down into the crevices and cracks between the stacks?

"I'll find you, Lizzie!" Carly cried. "I will!" Then the giggle. "But you won't get me. I know your tricks."

Who was Lizzie? JoJo's sister Elizabeth? Surely, she and her sisters didn't play hide and seek down here.

"I know you're in here!" she cried out at the ghosts. "You're all here now, aren't you? I can tell when you're around. I can *smell* you."

The light now shown in a flickering pattern on the floor beside the boxes only a few feet from where Rileigh was cowering.

"Mama!" the little kid voice cried out. "I see you. You won't get Carly. I won't let you."

Suddenly, Rileigh heard the sound of a crunch and then a crash and realized that Carly had brought the axe down on something. Something she must have believed was one of the ghosts that haunted the house... and haunted her soul. The ghost of her father or one of her sisters, or her mother. That's why everything down here was cut up and broken. How many times had Carly played hide and seek in this basement, hauling her axe around to kill the ghosts who were after JoJo?

"Missed, but I'll get you. I'll find you." Carly brought the axe down again. It wasn't three feet from the box Rileigh was hiding behind, and it ripped into the box, and the contents poured out of it. Cereal. Store brand Cheerios poured out onto the floor beside Rileigh. She squeezed back further into her corner, but she was, indeed, painted into a corner now. If Carly took two more steps, she would see her. Rileigh managed to roll over onto her side and lift the putter. It was all she had to protect herself from an axe stroke.

The axe fell again.

The flickering light got no closer. In fact, it began to dim.

"I'll find you all. I always do!" cried the little kid's voice. Then Rileigh heard the sound of the axe slamming down into some other surface.

Rileigh scooted out of her hiding place, trying to find somewhere better, something she could crawl into. It would be harder to find a moving target, she assumed, and so she moved, she crawled away from the sound of the voice, the giggles, and the crunching sounds.

After a while, her knees were bruised, the palm of her left hand was raw, the knuckles on her right hand where she clutched the putter were bleeding, but she kept crawling, watching for the light, listening for the sounds. Sometimes, she could see almost no light at all anywhere, while other times it seemed to be only a few feet away.

She crawled and crawled. Time didn't count here in this dark basement that smelled like dead bodies and was so full of bugs that her hands and knees were gooey from crushing them. Every moment seemed like the worst moment she'd ever lived, until the next. She could see no light anywhere now, so Carly and the ghost of JoJo were far away.

Or had she blown out the candle? How could she search for Rileigh in the dark?

Suddenly, the axe ripped down into something not three feet to the right of Rileigh and she jumped in surprise, making a sound. She knew Carly had heard her this time, so she leapt to the left into the open air she could feel in that direction and crawled frantically away.

The axe came down again right behind her!

"I'll get you!" The words came from right above her. "I'll *get* you."

Rileigh did the only thing she knew to do. She dropped to her belly and rolled sideways out of the aisle. Rags, old clothes, something cloth — a pile of it. Frantically, she dug her way into it, tried to bury herself, pulling her knees up tight against her body, cringing away from the axe slicing down and almost cutting her leg off.

Her breathing was ragged, terror-filled gasps, but she forced herself to stop, to hold her breath, to listen.

There was a crunching sound nearby — a cockroach crushed under a shoe. Then nothing.

Silence.

"I think I've found you," a little girl's voice purred out of the darkness right in front of her.

There was a scratching sound and then a match flared. And there stood Carly holding the candle. She set the candle down on the top of a box and stood looking down at Rileigh. "I always win. Mama got Elizabeth and Victoria, but she didn't get *me.*"

Mama?

"Are you saying your *mother* killed your sisters?"

Keep her talking, distract her. Rileigh turned over, moved as surreptitiously as she could to get the putter into a position where she could use it.

"Of course it was Mama. Everything was Mama. The bugs in the dark were Mama."

"The roaches?"

"You spilled your milk all over the table and I have to clean up your mess!" The voice wasn't Carly's anymore. It was the voice of a woman, angry and vicious. *"You come with me, young lady. All three of you!"*

"No, Mama, please don't, I'm sorry! I won't do it again." A little girl's voice, now, but not JoJo. Some other little girl.

"Stay down there until you can learn not to be so clumsy," the angry woman snarled.

The look on Carly's face then was terror incarnate, unlike anything Rileigh had ever seen on anybody's face.

"No, noooo!" she screamed. And then she began to swat at her own face and chest with her free hand, knocking away imaginary bugs. She banged her fist on an imaginary door and clawed at it with her fingernails. With a final, agonizing screech —*"Noooo!"* — she suddenly fell silent and her face went blank.

It was now or never. Rileigh ignored the agony in her side and her ankle and jumped up from her knees to a standing position just as Carly's eyes popped back open with awareness in them.

"Private Bishop, what are the two kinds of soldiers?"

"Sir! The quick and the dead, sir!"

"Which are you?"

Carly turned toward Rileigh, was lifting the axe into the air when the club head of the putter connected with her temple. Rileigh swung it like a baseball bat with every speck of strength she possessed. There was a sickening crunch sound and Carly's head snapped sideways.

Off balance, standing on one foot, the momentum of Rileigh's swing carried her forward and she slammed sideways into Carly's collapsing body, careened off it into a pile of boxes before crashing to the floor.

Agony lit up her whole side as what had been a cracked rib gave way. She heard the *snap* sound and shrieked, then lay where she had fallen, pain graying out the rest of the world. The light went out when she fell, but then she saw it flicker again. As she struggled for breath, it grew brighter. What...?

Then she knew. The tumbling bodies had knocked the candle off the box where Carly had set it — into a pile of broken cardboard boxes and paper. Christmas wrapping paper. The pile instantly ignited, sending out a bright flame that caught the box beside it — more wrapping paper — and in seconds there was a crackling fire.

Chapter Forty-One

RILEIGH DRAGGED HERSELF AWAY FROM THE HEAT. THE flames provided light, and that's what she needed.

As she crawled, commando crawling, in pain, the flickering light of the flames grew brighter and brighter behind her. She could smell the smoke, knew that all of the trash and junk that had been stored in that basement was as dry as tinder. She had to get out fast. But which way was out?

The pain in her side was a lightning bolt of agony with every breath, in or out. She stopped crawling, inhaled slowly, let it out slowly. She *had to* do this— she had no choice. She had to get up to her feet so she could see over the junk. With the firelight illuminating the room around her, she could find a pathway out if she could see.

Gritting her teeth against the agony, she slowly made it to her feet, crying now from the pain. The ceiling of the room was beginning to fill with smoke. *Moving* smoke. As she watched, the flickering light of flames produced a thick gray pall that moved rapidly across the ceiling. Rileigh realized the trap door back up into the house that she'd fallen through was serving as a chimney, directing the smoke out of the basement.

A chimney had to have an opening at *both* ends!

She turned in the opposite direction from the movement of the smoke and stared into the gloom. Squinting, she saw what she'd been looking for — a wall. There had to be an opening on that wall somewhere. The fire was sucking air through it and out through the trap door.

Rileigh began to make her way painfully toward the wall, leaning on the boxes and whatever was near, the room getting hotter and hotter, filling with smoke. The ceiling was covered in it now, and it was sinking downward toward the floor. Finally, she saw an opening in the wall. It wasn't a door, though, just an opening, like where a panel had slid away. The air was coming in through that opening, sucked into the room by the growing hunger of the blaze.

She hurried as fast as she could — bent over, with her arms around her body, limping. As she got closer, she could see something beyond the opening that made no sense. It looked like a tree. How could a tree? It was an artificial tree, a big one — a Christmas tree on a stand.

She staggered through the opening past the tree into the small basement they'd seen the night they searched the house looking for Hillary. The Christmas trees that lined the back wall concealed the secret panel that Carly — *JoJo* — had left open when she entered.

The door was on the other side of the room and she staggered to it and turned the knob. The door wouldn't open. It had closed behind Carly. Now it was held shut by a lock on the other side. Only one person knew the combination — Carly.

Rileigh leaned against the locked door and started to cry.

~

MITCH HAD BEEN LOOKING for Rileigh for what seemed like hours, calling out. She had just vanished... almost like. The guy from Ghosts R Us had showed Mitch how he'd vanished out of the dining room, through a panel in the wall. If there was a secret panel, there could be passageways, too. Carly'd lied about the secret doors, so she could be lying about the passageways, too. He would wake her up and find out.

He was able to find his way to the kitchen and the stairs to the third-floor apartment where Carly lived. He stomped up them and banged on the door.

"Carly, open up. It's me, Mitch. I want to talk to you."

Silence.

He banged again. "Open up, dammit!"

He tried the knob. If the door didn't open, he'd kick it in.

It opened and the lights were on.

How could the lights be on in Carly's room, when the electricity was out in the rest of the house... unless the electricity *wasn't* out at all. Unless Carly had killed the power to the other rooms in the house on purpose?

Why would she do a thing like that?

Looking around, his eye was drawn to the huge computer monitor on the desk, the one Carly'd said she used to watch movies. The screen was on — and though it was dark, it was clear it was divided into quadrants, like a monitoring station for a video surveillance system. He fiddled around with the keyboard for a few moments and was able to run the video backwards. Suddenly, the screen lit up with a picture of him and Rileigh at dinner tonight in the dining room. He clicked the unmute button.

There's a sudden clap of thunder.

"Like I said, it was a dark and stormy night."

Mitch stood there, watching the monitor, gobbling up the image of Rileigh smiling, the sound of her laughter.

Where was she?

All those cameras Carly'd said were fake, just to keep her guests honest — they were real. From this monitor, she could see what was going on in every room of the house. Suddenly, he had a thought. He ran the video back further and further, watching images blur on the multitude of screens. He stopped it finally on what he wanted— the date stamp for the night Hillary Schofield disappeared.

He fast-forwarded through images of her drinking, getting drunk, staggering out into hallway.

He stopped the fast-forward then when she staggered into the Persimmon room, the room full of dolls.

"Hey Victoria, E-liz-a-beth, Joc-e-lynn. Yoo hoo. Come watch. I'm going to break your precious dolls and... you... can't... stop... me."

She looked around, crying out at the emptiness, taunting the ghosts. Then she flew into a frenzy, smashing the dolls, tearing them apart, throwing them all over the room and out into the hallway.

He fast forwarded again past images of Hillary staggering around the house, yelling at the ghosts, finally collapsing at the foot of the stairs. He stopped the fast forward when she got up on shaky legs and started across the foyer, then stopped and turned around.

Approaching her was a figure in gauzy white, wearing a horrifying full-head Halloween mask — a doll's face, perfect and serene, missing one eye and its nose, with gore oozing down across it from a split-open skull above. The figure was holding a huge axe with dried brown blood stains on both sides — the axe that had been hanging on the rack above the mantel.

He recognized the figure. It was the one that stood in the background in all the photographs of tourists in the library. He watched in horror as the figure approached, watched Hillary back away.

"Get away from me, I'm gonna throw up!"

The figure raised the axe.

"You broke my dolls," it said, then it chopped down, cutting off Hillary's arm.

Mitch had to look away, couldn't watch the murder, but he did see the figure drag Hillary's body to the wall beneath the stairs, where a panel opened and the figure shoved the body in, then scuffed away the bloody drag marks on the floor.

Was Carly the gauzy figure with the axe? Well, if she wasn't, she damned sure knew who was.

Storming out of Carly's apartment, Mitch ran down the back stairs, the light from her apartment making it easier to see the steps he was taking three at a time. Once in the kitchen, he headed for the dining room. He had to find Rileigh! He ran from there through the other rooms, calling her name.

He'd only been looking for a few minutes when he smelled smoke.

RILEIGH MADE HERSELF STOP CRYING. It did no good, and her diaphragm shaking from her sobs shot agony through her broken rib.

Think!

She watched the fire approach the open panel leading into this part of the basement, fed by the chimney effect of the trapdoor she'd fallen through and — and *what?* The air was coming from here, this room.

Then her brain reconnected to her panicked mind and her eyes snapped to the fan grate beside the door. *Duh!* Carly'd said it was some kind of air return on the HVAC system. Rileigh moved to it, then carefully knelt and examined the grate in front of the fan blades. She pulled on it, moaning in pain, and it didn't give. She pulled on it again. Still it didn't give. Well, it would damned well have to give!

She grabbed it again and with all of her strength, sobbing in pain, she yanked and heard old rusty screws ping off the floor. She pulled again and was able to get the grate free from the wall on one side. That was all she needed, room enough for her to crawl in and wiggle her way through the fan blades to the other side.

The pain in her midsection dwarfed the throbbing in her ankle, but when she accidentally put her weight on the ankle as she started to crawl, the pain reasserted itself in a blaze of agony that took her breath away, and she had trouble concentrating. But she forced herself to focus. Squeezing past the grate, she slowly began to thread her way between the blades of the fan. The blaze behind her was crackling, flames licking through the opening, igniting the nearest Christmas tree. Flickering red light lit everything, casting a glow into the room on the other side of the fan. It was dark, of course. The electricity was out. Rileigh made for the darkness, the fresh air moving past her reviving her. She threaded her way, every movement a torment.

When she got to the grate on the other side, she shoved on it as hard as she could. It didn't move. The screws holding it firm were on the outside, so kicking it outward from this side should dislodge them. But she was facing the wrong way. There was no way in the tight enclosure to turn around. She'd have to go back, crawl in backwards and…

She slumped against the grate, then began to scream in frustration. Her voice formed words: "Mitch, Mitch, I'm here, Mitch!

～

"RILEIGH!" Mitch yelled. "Rileigh, where are you?"

He was in the library on the front of the house, the stink of smoke getting stronger and stronger, but he couldn't see any flames anywhere.

A strobe of bright lightning torched the sky and the brief flash lit up the whole room, revealing what he couldn't see with just the small beam of his flashlight — smoke was billowing up through the heating grates on the floor.

The fire was in the basement.

Somebody was down there.

He turned and bolted toward the kitchen on the back of the house. He heard a sound as he entered the kitchen, recognized it instantly as he raced toward the stairs.

"Mitch! Mitch!"

The steps led up to Carly's room on one side and down to the basement on the other. The sound was coming from there.

"Rileigh, I'm coming!"

Leaping down the steps, he skidded to a stop in front of the basement door, his flashlight sweeping.

"Here! Mitch, I'm here."

He turned the flashlight beam toward the sound. What he saw made no sense. Rileigh was behind the grate inside the huge fan."

"Oh God," he cried as he knelt in front of her. "What happened to you?"

She didn't answer his question.

"Get me out!" Her voice had the breathless quality of someone in pain. "Fire!"

He looked past her and could see it now through an open slot on the back wall, flames licking through.

But why was Rileigh crawling through — the door was locked! Only Carly knew the combination. Crawling through the blades of the huge fan was the only way out.

Mitch attacked the grate, grabbed the screen and yanked. It gave on the left side. The other screws seemed more secure, and he had no time to go find a screwdriver to remove them. He yanked again. Nothing. Again.

A screw on the top left side pinged off into the darkness behind him.

Grunting with effort, he pulled the screen down from the top, struggling to—

Two screws on the left side ripped free, leaving the right top corner hanging away from the wall.

Click!

Mitch heard the sound through his labored breathing and froze.

A look of instant terror gripped Rileigh's face.

"The fan turns off and on automatically based on... I have no idea what."

That's what Carly had said.

"But the electricity's *out!*" Rileigh gasped.

No. Carly had deliberately blacked out most of the house, but there was still power in her apartment... just up the stairs from here. What if her apartment and the basement were on the same circuit?

The fan blades started to move.

Mitch let out a sound, like a roar. Gripping the grate in both hands, he ripped downward, literally tore the screws from the wall.

The blade below Rileigh began scooping her body

upward as it started to turn. Mitch grabbed her arm and yanked her toward him, falling backwards with her body on top of him as the blades moved faster.

The fan whirred, spun and hummed to life. Within seconds, it was a blur of movement.

Rileigh moaned and he realized she was hurt and he gently rolled her off him to the floor. Then he knelt over her, showering her face with kisses.

He spoke words he'd been longing to say for months, whispered in her ear over and over. "I love you."

Her soft voice was hard to the hear over the roar of the fan.

But Mitch heard. "I love you, too," Rileigh said.

Chapter Forty-Two

MAMA WAS UP EARLY BECAUSE SHE WAS HAVING WHAT SHE called tummy troubles, her polite definition of diarrhea caused by something she ate.

It was happening to her a lot lately, she thought as she hurried into the bathroom to do her business and she knew why. Cooking all them strange dishes out of that cookbook. No wonder her stomach was upset.

She wondered if everybody else in the house was having issues too and was just too polite to say.

Coming out of the bathroom, she made her way slowly to the kitchen. It was barely light outside, but she was definitely up for the day. Might as well make a cup of coffee, sit outside and watch the light turn the night into day as it peeked over the top of Tucker Mountain. As she prepared to make coffee, she thought maybe she ought to take a cup on a tray to Rileigh, who still wasn't getting around very well on that crutch. She'd messed up that ankle again big time. Didn't break it, just re-sprained it, as if she hadn't sprained it bad enough the first time.

The doctor told her it would be weak and she needed

to wear an Ace bandage on it. But nothing would do but that she had to get into them pretty green shoes that matched that dress. Went off somewhere with Mitch dancin' and he brought her home all messed up, that ankle all swollen again and...

Mama pulled the tin of coffee down out of the cabinet and stopped. Or was that the way of it? No, that's not what happened. Rileigh didn't mess up that ankle going on a date with Mitch. She messed it up the night Shagbark Manor burned to the ground. She and Mitch had been in it, but Mama couldn't remember why. What had possessed Mitch and Rileigh to go spend the night in that haunted house? Mama shook her head. Seems like her girls was all the time doing things that didn't make no sense at all.

Rileigh hadn't just re-sprained that ankle that night, neither. She broke a rib, too! And oh my, did that hurt! Every time she breathed, it hurt. And if she coughed — or *laughed.* That poor child couldn't laugh or she'd cry at the same time. She and Mitch and Jillian used to cut up all the time, teasing and carrying on. Now, everybody had to be careful not to say something funny until Rileigh's rib healed. Lily didn't like them serious conversations, about all them dead people in the basement of that big old house, wondering who they was, and feeling bad 'cause their families wasn't never gonna know what'd happened to 'em.

She went to the refrigerator, got the little container of creamer out, and doctored up her coffee with it and some sugar from the sugar bowl. It had been a big deal when Shagbark Manor burned. That place was over a hundred and twenty-five years old, and every person in every historical society for five hundred miles in every direction got their panties in a wad over it. Everybody was blaming everybody else that the sprinkler system hadn't been up to code, so once it caught fire, there wasn't no stopping it. It was a damn good thing there hadn't been nobody in the place but Mitch and Rileigh when it burned.

Well, the two of them and Carly Farrington. Mitch and Rileigh made it out. Carly didn't.

Ever since then, Mitch and Rileigh was... different. Any fool coulda told they was sweet on each other before that fire, but mostly they tried to act like wasn't nothin' to it. But after the fire, didn't seem like they cared anymore who knew it.

Mama shook her head, thinking about poor Carly Farrington. She remembered Carly's grandmother, Grandma Josie. How she used to come to church and help out Bestowing Sewing at Christmastime, making quilts for poor families. Mama didn't know her well, but she seemed like a nice person. It was a shame her granddaughter died in the house that Grandma Josie's mama had built.

Lily picked up the coffee cup and walked through the kitchen slowly — she'd filled it too full of creamer and now it was like to spill — through the dining room and the living room to the front door, and opened it, but caught herself before she pushed the screen door open. That door squalled like a stuck pig at cutting time. You had to be real careful, ease it open like an inch at a time, and still the spring made little creaky, groaning sounds. She stood still, smelling the pre-dawn air, and dragged in a lungful of it. Fresh mountain air. There wasn't no other smell like it anywhere in the world.

Then she started easing the screen door open nice and slow, but it bumped into something that was sitting in front of it. Mama looked down and there was a box. It had been scooted up against the screen door. Mama stepped out onto the porch, reached down and picked up the box. It was about the size of a tissue box — square but taller than it was wide, wrapped up in that brown mailing paper. And when she saw the name on it, she froze.

Rileigh Bishop. That's all, just Rileigh Bishop.

Mama knew what it was! It was another one of them awful things that somebody was sending to Rileigh. Only this one hadn't come from the UPS or in the mail. Somebody had come up on this very porch and left it for her. Mama lifted her eyes and searched the dim yard fearfully, as if maybe whoever left it was still there.

Then Lily went from frightened to pissed off between one heartbeat and the next. She started to yell out at the top of her lungs, "Whoever you are, you leave my daughter alone — you hear me?" But she caught herself, didn't say it.

Mama stood looking down at the box in her hand. And she knew what she had to do. There wasn't no way in hell Mama was going to let somebody terrorize her baby again! One of them boxes had had a finger bone in it! Well, they wasn't gonna get away with it this time. Tucking the box under her arm, she went back into the house, easing the screen door open and closed so she wouldn't wake anybody up.

Lily was gonna hide the damn box. And she knew just where to put it where wouldn't nobody ever find it.

THE END

About The Author

Lauren Street has always loved a mystery. As a kid growing up in bible belt country she devoured every whodunit book she could get her sticky little hands on and secretly investigated all of her (seemingly) normal boring neighbors. Sometimes their pets and farm animals too. All grown up now and living in the UK with her thoroughly unsuspicious (and often unsuspecting) husband, she writes domestic psychological thrillers about families torn apart by secrets and lies. And she sometimes still peers over garden walls to check up on the neighbors.

Also By Lauren Street

The Bishop Smoky Mountain Thrillers

Hide Me Away

Fuel To The Flame

Closer By The Hour

A Gamble Either Way

Calling My Children Home

Too Far Gone

Here You Come Again

A Friend Like You

The Company You Keep

One By One

Come Back To Me

Replaced with Nolon King

Replaced

In Her Place

Irreplaceable

The Salazar Redwood Forest Thrillers

The Girl Who Couldn't Stop Dying

The Girl Who Couldn't Get Out

The Girl Who Couldn't Be Found